"You don't look like much," Billy said, meaning that I didn't look like one hundred thousand dollars. He was right. The shirt was clean; the suit was pressed; Gretchen was at her desk, pretending to be busy; but I didn't look like much. How could I? I wasn't much.

"Few of us do," I said. "You want looks, go to Paris. Paris looks great. You get indicted and you want to go home, hire somebody like me."

"They want to kill me," he said.

He got not argument from me. He was absolutely right. The attorney general was up for reelection, and he was in political trouble. Billy Ryan was a sitting duck. As the late Irvin S. Cobb said of resting waterfowl, levelling his shotgun at them: "Of course I'm going to shoot them now. You don't think I'm gonna wait 'till they get up, do you?"

GEORGE V. HIGGINS

Defending Billy Ryan

A Jerry Kennedy Novel

WARNER BOOKS

A *Warner* Book

First published in the USA in 1992
by Henry Holt and Company, Inc

First published in Great Britain in 1993
by Little, Brown and Company

This edition published by Warner Books in 1994

A CIP catalogue record for this book is
available from the British Library.

ISBN 0 7515 0034 8

Printed in England by Clays Ltd, St Ives plc

Warner Books
A Division of
Little, Brown and Company (UK) Limited
Brettenham House
Lancaster Place
London WC2E 7EN

DEFENDING
BILLY RYAN

ONE

The statutes of limitations have run. For noncapital crimes, the commonwealth's is six; the federal one is five. Nobody killed anybody, at least as far as I know, successfully defending Billy Ryan.

But then I didn't always know a lot, defending Billy Ryan, including, until much later, all who'd been involved. So there may still be a couple loose ends that I haven't spotted yet. Nevertheless, so far as I can tell, two of us who seem to have taken part in Billy Ryan's defense now survive to tell the tale. The other fellow's given his permission to report it on the provision that he will, if questioned by any other person, stoutly deny the whole of it, and say I made it up. So although he is my client, I violate no privilege in giving this account. And I've known him a long time. If you question him, he will do exactly what he promised, and deny every syllable. Cadillac Teddy's like that: as variable as a Maytime breeze, but he never makes a threat he's unprepared to carry out.

Maybe he will be telling you the truth. Maybe I am not. I think I am, but what do I know? Less and less as I go on.

I admitted it: "Nineteen-eighty-five was not a good year for
me," I told Colin Ryan. There didn't seem to be any point in
ducking the issue. "If it'd lasted maybe two or three months
longer, I think I would've ended up like Larry White did. Not
accused of bothering the Cub Scouts, probably, but some kind
of damned disgrace. I'm hoping this year'll turn out better."

He sat there giving me the kind of patient, sad look that a
jeweler who's known and liked you for years gets on his face
when he's taken his loupe from his eye and put it down next to
your wife's engagement diamond on one of those little blue
velvet pads they hunch over to do appraisals. Bargain diamonds
and battered Boston lawyers don't look good under strong white
light, decades after they were newly cut and mounted; dipped
over the years in strong detergents and being banged against
hard edges at bad angles, they lose some of their original fire
and get chipped. Their prongs bend, and the question isn't
whether they really need repairs, but whether their value justi-
fies the certain cost.

Associate Justice Colin Ryan of the Great Trial Court of
Massachusetts (its proper name is the superior court, but they
like the Great One better) thought about that in the seedy
splendor of the lawgiver's chambers, to the left off Courtroom
No. 6 of the New Courthouse (Depression era) of Suffolk
County at Pemberton Square, at the shag end of a February day
the color of a cheap beige vinyl-siding job, guaranteed to last a
lifetime, and considered the derelict before him. me.

I go back a long way. I know the lyrics by heart, and the
melody's familiar, too. "To this charge," the bailiff intones after
the jury has been sworn, "the defendant has said that he is not
guilty, and for his trial has put himself upon the country." He
pauses then and takes a breath, as though he had never in his
whole life read any words as preposterous as those he must say

next. "Which country you are, and you are sworn to try the issue. Jurors, harken to the evidence." Now and then, they do. So do your old friends, as volunteers—"officious intermeddlers" we call them in the law.

"You don't look good, Jerry," Colin said, the way people who have viewed the guest of honor at a wake say he looks so natural, being dead and all. "You don't look good at all."

I didn't want to shock him, so I didn't say I knew that. It doesn't do to shock judges by pronouncing their latest insight old news. They don't like it. If you are a member of the criminal defense bar in this town, and a quick look at the appointment calendar, checkbook and your secretary's vacant desk—she only comes in three days a week now, and doesn't really have enough to keep her occupied the third one—leaves some doubt in your mind about whether your practice is on the skids; if a glance in the washroom mirror at your bleeding eyes and forenoon stubble isn't enough to make you see you're on the road to hell; well, all you have to do is get yourself down the elevator of the Little Building and out onto the street, and pick up some gossip there. It'll be about you.

I read a book once about Washington where the man claimed it was the only town in the world where you can start a rumor in the morning and get it back, improved, over dinner that same night. For all I know he was right (I'm not one of that type of Kennedys, lacking the good judgment to have been born rich). It doesn't take anywhere near that long for damaging talk to circulate through the Boston trial bar. Ten A.M. and noon are about par for the course, unless it's really lethal stuff, in which case the cadaver of your reputation's ready for the medical examiner by 11:15. The thing to remember, when you swim in our lagoon with your dorsal fin exposed like ours are, for advertising purposes, is that we compete for food. Food in our line of work is money, the money being what we get for representing clients. If I get a client, you don't get him, and he gives me the money, not you. If I give you some pretext to badmouth my work, you'll use it to intercept clients. Healthy sharks eat wounded sharks. Blood in the water is blood in the water; the identity of the donating species is irrelevant. I knew what Colin Ryan'd heard about Jeremiah F. Kennedy, Esq., because I'd heard it myself. The trouble was that most of it was true.

"I know it," I said.

"You been drinking some?" he said.

It was not until sometime considerably later that I inadvertently—and uselessly, as far as Billy Ryan's defense was concerned (at the end I'd learned that almost everything I'd worked so hard to learn about Billy and his case had been optional almost from the day I started)—discovered the foundation of the Ryan family fortune. It had been no small change even before Colin's father, Billy, started building it even higher with the profits of bootlegging. Colin's grandfather, Buck Ryan, had been a central Massachusetts colleague of Old Joe Kennedy, the Gustin gang, and sundry other Massachusetts importers of beverage alcohol, who not only continued their diligent service to the public after the Eighteenth Amendment took effect in 1920, but charitably expanded their staffs and facilities in order to create employment for the jobless and serve consumers otherwise left high and dry. So the irony was lost on me when Colin asked his question. Just as well. I might've said something that would've steamed him and thus forfeited what turned out to be an offer of redemption.

I settled for a shrug. It is necessary for me here to explain some things about people, particularly men, who have become judges. This is because people like me who have to deal with them on a regular basis are able to do so only if we are aware of the change that has taken place in their earthly status, maybe in their eventual celestial one as well. In their own minds, that is. They take the same rattletrap elevators to their courtrooms that we bad guys and mouthpieces take, but not in the same cars or at the same times. They ride by themselves. After parking their cars not in pricey lots or garages some cold and rainy distance from the courthouse, but in the free spaces downstairs that they ordered reserved for their use. They spend their days seated in the same seedy courtrooms where their jurors sit, and they too are subject to chill draughts and wet heat, but they look down from their chairs on the rest of us. They declare the mid-morning recesses when they, not the rest of us, have processed the morning coffee and have to go to the bathroom. They also replenish both the fluid and solid calories, drinking more coffee and having the odd doughnut, just as we do, and neither one of those refreshments is any better or worse than the ones we ingest. But their coffee and doughnuts are brought to them in their chambers; we lawyers and clients must fetch our own and don't have any chambers, so we stand around munching and swallowing out in the hall. The commonplace is that a judge is a lawyer who once knew a governor, and that's right as far as it goes. The rest of reality is the past tense; a judge is a person who *used to be* a lawyer, and no one had better forget it.

In his previous life as a lawyer, Colin Ryan had been a good one. Not a damned good one, or a superlative one (few are, and I'm not among them except now and then, when I get the wind up), but a good and capable lawyer. We have one or two judges who were lousy lawyers, but turned out to be pretty good judges (a person whose deficiency is thinking fast while standing up demonstrates occasionally some skill at thinking slowly while sitting down), and we have some lousy judges who were cracker-jack trial lawyers (a person good at thinking fast on his feet can have some trouble checking his cultivated reflexes when sworn to sit down, shut up and listen). You never know how a lawyer will turn out on the bench, just as you learn very fast when you start trying cases never to predict how a jury will decide. If there is such a thing as reincarnation, and you entertain some irrational ambition to live another life in the future as a trial lawyer, try to be a horseplayer in your first one and a stockbroker in your second. You'll have a distinct advantage on those of us starting from scratch.

Colin started out in the Middlesex County Public Defender's office. Geographically, Middlesex is our state's biggest county, offering a rich and varied menu of evildoers to the rookie trial lawyer on either side. You get your suburban love-triangle murders from Lincoln and your drug-dealing killers from Lawrence; your organized crime guys from Lowell and Somerville and your batty hippies from Cambridge. If you can't learn in Middlesex County what the Jesuits at Holy Cross left out of the course in moral theology, you couldn't learn it on the docks of Macao.

Colin had learned it. He had also learned he didn't like it. Colin is finicky, which can be a real handicap for a trial lawyer. He hung on for three or four years, rinsing his soul out two nights a week as an adjunct professor teaching evidence and procedure at New England Law, pretending that made him respectable, but after a while it got to be too much for him. He also wasn't making much money, and while the members of the Ryan family have their faults, disrespect for hard cash is not among them. He resigned and went into private practice with a man named Dan Frears in Worcester.

I knew Dan. I didn't know him real well, because his practice was mostly civil and mine is almost entirely criminal, so our paths didn't cross much, but I liked him, and he had a good reputation. He's dead now, the victim of terminal fitness brought on by jogging one fine July dawn when the temperature at sunrise was a soggy 83 degrees. A lot of people—all males—that I've known and liked have done that. Not once have I approved either the activity that killed them or the fact that it did kill them.

When Dan was alive, which is by far the best time to do anything you may have in mind, and badgering everyone else within earshot to stop smoking and eating butter and to start eating oat bran and jogging, he hewed to a Darwinian theory of law practice: survival of the richest. If you brought the business in, you got most of the money the case brought. And if you didn't, you got thin and an hourly wage. If you were a decent sort, and Dan was, you tossed a few farthings to the fellow whose attendance at court led to the settlements of cases you brought in, but you gave him zilch in real compensation for his wearisome attendance at court that resulted in the settlement of your cases, and prevented him from hustling business on his own. Colin isn't stupid now and wasn't stupid then. He was no poorer in the Frears office than he had been as PD, but several people, emphatically including old Dan, were getting progressively richer on his sweat. He didn't like that any better than he liked defender's pay. He set his cap, as my mother used to say, on becoming a judge.

Generally speaking, a lawyer who becomes a judge believes the explanation is that God noticed his work, saw that it was good, and rewarded him. This is almost never true, but if you are a trial lawyer, it is a bad idea to suggest to a judge that it is false. I knew how Colin had become a judge: he had ascended to the bench because John Tierney, governor back then, wished to appoint his sidekick, Andy Keats, to the bench, and the only way he could do it was to team Andy's nomination with another one that Billy Ryan wouldn't dare or care to kibosh. But I wasn't about to tell that to Colin; when a judge becomes portentous, and plainly disposed to discourse at some sententious length upon your personal conduct and deportment, you sit there like the miserable wreck of a man that you are and you take it. Vowing revenge, of course, some day; silently vowing revenge.

"My brother-in-law's doing that," he said grimly. "Mark Frolio's doing that too." He shook his head. "My father, my family, my sister, we've done everything in the world we can think of for that kid, and if Marie doesn't have to kick him out pretty soon, well, I don't know what she's going to do. All the talent in the world. What makes you guys do this thing?"

Knowing little of State Rep. Marie Frolio, D., Norwich, I said nothing. I've since learned enough to know that if I were married to Marie, I'd drink Lynchburg, Tennessee, dry in a week. Jack Daniel would rise from the dead and bless the Lord for my existence on the earth.

"Well," Colin said in that practical tone that people use when they have no idea what they're talking about, "it must be something."

It was. It was my wife, excuse me, my ex-wife, deciding that first Roy and then Ace at the real estate office were, *seriatim*, the love(s) of her life, and then ditching me to play house with Ace. It was my daughter, Saigon, otherwise known as Heather; the nickname acknowledged the crucial part that her conception played in my exemption from compulsory participation in the struggle for freedom in South Vietnam. Heather took "a year off" from Dartmouth, with one year to go, when she "just fell in love with Charlie" in her junior year—read: Charlie knocked her up—and got married. Read: had to. The only problem that I have with Charlie is that I can't stand him. He's rich and he's good-looking, and he got a lot of money from his family, but leaving that aside, he ain't worth spit. Charlie could hold a conversation with a rock, and both of them would find it rewarding.

And then there was the government. If there is one thing a defense lawyer knows, it's that the government can get you if it wants to. Any government. Federal, state or local. Law-abiding private citizens do not believe this until some government sets out to get them, and they have to pay good money to a man like me to fight for them, but their disbelief is like unto the very dew of May; it evaporates fast. Along with their bank balances, cheerfulness, and the order of their lives. I knew what Mister Everson was when he called from the IRS: he was the scout, and the cavalry was right behind him. They cut me off at the pass and mowed me down: hair, hide, hoof and all. And Judge Ryan insightfully surmised that something must've happened. Can't fool him, boy, can't fool him.

"Yeah," I said. .

He coughed. Colin doesn't smoke, and it's against his religion to catch colds. Coughing for him is a device to gain time. I waited him out. "I need some help," he said.

TWO

Paste this in the band of your hat, and refer to it when in doubt: judges and cops do not need help. By definition. A cop is a person who gives help, not one who needs it, and a judge is a person who does not need help and never did. So when a cop or a judge says he needs help, he *really* needs help. So I said that. "Really," I said.

"Really," Colin said. He coughed again. "The grand jury's reporting tomorrow afternoon." No surprise there; grand juries usually report toward the end of the week so the prosecutors can grandstand for the media over the weekend. "They're indicting my father."

There was a surprise. Not that Billy Ryan was about to be accused of being a highwayman, brigand and general grasper— he had been universally acknowledged as a practiced professional in those trades in Massachusetts for many, many years, often with something close to admiration. Billy was "as cute as a shithouse rat." "The fox that bit him died."

"Really," I said again. No point in messing around with a formula that seemed to be working.

Colin nodded.

"For what?" I said. Partly, I was curious. But partly, too, I was ornery. Here was this ordinary bozo who got a black dress and a title, and therefore he could summon ordinary mortals to his chambers on cold, wet Boston days in February, and begin the conversation by disparaging their appearance and general deportment. I resented it. So I wanted to make him say what they'd at last caught his father doing, and humiliate himself by doing so. Plain meanness. It's one of my many failings. A full inventory's available from my former wife.

Now it was Colin's turn to shrug. I took some pleasure from that, too. The rain sluiced down the window behind him, and his underwear got smaller on his body, and for once, just for a little while, he knew and remembered what it's like to be in the wire-mesh basket with the hot grease up to your nostrils, the chicken wings due in next, and no rescuers in sight. It's good for a person to be truly scared. It builds character.

Colin sighed. That was a good sign. Resignation on the part of the person paying the retainer is the prelude necessary to extraction of a handsome fee. "Oh, bribery, mostly," he said. "But everything else they can think of. They're throwing the whole kitchen sink in."

Of course they were. They had it, too, and if they didn't, it was not for lack of trying. William F. Ryan, commissioner, Department of Public Works, Commonwealth of Massachusetts, at least since Noah built the ark: if they didn't have Billy for selling the apple to the serpent who peddled it to Eve, it was because the serpent had refused to testify against him. Professional courtesy and all that. If it was still nailed down, where you could see it every morning, Billy hadn't taken it. Most likely because he didn't want it, which meant he hadn't thought of a use for it yet.

"My," I said.

Colin looked disconsolate. "He needs a lawyer," he said.

Hard to argue with that. When somebody proposes to shove

you in the slammer for the rest of your natural, a good fierce lawyer is a handy thing to have around. And anyway, I don't argue with judges. That's against *my* religion. I said nothing.

"I have to help my father," Colin said.

Mine's dead. Good thing, too. If he were alive, it'd kill him to see what a mess I've made of things after all of his hard work.

"You're the sixth lawyer that I've called," he said. "None of the others'd take him."

Praise from Caesar is praise indeed. "Hard case," I said. "Can't say I blame 'em."

"We don't have much money," Colin said, now sounding disconsolate. "I think that's the reason." Another compliment; he'd called me because he thinks I'm a cheap lawyer. I am a cheap lawyer, of course. That's how I make my living: low prices, small cases and high volume. In the old and happy days, Mack took some pride in the modest prosperity we got from my hard and constant work for people who didn't have as much money as they had legal troubles, but that work never made us rich, and after a while that began to bother Mack.

"Hogwash," I said. "You've got about a hundred times what it'd cost to get a tiger with full stripes, the black ones and the white chest blaze against the orange coat, in the courtroom for your father. But you don't want to spend it, because you're fuckin' *cheap.*"

It's easy to talk tough when you've got absolutely nothing to lose, and that's about what I had that day. "The reason nobody wants this case is not money. You've got more money'n God has. And the reason you hauled me up here on a lousy day in the rain is because you've got a loser on your hands. And nobody wants it. They'd rather rub shit on their heads. You're desperate, Colin. Your father's desperate, because he doesn't want to spend his retirement years in the exercise yard at Cedar Junction, formerly known as MCI Walpole, with machine-

gunners watching his movements. You know all about that place, Colin. You send people there all the time. And you talk about how you hope they'll take this last chance to get rehabbed and all that, and everyone knows it's all crap. You included.

"Now all of a sudden it's different. You don't want your father taking tea with the boss cons, any more than guys on my side of the fence wanted our clients in there, either. But you sent them there just the same. Knowing what'd happen. And it did, in case you're not up to date on the case reports. Remember that cop case I had?"

The first cop I ever knew who needed help—at least from me—called me up two days after New Year's about nine years ago. He sounded calm enough. He said he was a sergeant on the Boston police force, and he had at least one problem. "Maybe two," he said. I asked him what they were. "Police brutality, for sure," he said, "and maybe child abuse. Two of the first, one of the second—child abuse, I mean."

"Could you be a little more specific," I said.

"Well," he said, "I didn't give my son his Christmas present, and he's not very pleased. Says he might turn me in." He laughed. "I think he's kidding, though."

"What was it?" I said. "And why didn't you? Not that stiffing a kid on Christmas is a felony yet, so far as I know."

"My brother officers took it away from me," he said. "It was a Louisville Slugger, thirty-one ounces, nice and light. Whippy, you know? He's not a very big kid. Bat-speed's a problem for him."

"And some other cops took it away from you," I said.

"That's right," he said. "Downtown Crossing. Christmas Eve. When all the stores were closing. So it was too late to get another one for him."

"Any special reason?" I said. "Did they give you some reason for this?"

"After they Mirandaed me, sure," he said. "Look, I had a pretty good idea what it was. I bought the bat at this store down on Summer Street, and I paid for it, and they put it in a bag, so I was carrying it up Summer to the subway under Filene's, and I saw these two fine young gentlemen having a disagreement with a lady about some bags. And it looked to me like the bags belonged to her, but they thought otherwise. So I approached the three of them, and I identified myself as a police officer, showed my badge, and suggested that the four of us, in the spirit of the season, of course, should have a nice, quiet, discussion about just what the hell was going on there."

"And?" I said.

"Well," he said, "the lady said she'd been Christmas shopping for her grandchildren, and what was in the bags were the presents that she'd bought. So that seemed to make it fairly simple, least to me. Whoever knew what was in the bags most likely was the rightful owner of the bags. So I held up my hand and said: 'Stop. Say no more.' And I invited the fine young gentlemen to tell me what was in the bags. One of them said I should go and commit a sexual act all by myself, and pulled a knife on me. So I used my son's Christmas present to emphasize my disapproval of what he said, and then I used it to persuade his companion that I wasn't happy with either one of them, and Santa wouldn't likely be, either."

"I see," I said.

"The two fine young gentlemen slipped and fell to the ground," he said, "and now claim that they were injured."

"And the old lady?" I said.

"She expressed her thanks for my assistance and went down the stairs to the subway before I could get her name and address. I rendered what assistance I could to the two young gentlemen, both of whom seemed to believe I had struck them with no reason, and so stated to the uniformed officers who came to the scene and confiscated my son's Christmas present as evidence."

"Did they arrest you?" I said.

"No," he said. "I didn't know either one of them, but we have some mutual friends, and they said they'd see to it that the young gentlemen received proper medical attention. Which I guess they must've, because three days later they came to headquarters with a large number of other people that I didn't see around Filene's on Christmas Eve, and all of them said I used my son's Christmas present to whack the young gentlemen around the head and ears for no good reason at all. So I got suspended with full pay, pending department proceedings, and a friend of mine says it might not even stop there, because this thing could wind up with me in court, sitting down and listening to people saying rotten things about me instead of standing up, like I'm used to, and saying rotten things about them. So I should get a lawyer."

"Have you got any money?" I said. Boy, I hate asking that question.

"Not a hell of a lot," he said. That's a very common response, which is why I hate asking the question.

"Oh dear," I said.

"Can I come in and see you?" he said. "This guy I know, that says he knows you, tells me you fight for your clients."

"And who might that be?" I said, not really knowing who it was. That's how I built my low-priced, high-volume practice: word of mouth, ex-clients doing unsolicited commercials for me within earshot of later clients.

"Fellow named Teddy Franklin," he said.

"Uh huh," I said. That figured. For years Cadillac Teddy's been doing for me what John Cameron Swayze did for Timex watches and Ed Herlihy did for Velveeta: promotion. "Done him a favor, have you?"

"He's always seemed like a nice guy to me," the cop said.

"Okay," I said. "Tomorrow at eleven. I've got two arraignments at ten, but I should be back here by then."

"Look," he said, "I'm right downstairs. Okay if I come up right now?"

"Oh sure," I said. I know when I'm whipped. And I know when someone else is.

Colin remembered that case. He'd been just as surprised as I'd been when I first saw my new client and discovered he was black, as his so-called victims were too, but that hadn't stopped him from all but ordering the jury to find the guy guilty as sin. Or from sentencing him to five-to-seven at Concord, where the legend is that ex-cops won't be bothered; the facts are otherwise —I had to get that one stayed by a single justice, pending appeal, and hurry like blazes to do it, or the reversal and retrial, which I managed to win, wouldn't have mattered at all (by the time the new trial date arrived, the complaining witnesses were in the federal jug for firearms-trafficking, which did us no harm at all).

"Well," Colin said. He cleared his throat.

I began to get up, half-rising from the chair and fumbling with my raincoat. Colin got a pleading look on his face, the same one he used at Boston College Law School when he wasn't prepared for Professor Jim Houghteling's class in civil procedure and wanted a quick glance at my notes. "Jerry," he said, "I need this."

"I know it," I said, standing up. "But you don't need it from me, as you've made perfectly clear. I'm a broken-down, washed-up, wreck of a lawyer, and you need someone who's eager. And cheap."

"What do you want?" Colin said, miserably.

I was firm. I had nothing coming in. If I went out with nothing, it was a wash. "A hundred thousand dollars," I said, "cash money. On the table. No 'later,' no 'next week,' no 'see ya next payday.' When the mazuma's on the mahogany, I go to work." My desk is not mahogany, but poetic license is allowed when you're shooting craps.

"Tomorrow?" Colin said almost timidly. I like that in a judge. Don't see it much, but I like it. Of course, judges like a bit of humility in lawyers, and they don't see much from me. "Any time you want," I said. "You know where to find me."

THREE

For all I know, the song is right, and it really is a long, long way from May to December. Then again, it may not be. What I do know for sure is that it's a longer way down the Lafayette Mall from Suffolk Superior to my office at the Little Building than it used to be when I started taking it, creeping up on thirty years ago. The Hare Krishnas in their saffron robes and braids, with their tambourines: they're all gone now, back indoors, I guess. There's still an abundance of bums—"Say mistah, you got any spare change?" "Yeah, I gotta couple quarters here I been meaning to throw away"—but they're different bums. Times change.

I guess I don't change with them. I meant to. It was on my calendar: "Things to do next week. Change w/ times." But somehow I never got around to it. There was always something else going on that distracted my attention, and I dealt with that, and then there was another thing, and another thing after that, and pretty soon my very own wife, the former Joan Mc-Manus, wasn't my wife anymore but a woman of fifty who looked pretty good until she got the notion she was eighteen again, and got horny for two guys who sweet-talked her into a real estate scheme that wouldn't've scared anyone who didn't know what *fraud* means. Then my daughter had married a jerk.

I paid for the wedding, as I paid for the divorce—about the same price, too: twenty-one thousand dollars I didn't really have on me, for veal birds with cream sauce served with champagne to a lot of people, many whom I didn't even know, much less like. Most of them were disgustingly young. My lawyer for his 16K at least said "thank you," which none of those young drunks and churls did; I thought it was decent of him. Heather said: "Thanks, Dad," and kissed me. On the cheek. My lawyer didn't kiss me. He just cashed the check. It cleared. As the caterer's did. Heather's mother was stony throughout both occasions. I guess that when none of your own cash-money's involved, and you have good reason to know the celebrations will pretty much exhaust what the host had left in his retirement fund after you got through with him, a dignified mien is expected.

It's a cold world, especially when you set out when you are young (but haven't yet found out you're foolish), to make your way by renting yourself out to people who decided to cut their paths through it by questionable means, and wound up getting caught. It always comes as something of a shock to the young lawyer to discover for the first time that a person who's accused of criminal activity is most likely just as willing to cheat and lie to his lawyer as he was—in all likelihood—to break the law he's charged with violating. The language of the court decisions that you have to read in law school; the code of professional ethics; the speeches you hear at bar association gatherings: all of them resound with lofty affirmations that the client must be able to trust his lawyer completely with his liberty, his property, and indeed his very life, or else the very foundation of our legal system will disintegrate. All that, of course, is true, but it omits the corollary that it really should include: the lawyer who reciprocates his client's trust is en route to disappointment, sometimes so severe it breaks his youthful spirit.

My spirit was not youthful—hadn't been for some years in fact—that afternoon when I'd left Colin. I was a man in need of money, which meant I needed work. But instead I'd treated myself to the luxury of treating a judge injudiciously, thus in all probability losing not only a case I most likely couldn't win, but a fee I sorely needed. Only a nitwit seeks ego-gratification from my kind of work. Regardless of the impressions to the contrary conveyed by books and movies, the first thing you have to get from practicing law is clients who can pay. They're the only ones who'll at least avoid deceiving you intentionally, which shouldn't by any means be taken as a guarantee you'll win but at least improves the odds, and at a minimum assures you won't get suicidal if you lose, because you will have some money.

Years ago I was appointed by the court—"the court" being in that instance Andrew Keats, who likes me about as much as I like him: not very much—to defend a miserable bastard who'd done everything the statutes prohibit except what the DA'd nailed him for: murder one. There were three outcomes in prospect on the day when I was silly enough to be in Keats's courtroom on another case that wasn't paying me much either, and the bastard was hauled in, shackled, manacled and chained, to be arraigned. He said he was innocent. Even worse, he said he had no money to employ a lawyer. Andy got this evil smirk on his face, and I got appointed. I got appointed because I was there. Life is full of misfortunes. Of the three possible that day, two were certain to come true.

The first one was that my client didn't do it—someone certainly had, very few persons being resourceful enough to shoot themselves three times behind the left ear and then climb into a Dumpster next to a chain drugstore in Tiverton, Rhode Island, to die—but he said it wasn't him. That's not a verbatim quote; he said: "It wasn't me." The second one was that he did do it, but the commonwealth couldn't prove it. The third was that I was going to lose a lot of money on the case, because when you are appointed by the very same court that has limited what it will pay appointed counsel to far less than it costs per hour to run a law office, and whose judges then routinely cut all counsel bills and stall your payment for defending evildoers, you are going to lose a lot of money on the case.

I lost one hell of a lot of money on that case. I was in the office in the morning, and I was there at night. I made Gretchen stay late, and Andy Keats, who also drew the trial assignment, offered to put me in the cooler four times for being too strenuous when I argued my objections. I went up the front and down the back of the prosecution witnesses, and when the smoke of the battle disappeared, I shot the survivors. The trial lasted six weeks. If it'd gone seven, either Andy would've lost his mind or I would've vaulted the bench and gone after him. In those days it cost me $1,350 a week to maintain my modest office. For those not quick at math, that is twenty-six dollars per hour. I was entitled to twenty dollars from the court, and knew I wouldn't get it. Try losing six bucks an hour for six weeks while trying to stay in business—ain't easy. Andy held up my bill for eight months, and signed off on it—after deducting thirty percent—only after I went to the bar association and said I would file a formal complaint next. I may also have mentioned the *Boston Commoner*, and my good friend on the city desk—who isn't there anymore and can no longer do me favors; he took a staff-reduction early-retirement offer and moved to Arizona. Too bad; everybody needs friends.

The jury returned with its verdict in my free-riding bastard's case. The foreman was a tall and lanky Presbyterian, I think, filling in for Cotton Mather, he being unavailable by supervening reason of death. When the jury was seated, the clerk, as usual, invited the defendant to rise, and as usual I rose myself, having no intention to serve the sentence but being willing to accept the blame for the decision that would lead to its imposition. My client whispered through clenched teeth that I sucked. I gave him no indication that I heard him, and stood placidly in the fig-leaf position, my hands clasped over my crotch.

"Mister Foreman," the clerk said, "ladies and gentlemen of the jury. In the matter of the commonwealth versus" my son of a bitch, "have you reached a verdict?"

Indeed they had. The foreman nodded firmly. "We have, Your Honor," he said.

"You suck brown wind," my client hissed behind me. "You're the worst lawyer I ever saw."

"What say you then, Mister Foreman and ladies and gentleman of the jury?" the clerk said.

"We find the defendant," the foreman said stolidly, "not guilty."

I turned to face my client. "Fuck you," he said. "You did nothin'. I told you I didn't do it. I never shoulda been here. Anyone could see that."

Such, such are the joys.

There is probably a colder wind than the one that comes over Boston Common on grey February days from the northeast, bringing rain and whistling down over the steeple of the Park Street Church before it tears down to the sidewalk and chaps an honest but foolish man's defenseless withers through his cheap flannel suit and all, but I'll be damned if I know where it blows. Siberia, maybe. Mongolia. No wonder Attila the Hun and Genghis Khan had such rotten dispositions: they weren't preternaturally surly; they were cold. I drive home these days and nights to my former summer "winterized" house at Green Harbor in Marshfield—Mack got the regular house, in Braintree; she sold it at once, pocketing the change, before the bottom dropped out of the Massachusetts real estate market. I did not say Mack is stupid. Some nights I light a fire so that I'll feel warm. It doesn't work. I haven't felt warm for years.

There weren't any lights on in my office when I got back after reading Colin out. This was to have been expected; I'd shut them off when I left, in deference to the Boston Edison. I think very highly of the light company but do not care to pay it a penny more than I absolutely must. It's depressing, though, to return to a dark office. Makes you think the lawyer whose name's on the door isn't doing very well, and things aren't likely to improve until he learns some manners.

I snapped on the lights and slumped inside, and in a little while a man who could've substituted for the weasel in any public broadcasting wildlife special you'd care to name knocked on my door and slithered wetly in. He wore a grey suit and a grey skin and a grey hat, and he had a brown attaché case. He said: "Mister Kennedy?" I said: "Yes," figuring he was from the Department of Revenue of the commonwealth, or the IRS, or the Ministry of General Miseries, and there wasn't any point in denying it. "This's for you," he said, and slapped the case down on Gretchen's desk.

"What's in it," I said, "gelignite?"

"Dunno," he said. "They told me to bring it to you here, and I done that, and I'm double-parked outside the side door on Tremont, and the cop was looking at me funny. So I'm leaving."

"From who?" I said.

He was surprised. He wasn't faking it. "Billy Ryan, of course," he said. "William Francis Ryan. The commissioner. You're the lawyer, right? This's what you asked for, and this's what you get. You know Billy, don't you?"

So I agreed and said I did, though my knowledge was limited to his name and reputation, and after the ferret was gone I opened up the case. Inside I found one hundred thousand dollars, in hundred-dollar bills, strapped as they came from the bank, and I left the case open on Gretchen's desk while I punched her number into the phone on her desk, so that I was looking at all that lovely money while the phone rang at her place, and then her answering machine came on, and her message was that neither she nor Harold could come to the phone just then, but if I'd leave my name and number, one of them would call me as soon as they got back. I said: "I hope the two of you had a nice shower together. I hope you found every nerve in each other's bodies. I'm going to the bank now with a whole bunch of money, and you get your ass in here tomorrow. I'm the lawyer, right? Man just told me so. We're going back to work."

FOUR

Somebody once said wisely that by the time you reach forty, you'll have the face you deserve, and most likely wanted all along. The law school graduation that turned Colin, Andy Keats, Tommy Grogan and me loose upon the world was also the first time I met Billy Ryan, well over forty by then; he could've been a pin-up illustration for the aphorism.

He had a face that looked like a headsman's double-bitted ax, freshly sharpened on both edges for a very special guest— Anne Boleyn, maybe. I'd known who he was, of course; very few law students in those days in Boston denied themselves the many pleasures of the human comedy reported in the papers mornings and evenings too, and Billy was a popular villain even then in the public melodramas. Seeing him close-up and watching how he used that weapon of a face, even on a happy day, at a social celebration—he most likely couldn't help it after all his years of practice—I had no trouble whatsoever believing that his public reputation as a merciless, relentless tyrant who saw what he wanted and took it probably didn't do him justice.

Of course from my point of view and that of the rest of Colin's friends, Billy did have certain advantages: power and money, for example, that none of us then had (and I for one never got). But I started to become sure even on commencement day that his mouthful of snaggled, yellowed teeth (no orthodonture for the offspring of backwoods bootleggers in his bygone childhood—assuming he'd bothered to have one—or for anyone else, either) must have served him well even with the harder guys. His hawk's beak; his tiger's jaws; his pale-blue, vulpine eyes; his gunnery-sergeant's crewcut of black hair just starting to turn grey in spots; topping off his light-heavyweight's muscled body most likely did him no harm with more formidable adversaries either. Billy Ryan's job had always been first to keep construction crews in line; while that graduation day I'd never heard a bear talk, and never have since, either, if I'd met a talking bear I would have expected him to sound a lot like Billy, and I doubted Billy'd had to raise that voice too often when he wanted something done.

Well, the decades had changed Billy some when he followed me into my office for our first professional conference the day after he'd coughed up the cash, as, of course, they'd changed me as well. He'd lost maybe an inch or two off his adult height —around six-one when I'd met him—and his belly'd gone a little slack on him. Jowls had appeared on the carnivore's jaw, some evidence, maybe, that too many potatoes had gone down the pipe with the beef and the lobsters and so forth, and the only remnant of the GI's brushcut was a lingering patch at the front, and some outgrowths above the ears, down the back. The hands were liver spotted, but they showed no sign of palsy, and they were still a boxer's tools. He was showing his years, but as I knew from chance encounters with him on the Hill and around town as they'd gone by, he'd defied them remarkably well. He was getting old at last, and he was in big trouble, but he hadn't lost his appetite for combat, and if I seemed interested in a good scrap with him that grim winter's day, he'd sure do his best to oblige. Or so he sought to convey.

I know why the TV and the movie people telescope the pretrial intervals after fictional lawyers acquire their fictional cases and clients; for the same reason they cut to the chase, and the gunplay, as fast as they can with the cop shows. They suspect that what we lawyers do when we prepare our cases would be pretty dull viewing indeed, and that if they showed that preparation as it really happens, the TV zappers would be clicking all across this Great Republic. Now I'm a lawyer, and when I get home at night from the day's skirmishes, whether with people or books, I don't always feel quite up to browsing through Montaigne's collected works, or even *Bleak House* for that matter. I'm beat, and I don't mind a drink and some "LA Law" one single bit. I think it's remarkable that the partners apparently manage to make such good livings while apparently spending most of their waking hours either getting laid on their office couches with their paying clients, making goo-goo eyes at each other in the file room, or doing what they can to work out their troubled marriages, because I never knew those activities to produce such handsome fees. I also have a lot of trouble understanding when the hell they get their work done. But maybe I'm just slow and inefficient, lost a yard off my fastball—or never had one—or just haven't figured it out.

The point is that I don't watch "LA Law" or any courtroom movie for lessons on running my practice. I learned that the hard way myself, and what I learned isn't what they do. I discovered long ago that I have to start work in the new case the day I meet the new client. It doesn't matter who the client is, or how much he's paid me to defend him, or what he's charged with doing, or how long his damned record is. What matters is the realization that any defense lawyer who's any good has at least two clients in each case, one of whom attends every trial: to defend the person who hired him, the lawyer must start by defending himself. Judges are now and then stern with defendants and spectators who disrupt proceedings, but those uproars are unusual. But it's not unusual at all for judges to holler at unprepared lawyers, and those judges are right. Ours is a serious business. Trial is the last blood sport, and to play it well we have to begin early, and stay late, by defending ourselves in our offices.

The first challenge is presented by the new client himself. The challenge is to persuade him, if possible, not to become your attacker, because once he does that you'll add to your problems when you and he go into court: you'll have a sniper behind you, along with the gunners in front.

That persuasion is not easy. This is because it doesn't matter how long you do it, you never get a detailed template you can follow when the next new guy comes in. Oh, there are some types, of course: the indigent client whose respect for you is precisely proportionate to the money he's paying—none; the paying client who by then's realized you may make him indigent, too; the client who's on the edge of a panic-collapse and needs a confessor or shrink at least as much as he needs you; the connoisseur whose many adventures in court have convinced him he's a great critic of lawyers; and last but not least among frustrating clients, the inveterate, long-playing, liar.

But then there are the ones who are *sui generis*, and boy, if any man ever had his own genus, William F. Ryan was that man. Oh, he bore a functional resemblance or two to many other clients I'd known—I'll get to those as I go along here— but that rock of a personality he'd been born with and improved set him apart from the rest. This man had been born demanding control; had been brought up to keep on demanding it; had gotten control when he was quite young; and kept it the rest of his life. Until, he now feared, this awful event. This sneak attack that might shift his power to me.

I was about seventh on the list of persons he'd compiled and resented as the suspects in his bushwacking the afternoon he came to my dingy office in the rain. At the top was the prosecutor who had had him indicted, understandably enough, and the next three were the people who had testified against him (we didn't know their names for sure then, or even what the charges were, because the indictments hadn't yet been handed up, but Billy had narrowed it down). After them came his son, Colin, who'd told him that he had to give me all that money, rightfully his because he'd stolen it fair and square, and my name was right after Colin's. Because I'd asked for his money and taken it. Colin being his son, he had a prayer of eventual restoration into Billy's good graces. So did I: unconditional surrender—or defeat in mortal combat—of the gentleman who'd had Billy indicted. Mine was not much of a chance.

But until I won it, against all odds, I was *persona non grata*, your regular lawn-party skunk. I, of course, resented that. I realize that clients dislike paying money to their lawyers, apparently believing that we're fed by ravens in the wilderness until they have need of us, but that doesn't make me cheerful when I encounter the attitude. Billy Ryan and I understood each other from the git-go. He didn't like me, and I didn't like him, and you can't ask more than that in a criminal proceeding. You want a friend? Buy a dog. Golden retrievers're good. They're friendly by nature.

"Colin said we had to come and see you right away. Not later," he said.

I nodded. "Colin's right," I said. "Man in your position should take all the good advice he can get." Colin looked apprehensive, not a bit the sharp smoothie he plays when he's in the black dress.

"I paid you a lot of money," Billy said.

"And I appreciate it," I said. That was true. Completely true. After that briefcase arrived, and I went to the bank, and I got the deposit slip that said "$100,000" to account of Jeremiah F. Kennedy, I went home and boiled myself until I couldn't stand the hot water anymore, and I went to bed and slept the sleep of the exhausted just until the morning came. Then I got up and I boiled myself again. I was as pink and fresh as a new-born babe the day that Billy Ryan met me.

"You don't look like much," Billy said, meaning that I didn't look like one hundred thousand dollars. He was right. The shirt was clean; the suit was pressed; Gretchen was at her desk, pretending to be busy; but I didn't look like much. How could I? I wasn't much.

"Few of us do," I said. "You want looks, go to Paris. Paris looks great. You get indicted and you want to go home, hire somebody like me."

"They want to kill me," he said.

He got no argument from me. He was absolutely right. The attorney general was up for reelection, and he was in political trouble. Billy Ryan was a sitting duck. As the late Irvin S. Cobb said of resting waterfowl, levelling his shotgun at them: "Of course I'm going to shoot them now. You don't think I'm gonna wait 'till they get up, do you?"

I said: "Yup."

He said: "You gonna stop 'em?"

I said: "Yup."

"Is that a promise?" he said.

"Close's as I get to one," I said. "I'll do the best I can for you. If I boot it, I boot it, and you go to jail. I don't."

He did not say anything. He looked like I might be on my way to getting to him, but I wasn't sure I was there yet.

"Look," I said, "there's no point in me kidding you here. All I know about the case is what Colin told me. But I know something about Mike Dunn. He's been a prosecutor ever since he got admitted to the bar. That was almost twenty years ago. That's at least twelve, maybe thirteen years more than a man can spend heaving folks in jail without having his judgment impaired, and Mike is no exception. If he wasn't righteous when he started, he sure is righteous now.

"There're only three things that he thinks about at least five times every day. I'm not sure what the other two are—probably his personal ambitions and how to accomplish them—but I know damned straight certain what the first one is, and so does every other lawyer who's defended a case he brought. It's that Saint Michael the Archangel realized sometime ago he hadn't finished the job when he booted the Devil and our first parents out of the Garden of Eden, so he got God to create Michael Dunn and send him down here to finish the job on the evildoers.

"The trouble is that Mike's brain's otherwise in very good shape. The first Saint Michael didn't bring a prosecution that he thought he might lose, and so when his self-anointed successor gets an indictment, you can bet the family jewels he doesn't think he's going to lose.

"That means the only prayer we've got is either to find something in what he's got that blows his case out of the water —and the chances of that are not good, because he's very thorough; you can bet he's mock-tried this whole thing to that grand jury, and decided that he'll win—or find something that he didn't get that does the same kind of damage."

Colin cleared his throat. "And how do you see the prospects in that line, Jerry," he said most deferentially.

"About the same as I see the ones of winning the state lottery," I said. "It happens. But it doesn't happen to many people, and when it's you going in by yourself, and having to win this particular jackpot, well, I wouldn't risk more'n a buck."

Billy Ryan was over seventy years old that day. "So I have to trust you," he said. He sounded almost vulnerable. Colin looked relieved. So, then, I did have him. Billy was a tough old bird, and I could imagine how much trouble Colin'd had to bring him to this point. But Billy was still an *old* bird. "What do I have to do? Just stay out of your way and keep quiet?"

"If that's what you do," I said, "we'll lose. Guarantee it. No, what you have to do from here on out is tell me the truth, the real and complete truth, no matter what I may ask you. And if what I ask you reminds you of something else that I would've asked you if I'd known, tell me what that is, too."

He sighed. "When do we start?" he said.

"We've already started," I said. "We started just now. So now I want Colin outta here. We're old friends, and I like him, but he's a judge, not a client, and I'm not in the habit of advising judges."

Colin cleared his throat. "No problem here," he said. "I do want to say one thing before I leave, though. Andy Keats's drawn the case, and he's made it known he plans to keep it."

When troubles come, they come not in single numbers, but battalions.

Four years later, Billy was dead, and I was driving Teddy Franklin to Norwich.

FIVE

It had been a mild winter for southern New England. The slopes on both sides of Route 495 mixed tawny grass and evergreen trees in a sunlit combination that suggested late April more than the reality of mid-March. Northbound traffic was light at 8:15 on Thursday morning, and I kept my new maroon Thunderbird SC steady at seventy-five, controlling it with my left hand.

"I suppose," Teddy Franklin said, "I suppose a learned counsellor like you doesn't have to worry about meeting up with cops that didn't hear they put the limit back to sixty-five, so seventy-five's okay. I suppose if you run across one, and he pulls you over, all you got to do is tell him it's okay. 'Hey, I am Jerry Kennedy, a learned counsellor of law. Apparently you didn't hear it's back to sixty-five, so ten more'n that's okay.' And he will say: 'Excuse me, counsellor. Didn't recognize you. Got yourself a new car, I see. Nice-lookin' suit, too. Tie, must've gone you good fifty. Got the monogram on the shirt cuff, I see. And you used to look like a bum. Hey, things must be going good again. Hope I didn't hold you up too much. Have a real nice day.' "

"You know what your problem is, Teddy," I said. "Your problem's that you're so illegal, most the time, for doing real bad things, you spend all your time on edge and the small stuff makes you nervous. This car is mine, all right? It belongs to me. By the time the lease ends, and I've worn the thing out, I will've handed over seventeen thousand American dollars for the lawful right to do it. I've got papers that prove this. If some cop pulls me over and says I've been a bad boy, the worst that he can do to me is write me up a ticket. Not like if he pulls you over when you're moving something quick, and he doesn't buy your story so you have to call me from the station. So relax."

Teddy shifted position. "Well," he said, "I can't relax, you know? I never can relax when somebody else's driving. It's the same when I'm with Dottie. When she thinks I'm stiff or something so she has to drive. Dottie's a good driver, and I know it and I trust her, but I still get just as jumpy. Because I'm not in control. I like to think: Well, if things get screwed up, I'm the guy that screwed them. If I could screw them up, then I can unscrew them. Whereas if someone else screws up, I'm not sure I can. I should've met you out there. I should've said: 'Don't think so, Jerry. You just go ahead. You go to your funeral, and I'll meet you at court.'"

"Not a good idea," I said. "You show up at court by yourself, someone's going to see you. They'll have someone *there* whose job's to see you. And the first thing that he'll do is run the numbers on it, plates and VIN, see if what you showed up in's got a bright history of its own."

"My de Ville's all right," Teddy said. "I bought that bastard new, and perfectly legit. They could run that thing to Wednesday. Nothing wrong with it."

"Which would just annoy them more," I said. "And then maybe instead of the grand jury just asking you some questions about Carlo, they also ask you where you got the cash to buy that car. Don't give 'em ideas when you don't have to, all right? You're a witness this time. Just doing your civic duty. But the only reason that you're one is because so far that DA doesn't have a hook to hang you on. Help you shouldn't give him."

" 'Carlo,' " Teddy said. He laughed. " 'Carlo,' 'Carlo,' 'Carlo.' All these years they're chasing Carlo. All these years he's laughing. I see Carlo one night, down in Providence. Me'n Dottie're having dinner, and Carlo comes in with some guys. Three guys and maybe three broads. Guys I never see. And I say to him, he comes over the table, 'Hey, Carlo, the hell you doin'?' The usual crap, you know? And he says that these broads're his niece and his sisters, or maybe it's nieces and sister, and the guys that're with them, their husbands. It's some kind of a family thing there. And I say to him: 'Jesus Christ, Carlo, what're you doing? These people know what they're doin'? The cops're all over you all of the time, and now they see you with them? They're gonna be saying, tomorrow morning, there's a whole new Mafia now.

" 'Carlo from Worcester's expanding. And now there's three dames around with him. Probably starting up whorehouses now. Ruin these ladies' reputations. Fine kind of uncle you are.' And he gets a laugh out of that.

" 'It won't bother them if it does,' he says, 'Teddy, they know all this stuff. They're like you and me—they know how it is with the cops and the crooks. Both kinds of guys make mistakes. But the thing of it is, the cops' one is always the same one, and their favorite now is with me: "He's the boss." Which both of us know is a laugh.' "

"The cops don't think it's a laugh, Edmund," I said. "The cops've been chasing Carlo now ever since they spotted him with some heavy hitters at the Marciano-Charles fight. And he hasn't disappointed them once. He still holds their interest, and he will until he's dead. Or one of these grand juries finally says: 'He's nailed. Now go get a new guy.' "

"I know that," Teddy said, "and Carlo knows it too. But that's what he was saying, right? Today I'm going out there because they are doing cars, and they know that I'm in cars. They can't prove it, but they know. And so they figure: 'If it's cars, Franklin must know, so we will haul him in here and say: "Okay, Franklin, spill your guts, or you go in the jug." ' Which scares me half to death, I piss my pants about it. And I say: 'I don't know from cars. What is this "cars" thing?' And they say, very serious: 'Don't jerk us around here. We know it's cars, and it's Worcester, so Carlo's running it. Carlo runs everything in Worcester, and he's going to the can.' Which makes Carlo piss his pants, just like I am doing. They think it's Carlo because they've always thought it's Carlo. They always think: 'Well, there's a boss. A guy who's in charge here. Somebody with the power.'

"And they're always right; there is. Just like some Cadillacs disappear, but any time a cop spotted me in a Cadillac, it's always been my Cadillac. And the next time he sees me in a Cad, he ignores me.

"Carlo's the man's Cadillac. They see Carlo, they don't spot the man. The thing they never realize is: it's not the Cad they see, and it's not the guy they see. It's never the guy they see. It's just like every other thing—there's someone running it, and they're always watching for him. The man knows this. First thing he did, he started running it, was get himself another guy, that they can always see. And Carlo is his guy. The guy that Carlo works for: Carlo is his guy. So, they *never* see the guy. *I* never see the guy. I know who he is, sure, but *see* him? No. They bumped into him, the drugstore, *they* would not see him even then. They would say: 'Oh, pardon us.' And then they would say: 'Do you by any chance know Carlo?' And he would just look at them, and say: 'I come in here for some rubbers. Who's this Carlo guy? I never heard of him.' And then they would go running off, looking for Carlo, because they don't know anything, and it would all stay the same. And that's all it is. All it is."

I had met Carlo by then. I met him one night right after I'd taken Billy's case and I'd put in a very long day at the office. The phone rang around 9:15, and it was Teddy. "*Counsellor*," he said, and I said: "Oh Jesus."

"No, no," Teddy said, "Got no problem. Just, I'm in town, had a couple things to do, couple guys to see, and I just finish up, and I'm hungry. Have some dinner with me. This isn't business at all."

I put him off. "Teddy," I said, "Like I told you, I'm still up to my knees in transcripts here." By then I'd received the Ryan grand jury transcripts from Mike Dunn, and I'd found some troubling stuff. If all of Dunn's witnesses stuck to their stories, we were in for a hard time at trial. "I can't go to dinner with you."

"Jerry, Jerry," Teddy said, "you gotta eat, right? You're not gonna get this guy Ryan off anytime before midnight tonight. Meet me at Tessio's, just down the street, we'll have some veal and some wine."

I was hungry. I was tired, too, and the fact was I wasn't likely to accomplish much more that night. Tessio's had very good veal. I'd been there many times with my late buddy Weldon Cooper. I went and I met Teddy. He had a semicircular banquette. He was wearing a sharp black suit and a white shirt and a narrow maroon tie. He looked like your basic well-to-do hood. "Teddy," I said, when I sat down, "we've got to do something about your clothes."

"What, my clothes," he said. "My clothes're fine. Your clothes looked like you slept in them." This was true. Improvement of the wardrobe had been on my list since Billy Ryan'd hired me. I just hadn't gotten around to it. "We're gonna have some wine," Teddy said, pouring a glass for me from the Chianti Classico Riservo bottle, "and then we're gonna have some veal, and talk about things, and you're not gonna mention the late wife and stuff. I'm tired of hearing about her. Just your cases, or what's on your mind."

"Or on yours," I said.

"Nothing on mine," Teddy said. "Nothing on mine except dinner." And that was when Carlo came up.

"*Carlo*," Teddy said. He stood up as much as possible in the quarters that confined us and stuck out his hand. Carlo wore a medium-grey striped flannel double-breasted suit, custom-fitted to his narrow waist, and a custom-made white shirt that set off his Caribbean tan beautifully. "*Teddy*," he said, offering a display of perfectly capped teeth.

"I'd like to present," Teddy said, flourishing his left hand, "my learned counsellor, Jeremiah F. Kennedy."

I stood up as much as I could and extended my hand. "Jerry Kennedy," I said. "Nice to meet you."

Carlo bowed. "Carlo Donato," he said. He took my hand in both of his and regarded me for a moment. "Teddy says you're all right," he said. "Says you did a nice job for a cop we know, just like you always helped him."

I was becoming uncomfortable. I was not aware I'd ever done a nice thing for a cop on the Mafia pad. "Teddy's not to be trusted," I said. "He gets everything wrong. I like most of the cops, except for the wrong ones, but I play on the opposite team." And my work is easier because the cops tell me things they wouldn't tell a lawyer who was on the Mob's pad himself. House counsel for the wise guys is not a job I want.

Teddy smirked at Carlo. "His memory's goin', Carlo," he said. "He still does good work for me, but the black cop he doesn't remember." He grinned at me. "The black cop with the bat? Remember that cop? The one with the Christmas bat?"

"Oh yeah," I said, "the brutality cop. Yeah. Now I remember."

"And I sent you him," Teddy said, "and you got him off. I told Carlo you did a good job."

Carlo shook his head. "And that's another thing you must've forgot," he said to me. "You can always trust Teddy. Teddy trusts you, says you're a very fine lawyer, and you've done very good things for him. And also he tells me that you've got a very big case coming up in the very near future. Hope you do well in it."

Teddy and I've been working successfully together for so many years that he's taken a proprietary interest in my career. Takes an interest in all of my cases. And in me, as far as that goes. As I do, of course, in his career, and also, I guess, in him. Dangerous business, having clients for friends, but if you got a little short of friends and went and did it, you should not embarrass them afterwards in front of their other friends and associates. "I'll do my best," I said, hoping that by being agreeable with this Italian film star I'd be able to get my hand back.

Carlo pressed it. "A friend of Teddy's is a friend of ours," he said. Important distinction there: he called me a friend of Teddy's, not a friend of the friends, but apparently by keeping Teddy out of the sneezer, I'd acquired some surrogate privileges I didn't know about. "If we can ever be of any help, well, you just let us know." Teddy beamed.

"Thank you," I said. Carlo nodded. He released my hand. When he had left us, Teddy said: "Very nice guy, Carlo. You could see he liked you." I did not say what I thought, then or afterwards.

"When we get out to Worcester today," I said, "I'd like it if you didn't see fit to explain all that Carlo stuff. What dumb clucks you think they all are. When you're in that room today. Just let 'em think what they want to think, all right? Humor the nice folks in Worcester. Answer the questions truthfully, you know the drill, just like all the other times. And just like all the other times, we'll be out of there in time to drive back to

Framingham, have ourselves a soothing drink and a nice steak at Ken's there, on Route Nine."

"You're paying," Teddy said. "For the grand jury thing, I'm paying you, but for the funeral, you're buying dinner."

"What about your witness fee?" I said. "You're getting mileage to Worcester, and you're going out in my car, and I'm the one buying dinner? Should go the other way."

Teddy settled in the seat. "I hadda get up early for this ride," he said. "I'm not used to being up this early if I've been to bed. And so I can go to church? Okay, this friend of yours is dead—he's not a friend of mine. That's why you're buying dinner."

"He wasn't a friend of mine," I said. "He was a client of mine. One I needed pretty badly when he signed up with me. It's his son that's my friend. That's why I have to go. Because my friend trusted me, and sold his father on it, and now the old boy's dead, and I have to see him off. Besides, nobody said you have to go into the church. You can stay in the car while I go."

"And do what?" Teddy said. "Play with myself while everybody else's inside, probably praying against me? No, I don't know these assholes, and that means I'm not letting them out of my sight one minute while I'm there."

"Well," I said, "that's also all right, too. Won't do you any harm, your infidel way of life, see how good people live. Might even convert you."

"Yeah," Teddy said, "well, if you're gonna do that, I wished you'd've converted me a little closer to home. Where the hell's this place, anyway? I never heard of it. I thought I heard of every jerk town between Providence and Montreal, but I never heard of this one. Who lives there, anyway? Indians and stuff? Guys with feather hats and hatchets, measuring my scalp?"

"It's about twenty-five, thirty, miles from Worcester," I said. " 'Bout the same from where we are. No one's ever heard of Norwich except people who come from there. Not nowadays at least. They used to hear about it, fifty, sixty years ago, back when Norwich Gear and the textile mills were booming. Big quarry business, too—lots of granite gravestones and big buildings still around, made from Norwich granite. But now the gearworks is closed down; too much foreign competition. The textile mills went south. The buildings were converted into yuppie condos; the young kids work out on the Pike in the electronics racket, come home every night to live cheap and drink white wine. What happened to the granite business, I don't know: guess nobody puts up granite buildings anymore, and they couldn't get by on just headstones. Maybe so many people left, not enough stayed to die."

"Well," Teddy said, "but your client did, right?"

"Only in a manner of speaking," I said. "Norwich for the last two-thirds of his life or so wasn't really where he lived—it was just the place he left every morning to go to Boston or out on the road; that was where Billy did his living. Don't get me wrong: it's pretty enough, nice town in a river basin, pretty hilly, can be steep, but there are some nice old houses, put up when there was some money, and most of the people who live in them are fourth, fifth generation. Lots of trees, quiet streets; cleancut kids who play ball, and the girls're majorettes and cheerleaders. Two Catholic churches, one for Irish, one for Not: you can get which one is grander, though Colin tells me 'Not for long.' Not many Jews. Some Protestants. A few minorities, but not many: it doesn't have any blue-collar jobs to offer, really, and it's too far from Boston for the really low-paid workers.

"So it's a sort of a backwater, I guess," I said. "Billy died there because it was the normal course of things for people of his generation. He was born there, went to school there, spent most nights of his life sleeping in the same house where his mother gave him birth—where else would he go to die? You'd've asked him how come he was dying back in Norwich, that's about what he would've told you 'Where the hell else would I?

I've been there all my life. You want me to go on a long trip just before I take the last, short one?"

"Well," Teddy said, "if you didn't win that case, which you didn't think you could, that was what he would've done. All expenses paid, room, board and everything. And he probably wouldn't've been out in time to go home when it was his turn came up to die, 'less he got a deathbed commutation. You did a lot of hard work to save him, Jerry, so he *was* home when he died. You shouldn't leave that out."

"Thanks," I said. "I was lucky."

"It wasn't luck, Jerry," Teddy said. "It wasn't luck at all."

SIX

As many times as I have been to the old New Courthouse at Pemberton Square—a great many, I can assure you—I have never ceased to be newly impressed and depressed by my surroundings. There's something daunting about having your case called in the Fourth Criminal Session of Suffolk Superior Court in the late-afternoon grey chill of a false-spring day, even when it's just the first of the preliminary stages. Dunn's office had already sent the indictment over to me, so that while there never had been any doubt but that I would waive the reading at arraignment, and Billy would say "Not guilty," the rest of the business that gathered us together that afternoon was strictly *pro forma*, too. For the lawyers, at least, just lawyering around in the customary way.

Still, although I'd made sure Billy understood all this, the surroundings and proceedings were sufficiently sombre to subdue even him. It's one thing to pick up rumors that you ought to be indicted, or are even going to be; Billy'd been hearing such reports about himself for most of his life, and although he didn't enjoy the gossip, he'd gotten used to it. And when the news came out, two days after I'd seen Billy for the first time as

43

a client, he still had a slender reed to grasp. There was still nothing he had then seen; there had been no court proceeding that would make it official to him that he was at last in the soup. Intellectually, of course, he knew it, but in his guts he could still deny it, think it all might go away, and defendants cling to that. But this was the day he had to confront his personal monster in person, and he didn't like it a bit.

All the courtrooms in Suffolk are stark, none ever more so than when Andrew Keats, associate justice, austerely presides, conveying by his bleak and dangerous countenance the desolation of the hour in which your client finds himself—in case it hasn't already crossed his mind. Andy once judged a case in which the defendant, a triggerman for the Mafia unjustly famous far beyond his actual exploits, appeared for sentencing on a plea on the sixty-seventh anniversary of his birth. He was already doing two lives, on-and-after, which gave him a prospective parole date roughly coinciding with his ninety-second birthday; Andy gave him another one, on-and-after the first two. "Your Honor," the defendant wailed, "I'm an old man. I can't do that much time." And Andy, sweeping off the bench, said: "Do the best you can."

My only substantial purpose in that room that first court day of Billy's was to file a motion for a bill of particulars. I had other motions—bail and that sort of thing—but I didn't expect the AG's office to resist them; for the particulars I'd have to give some reasons, and Mike Dunn or his minion would most likely make a fuss.

For the uninitiated: the bill of particulars is what you ask for when the prosecutor's been sensible and held down the indictment to the fewest possible words, thus limiting his exposure to its peremptory dismissal for failure to state an offense, while at the same time committing himself to proving no more facts than the minimum required. If the evidence is going to show that your client killed another fellow with a machine-gun, which is hard to do by accident, your crafty prosecutor is going to allege that your client did assault and beat the victim by means of a .45 calibre Thompson submachine gun (or Mac10, or Uzi, or AK47), and by said assault and battery did kill and murder him. It's up to you to ask exactly where they say he did it; what time of day or night; who saw it, if anybody did; and if the commonwealth has any evidence at all as to why on earth your client would get it into his fool head to blow another guy's head off.

In other words, you're doing the best you can to hem in your adversary. But he knows this, so you'd better be careful when you put those questions; more than one shrewd prosecutor has taken an opening provided by the defendant's motion for a bill of particulars and used it to allege a whole mess of gory detail that he never would've dared to put in the indictment, thus not only prejudicing prospective jurors—who always say, when trial time comes, they know nothing of the case though they "read something about it"—and making sure that when the actual jurors are impanelled, they will hear not only the murder charge, but the prosecutor's thoughtful gloss that the homicide was committed in "the usual gangland fashion." The stuff in the particulars that you ask for later on gets read to the jury.

The indictment in the case of *Commonwealth* v. *William F. Ryan*, et al., (those "others" being "John Doe, Richard Roe, and others to the grand jurors unknown, a prosecuting ploy to protect the commonwealth's flanks against the unlikely possibility that the defense might confuse the jury by showing that others not charged might have had some part in the wickedness) was about as straightforward as the form of the art permits. It alleged that Billy, being a "state employee" within the meaning of Massachusetts General Laws, chapter 268A, section 1 (q), serving with compensation as Commissioner of the Department of Public Works, "did directly and indirectly and corruptly ask, demand, exact, solicit, seek, accept, receive and agree to receive something of substantial value for himself and other persons and entities unknown to the grand jurors, for and because of an official act and an act within his official responsibility performed or to be performed by him, all in violation of MGL Ch. 268A, Sec. 3 (d)." Some other sections were mentioned as well.

The criminal statutes are alleged conjunctively—every possible way of violating the specific law is charged—but read disjunctively: if the defendant is proven to have committed an official act, *or* an act within his official responsibility, he's dead meat.

That pretty much covered it. Reduced to terms (Billy was also charged with conspiring with the other folks to do the things he was charged with doing, ballast for the main charges —if they got him on either it was as good for them as if they hooked him on both, because the punishment would be the same), Mike Dunn and his assistants had persuaded the grand jury to agree that Billy Ryan had engineered construction of a new four-lane road through Colchester. Colchester is—was—a wide spot in the road southwest of Worcester. No backwater town with a population of eight thousand or so, surrounded by eight square miles of wetlands, woods and land too poor to farm, except for the profit motives of Billy Ryan and his chums, has any need for a four-lane state road. But because Billy and his pals did have those motives, and had made damned straight sure they and their straws owned options on all the land abutting the accesses to and from that four-lane, Colchester was going to get that new road. The old rule still holds: if some official decision seems irrational, the first thing to do is find out whether somebody involved in its manufacture got some money out of it. If someone did, then others did, and then the sweet reason is clear.

As soon as the word of the new road got out, not one moment before they wanted it to circulate, Billy and his sidekicks promptly made their options available to developers, who snapped them up at prices that would've been laughable six months before. It was, as my late friend Mike Curran, unelected mayor of the Irish Riviera, once put it, "a classic middle." Either the purchasers declined a sure thing, because they had principles, knew what was going on, and would have no part of it (in which event they could look forward to watching their competitors grab the deals and become richer than they were, thus becoming stronger competitors), or they rose above principle and jumped at what was offered, knowing that as their own bank balances improved, their competition would necessarily become relatively weaker.

That was precisely how Billy Ryan, who'd never sought any elective office or any other appointive one, had gained his considerable power over the men—there weren't many women engaged in politics in his heyday, and if there had been, he would've made them beholden to him, too—who sought high office and obtained it. Andy Keats, slyly smiling from his perch, had gotten there by combining years of diligent collaboration with, and one day of miscalculation by, Billy, and it rankled me to see him gloating up here in his robe. He concealed most of it pretty well, but what showed was quite enough. Satisfaction's hard to take, unless you're the one who's taking it.

"Mister Kennedy," he said, and I stood up. "Your Honor," I said.

"Mister Kennedy," he said, "I am granting your motion for particulars in its entirety. Commonwealth will have ten days to comply." Mike Dunn and his deputy nodded and made notes, sensibly offering no bootless argument. I'd expected to get my motion granted, but not without a fight. That tactic lulled me into inattentiveness. "Your Honor," I said, "my next motion is for names and addresses of potential witness."

The passage of time tricks us all. We don't notice it happening. Mike Dunn had done more than proceed from appointed AUSA chasing Nunzio to election as attorney general of the

commonwealth in the years since we'd last collided. He'd gone
from being the smug little bastard of those days, product of an
upbringing much like Andy Keats's, husband of a wife just as
glossy and father of some polished children destined to be just
like the two of them, to being the polished and composed
young politician of today. Mike then was by no means stupid,
and he isn't stupid now. But *I'd* been a little stupid: I may have
warned Billy what Dunn was, but I seemed to've forgotten it
myself.

Smart people learn, and Mike's smart. He hadn't learned
how not to be smug, or how to avoid looking down upon the
lesser breeds without the law—in which category he reflexively
at one time included all lawyers representing them—but he'd
learned how to conceal his smugness and contempt. The process could not have been easy for him, since he'd acquired his
attitude of superiority during his early days as assistant United
States attorney by subpoenaing three of the defense bar before
the grand jury to grill them on the subject of where their (dirty
drug-smuggling) clients had gotten the lucre to pay them. This
provoked a great commotion and uproar about the Bill of Rights
—tar and feathers were mentioned; a rail was ordered up—but
he survived it, profited, and learned.

I doubt very much that he really moderated his views after
that frog-gigging, but thereafter he stifled them in his public
utterances. When he left the great grey building down in Post
Office Square to seek his party's nomination as attorney general, he was as cagey a rookie candidate as a blue suit ever fitted.
None of us who'd seen him up close and personal doubted for
an instant he believed he was destined to be governor, if indeed
he had to settle for so minor an office, but publicly in his first
campaign he'd convinced a bedizened majority that he sought
the AG's office purely out of goodness of heart and humility,
honesty, and just a smidgeon of *noblesse oblige*. There's nothing

our surly Massachusetts yeomen like better than a candidate who confidently begs for their votes on the ground that he's better than they are, and if you don't believe that, look at the pluralities racked up in the commonwealth by my unrelated kinfolk of the same surname.

Billy Ryan was Mike Dunn's next stepping-stone to Bigger Things. This meant there were at least three dynamics under way in Billy's case, only one of which was described in the indictment charging him with illegal finagling. The second was Mike's virtuous effort To Stamp Out Corruption, root and bloody branch. The manner was more subdued; there was a tinge of grey distinguishing the temples; but inside that finely tailored suit and muscled body, there still breathed the soul of Nemesis, Crusader Goddamned Rabbit. Mike'd gotten older, and he'd gotten wiser, too, but he was still opposed to sin, and disapproved of evil. The only difference between his old fangs-bared style and the way he was nicing me to death in Billy Ryan's case was his newfound suspicion that he might have more success by putting me to sleep than he'd had by goading me.

Now, you must pardon me. As Billy'd perceptively noted, and Colin had forthrightly said, I didn't look like a helluva lot when I took Billy's case. My former wife used to call me the classiest sleazy criminal lawyer in Boston, and then when we were getting divorced and fuses proved shorter than expected, she dropped the part about classiest. So be it. When I visited my stylish daughter and her trendy husband the first time, out in Colorado (it was a very short visit—one dinner was enough to suit me, and I made up an urgent matter that demanded I go home), I could see the pair of them storing up anecdotes for the slurping delectation of their prosperous friends; it was like they had Doc Holliday coming in for a weekend, tubercular as hell but still a pretty decent shot, "beat the hell out of the booze, said something about how he hadda meet Wyatt down by the OK Corral, and then he took off again. Like we figured he would."

I know they thought that and most likely still do, being too far away to've kept up on recent improvements, but frankly, my dear, as Rhett Butler should've said and didn't, I really didn't give a shit, and I'm not sure I really do now. If I have to finish my life without more than a perfunctory personal life—and the way I live, in the company I keep, that's the way to bet—well, that's the way it goes. I guess I wasn't put here in the husband-father role. I was put upon this earth to be an advocate. If I had represented the commonwealth *against* Billy Ryan, I would've gone at it the same way I did when I was on his side, balls-to-the-wall, and fought with every son of a bitch in sight who tried to say me Nay as I tried to send him away. When I represent a client now, whenever I have represented a client, I go into the courtroom all by myself, and I stand there in my rumpled suit—better suits rumple too, or at least they do on me—and evil temper, representing the noblest document ever drafted by the hand of man, and by God I know it.

Okay, this is boasting. But it's also what I believe. If you get in trouble, and you hire me, I will compel the serried ranks of government, row on row and rank on rank, to turn square corners and to prove that what they say you did, you did. Especially if I'm pretty sure you did it but suspect that they can't prove it. Thomas Jefferson and his chums back in the eighteenth century said that no man—we call them "persons" now—shall be deprived of life, liberty or property, without due process of law, and by the great horned spoon, if you hire me, you are going to get duly processed. They may hang you by the neck until you are dead, but when the trap springs, if you have any decency, sir, you will choke out the endorsement that I did my job for you.

The difficulty with that approach in Billy Ryan's case, given

Mike Dunn's new posture as the soul of fairness and so forth, was that the more I asked for, by way of discovery, the more he was willing to give. When I asked for the names of potential witnesses, he not only handed the list to me as I alluded to my motion, but when I subsided in momentary confusion he begged the court's indulgence to interject as well the common-wealth's voluntary provision of the statements made by the wit-nesses as well. I would be entitled to them, of course, but not until the buggers had taken the stand at the trial, and repeated them. He walked over to the defense table while he was still talking and put them on it in front of me, along with the grand jury transcripts, also mine by right to see, but not at the arraign-ment.

By furnishing them early, Mike was telling me something: he'd taken his case down to sixty fathoms and inflated it to test for leaks, and no bubbles had come up. This was intimidation of the very slickest kind, and also a neat finesse of any tactic I might use to claim prejudicial pretrial publicity—if something somehow found its way into the hands of the slavering media, Mike would be comfortably able to remind the press and court that his office was no longer the only repository of those confi-dential documents: "the defense has them as well."

He volunteered as well that two of the witnesses, including John Bonaventre, had undergone polygraph examinations, and that while he realized that results of those tests were not admis-sible in court, he was turning copies of them over to me. "The commonwealth has conducted no scientific tests," he said. "We are not in possession of any *Brady* material," evidence that would tend to show the defendant did not commit the crime, also mine by right, "but, of course, remain cognizant of our continuing obligation to provide it immediately to the defense, should any turn up." His smooth expression implied he ex-pected that to happen right after Jupiter collides with Mars. He completed his "interjection" by thanking the court for its time, pointing out that he hoped to have saved some by his performance, and sat down before I finished gaping.

Billy was a rookie at being a defendant, and he therefore lacked my grasp of what Mike Dunn had done to us. He just knew something was wrong. Back at my office he probed for the reason.

"It's very simple," I said. "He's sweating us to death. It's intimidation. There're two ways of going about it. The first way's to come on like a mad dog, so the other guy, if it works, gets the idea you'll give him rabies if he gets in your way. The other way's the route that Mike Dunn took today. The idea's to discourage us by showing us he's so confident we might as well fold up."

"Did it work?" Billy said. He was old, but he looked very young and lonely when he said that.

"Nope," I said. "The guy who prosecuted Larry White pulled exactly the same stunt on me. Handed me the whole file and dared me to get Larry off. And you know what happened in that case. I did. Look at it this way: Dunn's overconfident. You know what pride goeth before."

He left the office looking downcast, though, his own pride having gone before his formal fall, two days earlier, right in that same chair.

SEVEN

I did work hard on that case, just as Teddy said on the day of Billy's funeral. I worked damned hard, defending Billy Ryan, even by my own high standards. Mike Dunn was scarily serene. To beat him I'd need all the wattage I could muster, all generators at full capacity. The depressing thing was that the more work I did, the less progress I seemed to make.

I started with the statements of witnesses, given to the cops before they were paraded in before the grand jury where the transcripts were made, to find out what Mike Dunn had. And also, of course, whether any of the statements, compared to the testimony, showed that Mike and his staff had done a bit of missionary work between those two occasions to increase the zeal of the civilians. Until I'd slogged through what Dunn gave me, I really didn't know what to ask my client.

I didn't really expect that Billy would honor his promise to me: fully answer every question that I put, and volunteer the information that I didn't know enough to ask for. No client does that, no matter what the case, partly because few clients have any professional experience to tell them when something important to a trial has been left out or overlooked, and partly because what they'd really like to do is deny the whole thing is happening. But Billy presented an even more troublesome problem. Billy was charged with corruption.

I suppose that at one time or another in the course of criminal events there must have been a defendant in a corruption case who did not bitterly deem his indictment an outrageous abuse of authority committed by a cynical and power-crazed prosecutor, bent on advancement of his own career by sacrifice of another man's good name and reputation. I suppose this is because one of the things you learn over the course of some years at the criminal defense bar is that if a given act, no matter how reckless, dangerous, foolish or vicious, is possible, someone somewhere either has committed it, is about to commit it, or is making plans to do it later on. So it stands to reason that some defendant in a bribery case must have admitted to himself, if not to his lawyer, that he got hooked because the lawmen caught him taking illegal gratuities. But he was not my client, and I have never met him.

Robbers, murderers, thieves and even rapists will occasionally confide they have been caught fair and square—usually after they've gotten away with many similar prohibited acts over the course of several years, and long since philosophically calculated the risk of someday getting bagged—but corruption clients I have known can never bring themselves to take that long view. Private or public corruption: it doesn't matter whether they evaded the Fair Campaign Practices Act, Section X–10–B5 of the Securities Act (insider-trading), or trafficked in public offices. They're always, as they often say, shocked and appalled when they're charged. And, believe it or not, they really are.

It's partly because they are inexperienced, not at being naughty, but at being caught at it. They are, after all, almost invariably first offenders. A man who's been convicted of selling out a position of trust usually doesn't get another one (and thus a second chance to steal something bigger, but do it a little smarter with the benefit of the hard practice). They genuinely don't think of themselves as crooks. They mislead themselves with their own spotless reputations. In their own minds they are as upright and honest as their colleagues, friends and associates, not to mention their lawyers. When humble's called for, huffy's what the lawyer gets (which can be very trying).

But it's all understandable enough because those defendants usually are pretty much fungible with the happy-go-lucky people they see all the time, and have drinks with. It's just that their peers, doing exactly the same sort of thing, but being luckier or craftier at it, haven't gotten caught.

This is a crucial distinction. They've been proceeding on the public perception of themselves as honest men. Not on their actual integrity. When the perception changes—this happens when they get indicted—well, that makes all the difference. Existentially speaking, the new defendant the day after his indictment is not different from the man he was the day before, and he tends to be indignant that people seem to think he is, diminished and used up.

Billy Ryan was no exception. To him, a criminal lawyer was a rather shifty fellow whom you secured, through your son who was acquainted with such questionable fellows, to get a clumsy pal off the hook for something he'd stupidly done, or at least been charged with doing. It was one thing for him to summon Colin to draft me to get Larry White off the hook when all eight members of his pack of Cub Scouts simultaneously contracted virulent cases of the same sort of hysterical delusions that prompted little girls in seventeenth-century Salem to denounce innocent women as witches and thus managed to get them executed; Larry, after all, wasn't very bright. He looked like the kind of earnest, bumbling but good-hearted kind of guy you'd expect to find at the peak of his career sorting mail in the Norwich Post Office, working part-time as an undertaker's assistant in the McGillicuddy & Kilduff funeral home, and taking an active part in the life of his community by acting as a scoutmaster and assistant coach of Little League.

In Billy's mind that stood to reason. Sooner or later, he figured, Larry would be punished for one or more of his good works. The only questions on the point would be when it would happen and what would be the pretext. I do think Billy was mildly startled when the charges against Larry turned out to be child molestation, and I don't think Billy ever believed he'd actually gone and bothered the little kids, but I'm also certain Billy figured something bad was sure to happen to Larry before he reached the finish line, and if that was it, well, there it was.

Billy had never believed anything bad would ever happen to *him*. He'd gone through a long life cutting shady deals with pals on Beacon Hill (I knew more about his operations than he dreamed I did, because Tommy Grogan worked "closely" with Billy when Tommy was a state rep from Lynn years ago, before he became a lobbyist, and often became resentful over drinks at The Last Hurrah in the basement of the Parker House when he spoke of arrangements Billy had made with other reps, whereby they made a lot of money) and he had decided that he must be immortal.

Until the deal that landed Billy in my custody, he'd been right. He'd engineered no deals before that had enabled someone to say "gotcha." He sat there in my office after Colin left and said: "This's all political."

In the law we have what's known as the doctrine of collateral estoppel: you can't sue me when my dog gets loose and bites you if you've already let your dog run loose and he's bitten me. For Billy Ryan to denounce any action as "political" was akin to Mary Magdalene accusing some other woman of having loose morals.

For decades he'd protected his budget at the DPW by giving highly reliable real-estate investment tips to members of the Ways and Means, and Public Works committees on what plots of undeveloped land would be likely to appreciate remarkably when new state roads were built. That meant the new roads got funded and built, and the reps and the senators prospered. It wasn't anything new, any more than Magdalene's trade is, but the reason such crafts've flourished so long is precisely because they work so well.

All you need to go into the corruption business is an obscure office that confers power on its occupant, and is habitually ignored by the media and public (there used to be more of those offices than there are now, since the Watergate uproar made so many reporters rich and famous). That and a firm grasp of the rule that forbids writing down what may be said, saying what may be whispered, or whispering what may be conveyed by a nod. Billy had both of those things: the office and the rule.

Billy's problem that February day when he came to my shabby office, knowing I'd become one hundred thousand dollars heavier after he'd parted with that same amount, was that Mike Dunn, harboring no personal animus toward Billy whatsoever, had compared the benefits he could probably secure by nailing Billy to the detriments Billy would incur by that action, and had decided charity began at home. Mike was not the first person to contemplate such action. Billy'd been around a long time and was a tempting target for most of it; the rumors of his avarice were not fresh when Colin and I were in law school, and they were not secret, either.

But Mike, as the documents told me, enjoyed an advantage that none of his prosecutorial predecessors had possessed: he had Jack Bonnie by the shorter hairs.

John Bonaventre was not a bad fellow, as Teddy Franklin would say: "A working stiff, same as us, out to make the odd buck here and there." The trouble was that he'd been in too much of a hurry to make a lot of bucks. Those birds are not trustworthy, but Billy with uncharacteristic negligence had trusted him.

I doubt it had been a rare bout of rashness on Billy's part. I don't know why it would have seemed to be. It probably seemed to Billy like a perfectly normal decision to him. It was just like dozens of others that had caused trouble for no one. Taking note of Jack Bonnie's then-ascending career in the hierarchy of the house, his membership on the Public Works Committee, his manifest good fellowship with the speaker and particularly strong bonhomie with the majority leader—"He was thicker'n thieves with Gary Duggan then," Billy said sourly, with unintentional irony—Billy'd "let him in on something that might turn out to be a pretty good deal."

He'd suggested to Jack that an option to purchase eighteen acres of a woodlot in Colchester, part of Jack's district in Worcester County, would prove a prudent investment. When the new road went through, and an interchange went in there, it proved indeed felicitous. Jack made 60K or so when the shopping-center plans were announced (what Billy raked in was a good deal more than that; I never did find out how much, but that was all right, because it was none of my business).

The difficulty began when Jack Bonnie reinvested his profits, those and others, on the street. He turned them over to one of Carlo's boss's liege men. That, too, was a decision that would have looked all right at the time, but turned out to be an error of judgment. It's one thing to place your capital with a shylock and collect twenty percent a week on small loans—somewhat illegal, yes, but okay if nobody gabs. It's another thing entirely to choose the wrong loanshark, one who talks when he's grabbed by the cops on unusually provable charges of losing his temper, and hurting a deadbeat so badly the man has been retired to a wheelchair.

Having nothing much left to lose, and what he saw as a disproportionate penalty for welshing on a thousand-dollar loan, the crippled debtor made his lamentations not to the local police but to the state police who investigated bad conduct for the

DA's office. They found his attitude reasonable; so did the DA and the grand jury.

Whereupon, the witness interviews and the transcripts showed Jack's partner, having gotten himself into the whole scrape by egregiously exceeding the authority indirectly delegated to him (by someone Carlo most likely knew well, conduct uncommon among members of that otherwise-well-run organization), again behaved in a manner unbecoming to his occupation: he talked.

But, not having lost complete command of his wits, he did not talk about Carlo; he talked about Jack. Jack at forty-two was not game as big as Carlo, the trophy that the DA and the cops had had in mind, but in his own right he was still worth—in publicity—the effort it would take to bring him down. So they swallowed their disappointment and scooped Jack.

Jack in his sleek middle age had thus found himself unexpectedly looking at several years of taking his sun in the exercise yard in the penitentiary instead of in the skipper's seat of the twin-dieseled sport-fisherman he docked down in Cataumet. The prospect did not appeal to him. He began to think about people whom he knew who had done bad things, or at least things forbidden by statute. So treachery was at the back of his mind one afternoon when, while out on bail, he had some business underneath the Golden Dome and just happened to encounter the AG in the corridor.

Mike Dunn, whatever his faults, has always been a good listener, especially when the person speaking to him seems to have a substantial amount of dirt to dump on some third party whose name is familiar not only to Mike but to the community at large. That willingness to listen attentively was serving Mike well when I first got to know him many years ago. Then an assistant United States Attorney, he liked best listening to people who mentioned Nunzio DiNapoli's name a lot. When one of them uttered the name of my accountant, Lou Schwartz, as a

potential fount of information about Nunzio's various enter-
prises in the Boston area, Mike'd taken a strong interest in Lou.

But, just as Jack Bonnie's business partner had felt a strong
disinclination to chat with the cops about Carlo, Lou for similar
reasons thought it inexpedient to exchange the prospect of
some years of confinement in the Federal Correctional Institu-
tion at Danbury, Conn., for what he felt certain would be
Nunzio's certain displeasure at any betrayal sufficient to send
Nunzio to the slammer (cite no witness protection programs to
me; it's true that any sane man, forced to a choice between
tipping in a guy who'll kill him, or doing hard time, indeed, will
bow his head and go for the program, but a rational man who
has a different, safer, kind of higher-up to swap, one who won't
shoot him—and most pols are lousy shots—but whose smooth
hide is the price of short time for the rat, will hesitate a moment; he will swap the hide at once. You want to change your
name and disappear for the rest of your life, go to it, but most
people don't. Lou took the professional's view—what you lose
on the swings you make up on the merry-go-round—and went
away for knowingly falsifying Nunzio's tax returns).

Mike Dunn, having parlayed his willingness to listen first
into promotion to United States Attorney, and then into election as attorney general; never having seen any reason to take a
more standoffish attitude toward nervous crooks; being acutely
aware the *Commoner* was ominously restive about what its col-
umnists declared to have been his rather meagre first-term tally
of political thieves; had been most interested in what Jack Bonnie had to say.

After Mike's state police debriefed Jack, and made some
inquiries that seemed to corroborate what Jack had muttered to
Mike, Mike had called up the Worcester County DA and (no
doubt cordially) offered him the choice of going easy on Jack
come disposition day, so that Jack would feel comfy chatting
first to the AG's grand jury and then to a petit jury about his

partnership with Billy, or of sitting helplessly in his Worcester office and watching while Mike invoked the AG's statutory power as the commonwealth's chief law enforcement officer to supersede any DA in the commonwealth in control of any case —in addition to his other talents, Mike is also very good at reading statutes, and not bad at all, when his newest job doesn't leave him time to read much law, at finding other ladies and gentlemen who can read statutes too—and then went easy on Jack himself.

The DA sensibly chose to accept Mike's offer of a cracker-jack press conference at which both of them bragged about the "joint investigation of corruption" they had shrewdly engi-neered. Jack Bonnie's day of sentencing—on pleas of guilty to some rather nasty charges of extortion, accessory before the fact of mayhem and so forth (that I projected could have netted close to forty years in on-and-afters, say, twenty-five to be served at Cedar Junction)—was relatively painless: five years concurrent on all charges (meaning: out in three, max). But *all but six months* were *suspended*. And those six months were not only to be spent in the House of Correction at West Boylston, far cheerier than fifty times six months in Cedar Junction hospi-tality, but deferred until after he performed his handsprings and cartwheels for Mike Dunn.

I have to say this for Mike Dunn: when he buys the horse, he makes sure he gets the whole horse. If Jackie sang pretty for Mike, that West Boylston vacation would be reconsidered, and Jackie was going to walk. Jack Bonnie had every reason in the world to do what Mike Dunn wanted, and say what Mike wanted said. And a whole bunch of reasons not to displease Mike. While I hadn't attended his dress rehearsal in front of the grand jury, there wasn't much doubt in my mind that he'd been in good voice that day; the mere existence of the indictment proved that.

Late on the March night that I finished the Jack Bonnie

volumes in the transcripts and documents, I made a decision I regretted: I decided to wrap up the long day by glancing at Dunn's list of witnesses. I shouldn't've. Like all the others, Jack Bonnie was listed by name and address. But their addresses appeared to be those of their homes or places of business. Jack's was "c/o Asst. Atty. Gen. Dermot Barry; Chief, Corruption Unit; Criminal Division; Dept. of the Attorney General; 20 Ashburton Place; Boston." Right. Jack might not have been ushered off to a safehouse under twenty-four-hour police guard, but he'd been relocated, and the only people who knew where he was, and could tell me, were the very people whom I did not wish to have standing around, looking bored and filing their nails while I tried to hammer Jack pretrial into some inconsistent statement that would give me a shot in the courtroom. Scratch that idea.

It was after midnight when I made it back to Green Harbor, my cold house and bar, that Teddy called me for some sort of conversation about some minor problem of his. It was so obviously trivial, and I was so exhausted and fed up that I cussed him out for bugging me. He was taken aback and asked me how the hell many live rats I'd decided to stick down my shorts. I'm sure I told him what was on my mind. I told him why and what a problem Jack Bonnie looked like he was going to be for me and Billy Ryan. Teddy told me to shut up and go to bed. I took his advice.

EIGHT

Like most of the lawyers I've beaten, and all of the lawyers who've beaten me, I consider that when I've completed my review of the documents provided by the other side, I've done about a third of my preparation for a major trial. The next step is field investigation. I don't have the same attitude about cases that both sides know are destined to conclude in plea bargains, because there isn't much point in scrounging around after trivial inconsistencies in prosecution testimony when they couldn't possibly matter, and I can't afford to spread it when that offense that's been charged is minor, even if it is going to trial: clients up on petty larceny, shoplifting, even first-offense stolen-car charges seldom have the cash to pay for much investigation; if they did, they wouldn't have skimmed their employers; boosted a few cashmere sweaters; or stolen a nice car not for resale but for their own personal use. But in major cases, such as Billy's certainly was, pretrial field investigation is not an option but an imperative. If it was going to eat up, say, twenty thousand dollars of the fee he'd paid me, well, that was only a good investment.

There are two kinds of field investigation. The first variety is the government brand: state police, FBI, IRS, DEA, what those outfits do. All of them howl to the press from time to time that hordes of criminals are escaping scot-free because the law enforcement budgets are too skimpy to allow them to hire and deploy sufficient numbers of skillful and hardworking people to capture all of the wicked. I don't doubt this is true, but it doesn't change the fact that there are more than enough cops out there to run down a given citizen to whom they've taken a dislike, and no citizen, however wealthy he may be, can muster enough private troops to meet the cops with even odds. So while the first kind of field investigation that I do somewhat resembles the government kind, the difference being that mine is a search for evidence that might help my client, and theirs is one for evidence that would sink him, the evidence I'm after in this mode is a lot more limited. I start with what I know about the government's case and see if I can find something wrong with it. Or, if my client's claimed he didn't do it, I'm out to determine whether I can find some document or person who will back him up.

When I say "I do it," I don't mean I usually do it myself. For the first kind of field investigation, my usual practice for many years was to call in Bad-eye Mulvey, tell him what I wanted him to find out, and send him out to get it. I am not insulting the late Sergeant Mulvey, then-retired after many years as a detective in the Boston Police Department. He had been born with his minor disability, a lazy eye, acquired the nickname from his childhood friends, and not only answered to it most of his life but identified himself with it. He would leave messages on answering machines (on which he refused to leave messages: "What I get for you is confidential information, Jerry. Never can tell who might come in and play it back"): "Tell him Bad-eye called." Neither the impairment nor the name it gave him seemed to bother him at all.

To work successfully with Bad-eye, you had to be very specific about what you wanted him to track down. He was as reliable as could be at coming up with the data you sent him to get, sparing neither his dwindling hours on earth nor his shoe leather, delivering on time and in detail, regardless of his own comfort or convenience. A slow-moving, slow-talking, old-tweed-jacketed turtle of a man whose manifest harmlessness accounted for much of the willingness of strangers to answer his (my) questions, locate documents for him and even photocopy the ones that he sought to save him the time-consuming bother of copying them all down by hand. This was most likely because of his placid, stolid demeanor; it suggested when he arrived that he had all day to hang around all day and would be happy to return the next day, the morning papers rolled up in his jacket pocket, until you found time to see him or give him what he wanted. While he sat in your reception area, carefully reading the papers, he would sigh from time to time, every so often humming off-key, "When Your Old Wedding Ring Was New," the only tune he seemed to have in his head, driving your receptionist nuts. Bad-eye knew what he wanted, because I had told him, and he was not about to leave until he got it. That's why he got steady work from a number of us, whose practices would not support in-house staff detectives, sensibly reciprocating by charging low rates we could afford.

But Bad-eye wasn't good at two things. One of them was the investigation of marital matters he deemed squalid, such as mine. The other was following up on unexpected leads supplied by his work in the field.

For example: some years ago I sent him down to Fall River to ascertain whether a client I'll call "Cisco" had spent the whole evening blamelessly, though not temperately, in the Portuguese National Club the night Bink's Liquors in the Saltmarsh Mall in Danvers—call it seventy-five miles away—was held up just before closing at 10:00.

Bad-eye's report, promptly turned in two days later, told me

he interviewed the bartender on duty "the night in question"—
they could make Bad-eye retire from the force and turn in his
badge when he reached the mandatory age, but they couldn't
make him turn in the written diction he'd acquired in his years
of service—as well as two or three of the regular customers, and
that they were unanimous in support of my client's alibi. It told
me that the bartender's sister had married Cisco, but divorced
him, in part because he spent more evenings at the club than he
did with her, and that the regulars corroborated this by stating
that Cisco was indeed in the club every night, and the night of
the holdup was no exception, or else they would have remembered it.

That made Cisco's alibi look pretty strong, giving me the
uncommon—not rare, but not common, either—notion that
for once I had a decent shot of walking my defendant when the
case came up for trial in Essex Superior Court. There was a
spring in my step and a melody in my heart when I went to visit
him at the House of Correction in Billerica, where he was being
held in lieu of fifty thousand dollars bail (set in consideration of
the fact that while he had never been convicted of a felony, he
had jumped bail on a charge of unarmed robbery two years
before, and the district attorney suspected he was on the way to
becoming a real bad actor).

Only when I observed Cisco's odd shiftiness in the face of
my good news, my explicit expectation that four witnesses backing up his alibi ought to give him a pretty decent shot at acquittal, did it occur to me that maybe I hadn't asked Bad-eye to
resolve enough questions. Bad-eye's next report, detailed and
thorough as the first, informed me that Cisco in fact had initi-
ated the divorce proceedings to dissolve his marriage to the
bartender's sister, citing adultery and desertion as grounds; that
the bartender and two of the three regulars mentioned by Bad-
eye had sided with Cisco in the proceedings, fully backing him
up; and that the corespondent in the case was a Fall River

licensing inspector who had twice shut down the club for periods of seven days on the grounds that he had observed illegal games of chance in progress there, and who'd been allowed to resign from his job as a result of the scandal caused by Cisco. Who appeared to have had no objection at all to his loving wife's long-standing shared living arrangements with the inspector until after the club's second shutdown.

That severely shook my confidence in the truth and veracity —we lawyers like lingo ourselves; we always say "truth and veracity," just as we always refer to what the dictionary defines as "shameless depravity" as "moral turpitude," when "turpitude" would do the job—of Cisco's alibi. Not to the point at which I'd dismiss it entirely; just to the point at which I retreated from my bold intention to wheel those four birds up to the witness stand at trial, and settled on the more prudent course of confiding to the assistant DA, few of whom are real stinkers or greatly interested in multiplying trials when they've got great backlogs of cases, that I'd found four witnesses who'd testify that Cisco was seventy-five miles away the night Bink's receipts got diverted from the night depository by a young man with a gun who looked a lot like Cisco. And then I asked the ADA what could be done on a plea. As I generally do, in most of my cases: try to work something out. As Teddy Franklin's said many times: "Most guys that get in trouble, they got this habit where they see everything in black and white, you know? And they should forget that. Because most of what is going on is in the grey. And that's because there's more of it. More of the grey, I mean. So that's where your margin is, and you got to work the margin."

Teddy's right—he must be—but Teddy can be sure; he deals in the same sort of business all the time. He knows, before he goes out scouting, that somewhere between New Haven and the Canadian border is the automobile he wants, and there will be a margin. If he looks long enough, he will find the car and then calculate his leeway. I can't have that confidence. Every case is different. I can't be sure in any one of them just whether what I need to win it even exists, or what my chances of getting it might be.

In the Ryan case, the transcripts suggested to me only one possible location where I might find what I wanted: it was where Jack Bonnie was, and with him I had no margin because of all the cops around. The problem was squared. I didn't know what I expected to find out about him, so I couldn't sic Bad-eye on him, and I didn't know where the hell he was, even if I could have. I knew where he'd been, and I knew what he'd said, at least about Billy Ryan, but I didn't really have the foggiest notion of how to go about looking for a hole in the story he'd told.

So I compromised. I called in Bad-eye and asked him to scout up every record in the State House of Bonnie's term in office; every piece of paper Worcester had on him; and everything the cops might have; and I expected nothing. It was time to go to the second kind of field investigation. I would go to Norwich.

NINE

The less-sophisticated people whom I personally interview in the second kind of field investigation seem to assume that the primary purpose of my visit is to find out whether they possess some evidence, unsuspected by the cops because they never came around and asked for it, which will, all by itself, split the prosecutor's case like a ripe melon. They are almost invariably apologetic to admit they don't, and I do nothing to relieve their embarrassment. They have obviously watched and enjoyed a lot of "Perry Mason" shows, and there's no help to be gained by either me or my client in ruining their future pleasures by telling them the real world's different. Just by showing sheepishness, they've given me about the best result I could reasonably expect, especially in a small town like Norwich. They didn't hate him or despise him, and they did feel sorry for him. I didn't have to worry that they'd suddenly show up in Mike Dunn's case and define my client as a bastard to the world.

The more-sophisticated people that I call upon realize they don't know any facts that would serve as evidence. They presume that I'm out reconnoitering for possible employment as character witnesses. They're mistaken too, but I don't correct them, either. I see no purpose to explaining that I don't think character witnesses serve much defensive purpose. And they can really hurt my man, not because they'll call him a dirty dog but beacuse if I summon three nuns, four priests, and a minister and rabbi (for a little balance) to testify that my client, charged with larceny and then lying about it, is the soul of honesty, that allows the prosecutor to bring in four or five cops and three assorted enemies who will testify my client surely would have invaded Poland if he'd had his own army and Hitler hadn't beaten him to the punch. I think character witnesses add at best nothing but tedium to a trial. The only time I ever use them is when the time comes for sentencing, and I think a bunch of pleading letters from old friends and community leaders at least can't make things any worse. So I thank those friends of my clients that I've found, and explain that, of course, while I haven't yet made any decisions about whom to call to the stand, I'll certainly keep them in mind.

Bad-eye, dead these three years and some, never did quite understand what I was up to when I didn't call him and went out into the field myself. His feelings were a little hurt, and when he found out what little new and helpful evidence I usually brought back, he had trouble concealing his opinion that when it came to investigating, I was pretty good at lawyering. I didn't try to explain to him that when I went out in the field, lawyering was what I was doing. He'd been a cop too long to understand that in addition to the kind of field work that gathers potent information, there's the kind that helps to neutralize facts adverse to my clients, more of an exercise in anticipatory damage control than one of preparation to attack. There's no point in euphemisms here: what I'm doing is brown-nosing, because if people in his hometown like my client, and like me, the word of that in this age of easy communication will soon get around, and you never can tell who might hear it, whose sister-in-law's on the jury.

So my unstated purposes on my two pretrial trips to Norwich were first to ascertain whether Billy might have some bitter, lifelong enemies lurking out there in the weeds, ready to get
even by volunteering their services to Mike Dunn if the media
before the verdict seemed to be treating Billy with too much
deference—he probably did, but I didn't come across any, and if
I didn't find them in the places where I looked, they weren't big
enough to hurt him—and second whether, just by chance, he
might in the course of his long life have perhaps committed one
or two charitable acts big enough to rebut any testimony Mike
Dunn and Dermot Barry might elicit to show in passing that he
was slightly more grasping and greedy than Ebenezer Scrooge.

I didn't do too badly. I used my previous exploits in poor
Larry White's behalf, and a few other war stories of mine, to
ingratiate myself with several gabby people, and I came back
with one significant charitable act and one piece of information
useless to Billy's case but very useful indeed to me as Billy's
lawyer.

With the Kilduffs, Jim and Emily, of McGillicuddy & Kilduff, she being the granddaughter of the founding McGillicuddy and he by matrimony having been admitted partnership
in the funeral business she'd inherited, I relied principally on
the reminder that I saved their part-time employee, Larry
White, not only from disgrace but from a long time in a bad
place surrounded by a lot of thugs who don't like child molesters.

"Larry isn't a bad guy," I assured them, because, of course, I
knew they agreed. "Just an ordinary ragamuffin-kind of guy
who'd blundered into a bad situation. He didn't create it."

"He was absolutely devastated when they indicted him,"
Emily said. "He didn't know *what* to do."

"Few of us would," I said. "Man's spent his life down at
the post office, used his mornings off to help you folks run funerals . . ."

"And done a good job of it, too," Jim said. "Does what we tell him and that's what we need."

". . . and generally behaved himself," I said, "and all of a sudden all these Cub Scouts are saying he fondled them. He didn't think that was fair."

"Neither did we," Emily and Jim said together. "We were afraid he might kill himself," she said.

"Neither did I," I said. Very important to make it clear to a defendant's friends that it wasn't just money that made you take his case: it was also your outrage that he'd even been charged, and your determination to correct the injustice. "Because he hadn't done it. The day he came in to see me, he looked like he'd been whacked on the head with a lug wrench. That's why I took him on."

Well, partly. I also took him on because Colin called a recess one day when I arrived in his court to argue against a revocation of probation and commitment to jail of one of my genuine evildoers, and announced he would see me in chambers. By myself. That is never good news when the judge says he will see you by yourself in his lobby, because it always means he wants you to do something that you will not want to do, wouldn't do if a judge didn't ask you to do it, and won't get paid for after you've done it.

Colin told me quite forcefully—at least by his mild standards—that his father had known Larry "casually" (Colin certainly didn't want to give me the impression that his father was in the habit of hanging around with people he suspected of being child molesters) for many years and was very worried about what Larry might do under this new pressure. Colin has a flair for meek dramatism, but after I had seen Larry I also wondered whether he might attempt suicide—although he was such an ineffectual bird he most likely would've foozled that too. Colin assured me that Billy was "very anxious" that I take the case on, telling me "how impressed Dad was the day he met you at graduation," which was arrant bullshit, and that he would not rest easy or give Colin any peace until he was satisfied that Larry had a good lawyer. Meaning he'd made it clear that *Colin* wouldn't rest easy until *he* got this townie jerk a free lawyer.

There was no compliment in any of that, and I didn't take one from it. "Good lawyer" meant "any poor clown with a law degree and a bar ticket who's dumb enough to take the case, so's my father can tell Larry he got Larry a good lawyer."

Colin told me he wanted me to interview Larry and determine whether he had in fact bothered the Cub Scouts, and that if I concluded he hadn't, to defend him. He explained that Billy didn't hold with grown men groping little boys, in case I might have imagined so preposterous a thing, and was not only fully resigned to the notion that they should go away and be bothered by other grown men for several years, but in favor of it.

So my mission was clear: I was to judge Larry's case myself, and, if I found him not guilty, was to move heaven and as much of the earth as might be necessary to get him acquitted by a jury of his peers. Colin chose not to raise the subject of my fee for this service, and who, if anyone, had plans to pay it. This reticence suggested to me that neither he nor Billy had any plans to pay me, and that if I couldn't get a fair wage out of Larry, that was my tough luck. Since I had had a fair amount of experience defending civil servants who'd discovered to their displeasure that the government didn't pay for their defenses against criminal charges with the same ready generosity that it showed when confronted with medical and dental bills, I thought it unlikely that Larry would appear in my office with a fat roll of greenbacks he had saved up at the Postal Workers' credit union in case of the kind of emergency in which he found himself, which meant that I *wasn't* going to get paid, always doleful news for the lawyer in private practice. I guess the public view is that we live off our trust fund and play bridge to while away the hours until our clients need us, and the fees are just our tips. Okay, but when a judge displays that view, well, it can be annoying, and I would've liked to tell Colin off.

The trouble that day was, I couldn't. As Colin knew very well, I didn't want my genuine client, who had paid me, to be violated. He did have a disagreeable habit of robbing at gunpoint gas stations and other business establishments that are open late at night and seldom have more than one frightened, young employee on duty whenever he became a little strapped for cash, but he had nevertheless compensated me fairly for representing him, conduct that always stimulates feelings of warm friendliness and lawyerly concern in my charitable breast. I didn't want to piss off the judge about to sit on his case. So, only hedging my bets a little bit, I said I'd talk to Larry and see what developed.

Then we went back out into the courtroom, and in due course my genuine client's case came on to be heard. Colin listened patiently and intently while the prosecutor gave him a whole list of pretty good reasons why my customer should go to jail right off and stay there for a good long while so that he might meditate upon his many sins and maybe decide to turn over a new leaf. Which, given his record, did not seem to be very likely in the prosecutor's estimation but was worth a try, at least. And anyway, if he was off the street and securely locked up, part of the crime wave would be stemmed. I must confess that even I found much good sense in the prosecutor's argument.

Then I stood up and assured Colin that my pal was a fine fellow who only knocked over gas stations, convenience stores and suchlike in the dead of night when the fit was on him, and that he had promised me solemnly that he wasn't going to do it anymore, and that neither one of us understood how on earth the policeman who'd arrested him in the parking lot at the 7–Eleven on Adams Street in Quincy at 11:48 P.M. on the night in question could possibly have spotted the fully loaded .38

Smith and Wesson revolver under the passenger seat without having conducted an unlawful search, not based on probable cause. Or how, having seen it, he could have leaped to the conclusion that it belonged to my client, whom the cop had recognized right off "as a known felon," and that he had been planning to use the .38 to knock over the store as soon as the last stray customer left with his strawberry Slurpee and prepackaged ham-and-cheese sandwich.

Colin listened to me as patiently as he had heard out the prosecutor. Colin always listens patiently to every lawyer, because he used to be one himself and has at least managed to remember that clients are easier in their minds and do their time more peacefully when they're satisfied that their lawyers have been granted a fair hearing by the judges who then do mean things to them. Then Colin violated my man and turned him over to the policemen who were on hand there to receive his surly soul, and he was carted off to the Norfolk County House of Correction to recommence service of the remainder of the seven-year sentence he had gotten on conviction of robbing the Gulf station at the corner of Washington Street and Route 1 in Dedham four years before.

I shook hands with my client and wished him all of the best —he did not seem optimistic, but appeared satisfied with my work; you do the best you can—and went back to my office to wash up and contemplate my own sins. Larry called me while I was regretting my oversight in not going to medical school and acquiring a useful skill, such as brain surgery. I saw him the next day. A sorrier excuse for human masculinity you could not imagine. He told me with regret that he did not have any money. Surprise, surprise: life's just full of surprises.

"But why did those boys say those things," Emily said. That was a good question. It had occurred to me. I did not have an answer for it. The best I could do was a guess. The guess was that some public-school teacher with the best of intentions had essayed to repair any possible parental failure to instruct impressionable children about the hazards lurking in the great world beyond the hearth and had done it so vividly and graphically that one of the boys had decided that it must have happened to him, and therefore, of course, to his friends.

There had to be a culprit, of course. Even a kid knows you need a villain for a shocking story. So the kid looked around for a likely nominee, and there was sitting-duck Larry, mid-forties and childless, given to using his brown-and-tan Volkswagen van, as well as his meagre earnings, to take Cub Scouts on weekend hikes in the White Mountains of New Hampshire, cabins and campfires for boys. "Aha," said the satanic little kid, "Larry did it." When Larry'd done nothing at all.

"I never did figure that out," I told Emily. "Kids sometimes imagine some things. They're dangerous people to have on the stand. You never know what they'll say. But they're also prone to forgetfulness. If you don't make them cry, they'll be honest. The question that bothered me then, and the question that bothers me now, is how the prosecutor convinced himself that what they told him was the truth."

Almost from the giddyap I was convinced that those boys were reciting by rote. Witnesses adult or witnesses children never agree on details. One recalls a blue car; the next one says "green"; and the third one is firm on "turquoise" maybe only because he likes that word. We settle on things—"Well, it must've been that"—that we don't remember at all. But those boys were different. All very firm. No question in their minds at all. Larry picked them all up, in their blue shirts and gold scarves, and loaded them into his van on a lovely Friday afternoon. He drove them up Route 93 to North Woodstock. There was a cluster of condos there in the White Mountain National Forest. The heat wasn't on in the one that they used. Larry lighted a fire. They ate franks and beans that he cooked on the gas stove. He read them a Sherlock Holmes story, "Silver

Blaze." The one about the racehorse that got away, only it didn't, and the jealous neighbor painted it and tried to palm it off. The boys all got into their own sleeping bags after they put on pajamas, and slept around the fireplace. Around 2:00 A.M., Larry came out of his bedroom and stoked the fire. Then he went around and pawed them, *seriatim*. After that he went back to bed. The next day they went hiking as planned. That night they went out for pizza. He didn't bother them that night. The next day they went home. And charged him with child abuse two weeks later.

Joseph was a fidgety witness. I couldn't blame him. He was eleven years old at the time. I've been a fussy witness myself, ill at ease, not well spoken, drawing blanks when someone's asked me something I know very well. Mack's lawyer in the divorce case was very acute in the identity of such weakness; he was like the divine wind when it came to shooting me down, and I'm abashed today to say he wasn't really all that good. He didn't need to be; I was that bad. There were times in that proceeding when I looked like a perfect fool, and knew it. So I was sympathetic to Joseph. As it's best to be when you have a fresh-faced, decent, good kid to cross-examine and you'd really prefer that he didn't send your poor helpless client to jail for committing indecent acts. Because if he is, he will have things done to him that the Marquis de Sade never dreamed of.

"Now Joseph," I said in my best and most-practiced paternal fashion, "I have to ask you some questions here, and you know I'm Mister White's attorney."

"Yes sir," he said thoughtfully.

"And so it may seem to you now and then that I'm trying to upset you. Make you angry, or mad, or maybe even to forget something you remember very well. And I don't mean to do that, all right? If something I say sounds to you like I want to start a fight, I wish you'd say that: 'Mister Kennedy, are you trying to start a fight?' And then I'll know I didn't phrase my question very well, and I'll do what we call 'withdrawing it,' and we'll start all over again. Understood?"

God bless him, the kid grinned at me. "Understood," he said. Judge Andrew Keats yawned audibly and said: "Are we about finished with this little *pas de deux*, Mister Kennedy? We do have to move along here, you know."

"Certainly, Your Honor," I said. "I thank the court for its indulgence thus far." I had a hunch. I almost never act on hunches, except when they're so overpowering it would contradict every instinct that I have to ignore them. This was one of those times. "Joseph, tell me this: did Mister White ever touch your private parts, or otherwise harm you in any way?"

The kid shook his head. "No," he said, "he didn't."

"But your friends," I said, "your friends said he did. They told that to the police. And that he did it to you and to them, too. In the middle of the night. In the condo."

"I don't know," the kid said. "I don't know what he did to them. But he didn't do anything to me. It was Timmy's idea. He was the one who thought it up. He said Mister White was a jerk, and a queer, and that was why he was always doing things *for* us, because he wanted to do things *to* us."

"But," I said, "he didn't do anything to you at least."

"No sir," Joseph said, "and I was awake when he came out to do the fire. I was getting cold, and I woke up, and I saw him come out and put some more wood in the fireplace, and then he went back to bed, I guess, and it started to get warmer but I was still a little cold, so I moved my sleeping bag right up close to the fire, and then I went back to sleep."

"Now Joseph," I said, "think back very carefully here: when Mister White came out and put more wood on the fire, did you see him touch anybody?"

"No sir," Joseph said, "just the wood. And the tongs and stuff. He didn't touch any of us."

Quit while you're ahead. "No further questions," I said. I sat down. The jury was out twenty minutes. Not guilty. Larry White was not guilty. He walked.

"Larry wears a wig now," Emily said thoughtfully. "For formal occasions, at least. When he works here, and when he takes up the collection at Saint Matthew's. I wonder why he does that."

"Disguise, most likely," I said. "That was the kind of charge you can get acquitted on, but in the town where people know you, you're never not guilty again."

"Is Billy Ryan's case like that?" Jim said.

"If we're as lucky as Larry White and I were, it will be," I said. "If we aren't, it'll be a lot worse."

"What do you think the chances are?" Emily said.

I lied through my teeth. "I never predict what a jury will do," I said. "Not even to myself. I've been at it too long for that."

TEN

"Is it always like that?" Jim said. "In your line of work, I mean?"

By then I'd been invited to stay for dinner. This was an act of mercy, since for the better part of a month I'd been on my usual post-divorce, pretrial crash diet of fast-food cheeseburgers, potato chips, canned beer and rivers of coffee, woofed on the run; I know the decent restaurants remain open for business while I'm going all-out on a case, and while I'm no Escoffier I do know how to broil a steak and bake a big potato, but either method of getting a decent meal takes more time than I'm willing to spend. So, after nearly an hour of smelling Jim's prime rib of beef roasting, I was almost faint with hunger. I would've discoursed on the writings of St. Augustine, about which I know very little, if that'd been what it took to earn some honest beef.

"Usually not," I said. "Most clients plead guilty, mine and everyone else's. Most times the government can prove what it says my client did, so if he saves them the trouble, and the court some time, the punishment he gets is lighter.

"Billy's case is different. He's got to go to trial. Most people in his kind of situation do. If they're found guilty by the jury, they're ruined. But they're also ruined if they're found guilty on a plea. So they have to take their shots."

Our system of criminal justice purportedly excludes status offenses: prohibitions of, and punishments for, being rich, poor, middle class, unemployed, professional, amateur, or being a member or nonmember of a given ethnic or religious group. Righteously we protest that we punish only acts, acts that are disruptive of the peace and good order, destructive of the common weal, or atrocious and barbarous by all civilized standards.

This is true as far as it goes, which isn't very far at all. In operation, the criminal law and the people who enforce it permit the moneyed to do certain things—such as enjoy moderate (weekend) use of recreational drugs, provided they are sophisticated enough to know how to obtain their Andean marching powders without resort to street pushers—for which they punish those without the money or discreet connections. And by the same token, the enforcers permit the poor—*i.e.*, blacks and Hispanics—to employ sharp kitchen implements for the settlement of domestic disagreements over such subjects as spousal fidelity or paternity without too much fuss, but vigorously capture and prosecute highly reputable persons ("community leaders") who pound on their spouses while drunk. A laborer has a pretty decent chance of cheating on his income tax and getting away with it; an orthodontist does not (reasonable enough, I suppose; what the government loses to the laborer in taxes on under-the-table income wouldn't pay for the cost of catching him, but the tax, penalties and interest on what the orthodontist hides will pay the salaries of two auditors for a year).

Life's a trade-off. A middle-echelon gang-messenger from North Dorchester enjoys favorable odds of success as he sets out on a gun-running trip to Florida, where any drunk recruited fresh off the sidewalk for a sawbuck can buy half a dozen fine 9 mm. semiauto fifteen-shot double-stackers over the counter at the store, if he's got the money; the well-known kidney specialist from Weston had better expect trouble if he decorates his game room with the hides, heads or tusks of species declared endangered, *because* he's got the money, and people envy him. Envy accounts for many prosecutions instigated in the name of what is Right and Just. If you stick your head up high enough, someone will be tempted to cut it clean off your neck. If your situation, when you're caught, would make a stranger think you ought to've known better than to get in that big mess, you probably should've.

When envy is the root of the proceeding, the government's pretrial public gloating suggests the reality that forces the victim of the indictment to try the case: his entire life and career, significantly damaged by the mere accusation of wrongdoing, will be utterly destroyed if he's convicted, regardless of whether he throws in the towel or demands that a jury decide. So if that client has any shot at all, he simply can't deal.

The real charge against Billy Ryan, as opposed to those stated in the indictment, was not that he had violated Massachusetts General Laws, chapter 268A, sections 1, 2, 3, 4, 7 and 8 —that he had willfully and with malice aforethought employed his official position for the purpose of personal gain, or that, as further detailed in the bill of particulars I demanded from the AG, that he had gone into lucrative cahoots with Jack Bonnie, John Doe and Richard Roe. It was that he held a status, as powerhouse, longtime, Commissioner of the Department of Public Works, which he had carefully used to get rich, and had thus made himself a public figure not only of some odium but of trophy-head magnitude. His history of prominence had counted heavily in the AG's decision to watch him till he slipped, and then nail him, just as it had prompted many of Mike Dunn's predecessors to watch Billy as though they had been peregrine falcons who'd mistaken him for a fat pigeon.

"So my problem as his lawyer," I said to the Kilduffs, "is not only to get to know my client as well as I can, but since his public reputation really is a large factor in his case, to get to know how other people, people who've known him a long time, what they think of him. By the time I meet my client for the first time, he's got a lot of history behind him, especially when he's as old and's been around as much as Billy. And the man I see in my office is probably different from the man he was in ordinary, daily life, the man his family and friends knew before his ego got shaken and his personality got bent by what's just happened to him. I defend the guy as I know him, of course, because that's the guy the jury's going to see—and no matter how the case comes out, he'll never be his old self again. But it helps me to know as much as possible what that old self was like. And you people've known him for a long time, Billy and his family."

"Just professionally," Emily said. Emily wasn't going to sit there and let me call her a gossip, at least not without resisting. "When he'd come here for wakes, which naturally he did a lot, knowing so many people, family'd lived here all their lives, but we're always pretty busy when we've got a case, that was all we saw him. And we're busy when a wake's on. Don't have much time for small talk with the friends who come to call."

"We were never social friends," Jim said.

"But this is a small town," I said. "If I know anything about that kind of town, and I do because my ex-wife and I both came from that kind of background, anybody whose family's lived in one of them for a long time is pretty well known to the other people whose families have also been there a while. I'm not going to put you up on the witness stand and ask you what you know about the Ryan family. But it'd help me to know what kind of people they are. Because to some degree I represent them, too. They've got their own investment in me, along with the one he's made himself. Someone they love is in danger, and I've been entrusted with protecting him. If I do something that upsets them before the trial, or even worse, during it, my client's going to get even more rattled than he is right now, and I don't want that to happen."

"Well," Jim said, "the wife's Fannie."

"Her name's actually Frances, I guess," Emily said. "But I've never once heard anyone call her that. She's what my father used to call 'a good soul.' "

"She hasn't had an easy life, with Billy," Jim said. "I don't mean they lacked for money, far from it. Or that he was mean to her. But there's no question about who raised those kids, making sure they got good marks in school, with him gone all the time. He put up a good show, at Sunday Mass and so forth, leading Fannie and the kids up the aisle to receive, but when it came to home life, he spent a lot more of his time away from it than he ever did in it."

"The only one of his children that I know—heck, that I've even met more than once—is Colin," I said. "Went to law school with him."

"Colin's the second one," Emily said. "Doctor John's the oldest. Then, after Colin, there's Patrick, the general, and after him is Marie, the state rep. And grandchildren, of course. Eleven of them. Marie and Mark had two, and Patrick and his wife had the three, and so did Colin and John and their wives."

Jim laughed. "Until they started getting grown up," he said, "the only ones you could tell apart from the others, who their mother and father were, were John and his wife's three. Red hair and freckles, all three of them. Now, of course, Patrick's oldest, well, she's a regular little sexpot, and she knows it, too. Fifteen or sixteen by now, I'd guess. No surprise, really. Patrick's wife's a fine-looking woman, best of the three daughters-in-law. But I tell you, they must have to call an extra squad of MPs to that house up there in New Hampshire, when the guard has its regular weekends. Some of those young privates, my, get a look at that? Pretty tempting. Especially when it's the daughter of the commanding officer. Get *her* out in a meadow."

"Now Jim," Emily said.

"Any family problems that you know about," I said, taking another piece of the beef.

"Well, I sure wouldn't want to be married to Nancy," Jim said. "Colin's wife, I mean. She's uglier'n sin."

"Now Jim," Emily said, "she's a good wife and a fine mother. Everyone says so. She can't help how she looks.

"Marie has some problems," she said to me. "She was here one night for some wake or another, and she kept getting drinks of water, and then going down to the ladies' room—it had to be that, because she doesn't smoke—and then coming back up. And, it seemed like, two or three minutes later, she'd get another drink of water and go back downstairs again."

"Doctor John put her on some drug, I think it was that night," Jim said. "What'd they call that stuff, Emily? Something began with P."

Emily frowned. "Preozine?" she said. "Preozac?"

"Prozac," Jim said. "Prozac, that's it. I don't know what it's supposed to cure, but that's what John put her on."

I did. It's the boutique medication for obsessive-compulsives who get into fugue states and wash their hands repeatedly, or conduct their conversations as though all of their comments had been recorded on a tape loop: it reaches the end, rewinds and begins again. "I'm not a doctor," I said. I didn't need to be one to know for sure that now I didn't want Marie anywhere near Andy Keats's courtroom at any time during Billy's trial. Bad enough that she was a state rep, whose very presence would silently remind every juror that Billy Ryan was a lifetime power politician, but if she was also three degrees off the vertical and liable to do anything, well, that made it even worse.

"Miller Benjamin," Emily said, "he's the druggist. Why Doctor John sent her to Miller for that prescription is something I'll never understand. Everyone knows that Miller can't keep his mouth shut. John could've just waited 'till the next day and gotten it himself when he went to the hospital. Chief of surgery at Assumption? Nobody ever would've said a word."

"Maybe John didn't think she could wait that long," Jim said. "She was running for reelection then, keep in mind. There was a campaign on. Somebody'd spotted her the next morning, some candidates' breakfast or something, that there was something kind of funny about her, well, that could've blown the election. And you know how the Ryans are about power. If you've got it, even if maybe it'd be a whole lot better for you and everybody else if you just let it go and went home, you're not going to do that. Put up the best front you can, no matter what it costs you."

"I think it was more likely her marriage," Emily said. "She and Mark, Mark Frolio, they haven't had an easy time." Her lips tightened over her teeth. "He drinks," she said.

"I'd drink, too," Jim said, taking his third piece of beef, "I was married to her. And that family of hers."

"He knew what he was getting into," Emily said primly. "He'd met them all when he and Marie were in law school. I think he drinks because he likes it. My father always said that's why my uncle Edward did it. In and out of one hospital after another. Always: 'this'll be the one that gets him straightened out.' And none of 'em did. None of 'em could. That was what Dad said. 'It isn't medical,' he said. 'He drinks because he likes it. You tell him it's killing him? He knows it's killing him. Man plain doesn't give a damn what it's doing to him. He likes to drink, so he does it. Some day he will die and someone will bury him. And that'll be good news for all his silly relatives who said the booze'd finally kill him and by God it finally did. But Ed won't give a damn what they think or what they say, not that Ed does now, because by that time he'll be dead.'"

Jim shook his head. "I don't think he did," he said. "I mean: I don't think Mark did know what he was getting into. The family, sure, but there's no way he could've known that Patrick'd make such a mess of Ryan and Son Real Estate—Billy added the 'and Son' when Patrick resigned from the army and came home with no job in sight, and Billy'd always bragged he'd never put a relative on any state payroll—he'd have to go back in the service and turn it all over to Marie. Or that Marie'd decide to run for the house, and leave Mark stuck with the whole shebang. I think when he married her and came out here, what he bargained for was that they'd open up their law office and get lots of business, all the deeds and so forth from the real estate operation, and in time, the bank work, plus a good deal of other stuff because this was Norwich, and her maiden name was Ryan. And he'd sit out here and have himself a nice comfortable life, much better'n he ever could've gotten on his own, and he thought that would be good." He paused and smiled. "Just like I did when I married you," he said.

"It was not the same thing," she said.

"No," he said, "it wasn't. For one thing, when I met you, I was fourteen years old, way too young to've started scheming how to marry some boss's daughter and inherit the business. Besides, I was going to be a Navy fighter-pilot then if I couldn't play for the Red Sox. Or maybe it was: a cowboy. I forget. But I sure didn't plan any of this, the way it's turned out for us. But Mark was a little bit older than that when he met Marie. Eight or nine years or so older, and that's old enough to be thinking: 'Well, how can I get what I want,' which in his case, I think was an easy life, with money, 'without taking too many risks?' And that's what I think Mark did."

"Well," Emily said, "if that's why he married her, I think he deserved what he got. Fortune hunter. She was right to put him out. If the drinking wasn't enough, well then, that would be."

"I don't agree with you there either, Emily," Jim said. To me, he said: "She's put him out either four or five times. He's got a place somewhere west of here, and that's where he lives, for the most part. But he's still at his desk at Ryan and Son every morning—it'd go under without him, but even with the market down, he's still selling properties—and they still put up the front. All together with the kids and the rest of the Ryans for Mass, holidays and so forth, just like everything's normal." .

"Four or five times," I said.

"The Ryans don't believe in divorce, I guess," Jim said. "Especially the one that's in politics, and she's the one that seems to need one."

"Oh Jim," Emily said, "divorce in politics doesn't matter anymore. It's not nineteen-fifty-two anymore, when Stevenson was running. She doesn't divorce him because she feels sorry for him. Where would he go? What would he do?"

"Anywhere else," Jim said. "Anything he wanted. It'd be better'n what he's got with her. Making a profit for the Ryan family, and getting the back of her hand for it."

Recall now my first purpose in field investigation: to ascertain whether there are any snakes unknown either to my client or to me, lurking in his familiar weeds. Mark Frolio sounded like he might be a serpent. I made a mental note to wait a week or so and then call him at his office. When you stumble onto a lead that could mean there's a viper waiting for you in your client's family, you don't track the guy down the day after you pick it up. That'd make him think you were worried about him, and he'd start thinking about who it was who had told you what it was that worried you, and what that information might have been. Mark Frolio, if he was smart enough to have made it through law school and the bar exam—to this day I do not know how I passed that bar exam—would not have much trouble making the connections if I called him the morning after I'd had dinner with the Kilduffs (and be sure that he would know, by next midday at the latest, that I'd been in town, and fed). And if he got mad enough at them to confront them, that would give me, and thus Billy Ryan, three new enemies in Norwich. I suspected Billy was already well supplied, although none of his had cropped up. As far as I knew, I didn't have any, except perhaps for the embarrassed parents of the Cub Scouts whose sons' testimony I'd exposed as lies at Larry White's trial, and they were powerless in Billy's case; I didn't want any others.

"You should, ah," Jim said over coffee, "you probably should see Frank Martin."

"Yes, he should," Emily said. "You definitely should see Monsignor Martin."

"Father Shaw mentioned him to me when I saw him this afternoon at the rectory," I said. "Used to be the pastor here, right?" What Father Dennis Shaw had said was that Monsignor Martin, one of the people Billy had grudgingly suggested I visit, not because Billy thought any of those he named would dare to badmouth him but because Billy resented me poking around in his past, "is probably the most self-centered old windbag God ever called to Holy Orders. If anything good ever happened in Saint Matthew's parish, before Frank came or after he left, if you listen to Frank, well, he did it. And anything bad? Someone else was to blame. Make Frank tell you about the bells, and see how his story squares with mine."

"He lives at Regina Cleri now," Emily said. "On Beacon Hill there in Boston. They made him retire. He didn't want to. He said it was a fine thing to do after all he'd done to rebuild Saint Matthew's after the fire just destroyed it."

"The monsignor knew the family quite well," Jim said. "Much better than we do. I gather that's what interests you."

Well, yes, but then when you have nothing, and you desperately need something, everything in the world interests you.

ELEVEN

I couldn't possibly overstate the sore-thumb problem of Billy's reputation in his case. I've made some friends on the other side of this business in more than a quarter century at it (thus contradicting another one of those "Perry Mason" canards: Perry and DA Hamilton Burger may've hated each other, thereby heightening the drama, but in real life few defense lawyers and fewer prosecutors permit themselves the luxury of despising each other; personal animosities interfere with the orderly conduct of business). To a man they've cheerfully admitted that there's nothing a prosecutor likes better than listening to the trial judge tell the jury that they can draw "no inference unfavorable to the defendant from his decision not to testify." The prosecutors also like the judges' warning that the jurors must not allow anything they've read in the papers or seen on TV, before or after they started the case, "to influence your judgment of the evidence in any way."

Twenty years or so ago there was a kid in Middlesex then with the face of a Vienna Choir Boy—he probably looks like Bluebeard now—and the heart of an assassin who put it very nicely over beers one night in the old Esquire Lounge: "The only beef I've got with those instructions," he said, "is that the judges only get to give them once or twice a trial. I had my way, I'd have 'em start and end each day by reminding those good men and women that they can't decide the rat is guilty just because the papers say he's Jack the Ripper, and he's such a lying bastard that his crooked lawyer hasn't got the guts to let him take the stand. Tell 'em and tell 'em and tell 'em again— that's the way I'd like it. Because every time you tell 'em that, they say: 'Oh yeah? Up yours.' "

Billy was going to have to take the stand in his own defense. I think I would've had to have him wrapped in a wet sheet and covered it with a thick coat of plaster of paris to prevent him from doing it, regardless of the tactical realities, because he was spoiling for a fight with Mike Dunn, and he wasn't really content with my assurance that I'd be his champion. The law was one thing; this was also a personal thing that could only be settled in hand-to-hand combat, and Billy thought only he could do that. But even if I could've had him shot with half a dozen tranquilizer darts, immobilized and tagged for the duration of the trial, the tactical reality was that if I did, I'd lose. There was just too much about him out there in the wind, decades of innuendo, defamation and contempt, and for the jury it would resonate in the evidence like the bass undertone on a fifties rock-'n'-roll record, unless someone put it to sleep. The only person who could do that was Billy. He would have to get up on his hind legs and put his left hand on the Bible, raise his right hand, swear to tell the truth, the whole of it, and nothing but the same, and then sit down determined and pre-pared calmly to convince those twelve good men and women true that while Dracula might be alive, and roaming around nights, he was not in that courtroom, charged with corrupt deal-ings.

When Billy did that he was going to get eaten. I've never been a prosecutor—a gap in my experience I've sometimes regretted; it stands to reason that if you get tunnel vision from never being anything *but* a prosecutor, you must develop some kind of judgment disability from exclusively defensive work, but while I've flirted with the odd special-prosecutor opportunity from time to passing time, I've always ducked them on the grounds my clients would get mad. Still, I know what a prosecutor does. A prosecutor waits. He licks his chops and *waits*, for a nice big fat defendant to get up on the stand. Especially a nice big fat defendant who's spoiling for a fight. "Ah," says the prosecutor silently to the jury, rising from his chair and buttoning his grey suitcoat, his face as blank of emotion as a six-year-old's at First Communion class, "would you jurors like some pie for the afternoon recess? Go good with your coffee, right? I'd suggest mince pie. We'll have the mincemeat for you right here, soon's I finish with this guy."

Why do you think those executioners in suits were so forthright with me, the enemy, about their fondness for those jury instructions? Keep in mind now that when I said we're not generally unfriendly toward each other, I just said that we don't sneer. I didn't say we never tried a little psychological warfare on each other, all in good fun and a day's work, of course. Having a suspicious mind, I think they were trying to mousetrap me, just as I try to mousetrap them, when the opportunity comes up, into muting those instructions by throwing fresh meat on the stand. Where they could then eat it. I will never understand why a perfectly intelligent but untrained civilian, one who would never try to do a kidney transplant or a cardiac bypass, or even change the oil in the family car, will get it into his fool head to argue with a lawyer.

But they do, they all do, and I knew very well that Billy would be no exception. Oh, he would absorb my prepping, and agree to all my terms, and on direct he would be meek as mother's milk, play the senior citizen with grave, serene aplomb. But when Dunn or his designated hitter (who turned out to be Dermot Barry, just as Jack Bonnie's "care of" address had portended) got him on cross, Billy'd bridle, and then bristle, and then finally explode with all the pyrotechnical effects we all hope for on the Fourth.

So I needed some soothing stuff in reserve, for follow-up on what was sure to be the rasping cross-examination Billy would undergo. Not character witnesses, for the reasons I've given. No, what I needed was one or more witnesses who could testify truthfully to Billy's performance of one or more impressive and completely spontaneous acts of charity, thus rebutting what I was sure would be Dunn's chief emphasis during Billy's cross-examination: Billy's greed.

Dennis Shaw gave it to me. It was not the "Open, Sesame" that would walk Billy right out the courtroom door as soon as I got it into evidence, but it was better than anything else I had. "Oh, yes," Shaw told me, nodding, the late March sunlight shining on the varnished wainscoting of the office, "I'm not saying Billy still won't get the next room to Barabbas when he goes to the hereafter, but he did do one extremely generous thing for Saint Matthew's that he didn't have to do. He got the bells for us."

Those bells were pretty much all I had. You go with what you've got in my line of work. I went to see Monsignor Martin.

"Oh, I had a terrible time with that man," Monsignor Martin said to me. "He is truly an awful man." We sat in a small, panelled, conference room on the first floor of Regina Cleri, and I gathered he would not be eager to testify in open court to my client's superb reputation for telling the truth. I had no intention of calling him or anybody else to do any such thing, of course, but I prefer not to allow such prospective witnesses to make those decisions; I like to make them myself. I said as much. The monsignor was shocked. "Of course I'd testify," he said. "I never said I wouldn't."

"But you said he's a terrible man," I said.

"And he is," the monsignor said. "But he's not a bad one, not by any means. And this is a terrible thing that they're doing to him now. Anything I can do to prevent it is a thing that I will do. Do you know what it is he asked me to do?"

I did not, and I said that. "I thought not," he said. "He asked me to bury him in Latin.

"'Back when they changed it over,' Billy said, 'what was that, anyway? Thirty years or so ago?'

"'More than that,' I said. 'Seems like yesterday, or else it seems like a century.'

"'Yes,' he said, 'well, I didn't like it then, and said so, and I don't like it now. One thing I want you to do for me is bury me in Latin.'

"I didn't say anything for a while," Martin said. "It took me a moment to gather my wits. Then I said: 'Not that I wouldn't like to do it, Billy, but you must know I can't. I'm not in that good odor as it is down there in Brighton. Haven't been for years. When I was still active, I complicated their lives, all that ecumenical slop that they started peddling then and're still pushing today. I don't know exactly what would happen if I did something like that now, what they could do to me, but I'm an old man now, and it wouldn't take that much, and they would think of something that would do the job.'

"They knocked the wind out of me with that Red thing," Martin said. "I never said it, but I always wondered if maybe that so-called 'electrical fire' wasn't set for me at Saint Matt's. By those people you attacked. There's a way to do that, I understand, if you can get at the wiring. Wouldn't've been too difficult then, when the church was never locked."

"I'm not familiar with the 'Red thing,'" I said.

Martin looked sadly at me. "No," he said, "no, you wouldn't be. It was forty years ago. You were just a kid then. The cardinal, Richard Cardinal Cushing, was dead-set against what he called 'godless, atheistic, communism,' and I became inflamed. I was just a kid myself then, barely in my forties, and I thought that if I took a hard line, harder than the cardinal's, but not in disagreement with it, well, that he would like that. And I did. In my sermons. At communion breakfasts, that sort of thing. And after a while, word began to spread around the area, what I had to say on that issue, and I was invited to conduct a half-hour radio show on issues in the news. It was just a small station, only five thousand watts, out in Cardiff. You couldn't even get it in Norwich during the day—only at night. But that didn't matter. The anti-McCarthy people found out about it, and they got someone to record what I was saying, and then they went to the cardinal and complained. Not that I was anticommunist, which I was; that I was anti-Semitic, which I was not, and am not to this day. And, well, they had a lot of influence at Lake Street. The cardinal listened to them, and it didn't matter whether what they had to say was true. What mattered was that he would go to those rich liberal Unitarians—no better than agnostics themselves—and the Jews, when he had some project in his mind and couldn't find the money in the archdiocese, and they would help him out. So if they were unhappy, they had to be calmed down, and the way to do that was to silence me.

"He never did tell me not to speak out," Martin said. "He called me in and sat me down and said he'd heard what I'd been doing, and, of course, the threat from communism was so great that we all had to be on our guard. But he urged me to be, well, 'more discreet' in what I said, and the minute he said that, well, I knew I was to stop.

"And I did stop," Martin said. "I could only hope that by giving up the radio and speaking of other things at public events, I could buy enough time for the damage to be forgiven

if not forgotten. But I was wrong. Those people who'd complained about me held their grudges. So when Saint Matthew's
burned, well, I did have my suspicions. Some conspiracy, not
that I hadn't been completely silenced by then: to punish me
for what I'd said before. Sheer vindictiveness. But the fire marshal said: "It's not arson, Monsignor." Old building, old wiring,
and so on. I thought he was incompetent, lazy, the whole thing
on his mind wasn't to find out how it started, how it *really*
started, but to finish up his chores there with as little work as
possible and go on to the next thing.

"Essentially what Billy did to me after the fire," Martin said,
"was tell me it didn't matter in the long run whether the fire
was accidental or it had been set. In either case the insurance
was the same: not enough. 'The important thing,' he said, 'is
that that church has got to be rebuilt. And you're the only man
who can do that. It's going to take all of your time, all of your
energy, and you can't be distracting yourself with any other
questions.' And he was dead right. What a good head that man
had on his shoulders. We need men like that. Even when they
are so damnably hard to deal with.

"When we had the fire," the monsignor said, "the original
bells were ruined, damaged beyond repair. The men who came
in every year to clean them up—there just isn't any way to keep
the pigeons out of a belfry, and bats too, I suppose, and they
make a terrible mess with their nests and so forth. If you just let
it go, you'd've had corrosion, and probably a sanitation problem. Anyway, the cleaners came and inspected the bells after
the fire, and told me they were cracked and couldn't be fixed.

"Well, the price of replacing them, even with smaller bells
that wouldn't've sounded anywhere near as beautiful—or as
loud, either, although some of the Protestants in Norwich might
not have objected too much to that; there'd always been a certain amount of grumbling from the neighborhood during Lent

—was just staggering. Far beyond the amount of our budget to repair the building itself. So I went to the cardinal and all but got down on my knees, begging him to help, but he said, well, it was hopeless. Hopeless in Saint Matthew's case, at least, as long as I was still the pastor, because the people he'd normally approach in that kind of an emergency—those rich Jewish people who gave to all kinds of charities, hedging their bets, I suppose, a few wealthy Protestants with old family money—were exactly the same people, liberals and so forth, who hated and despised me for my stand on the communist thing. 'They remember you, Frank,' he said to me, 'and they don't like what they remember.' So that was that. He said the only hope I had was to go back to my parishioners and tell them the whole sad story, see if they could come up with more money.

"Well, he might as well have told me to fly over the church every Sunday and see if people would come and pay to see me do it. The quarries were on their last legs. Norwich Gear was shutting down. People were losing jobs they'd held for thirty, forty years. The new industry out along the highway hadn't really come into bloom yet, and even if there had been that possibility, the people from the gearworks wouldn't've gotten those jobs—they were too old, most of them, to learn a whole new kind of work. All that technical gibberish probably would've been too much for them even if they had been young enough to start all over again. As it was they'd been pretty hard pressed, even before the fire, to keep up the church, and the school, the convent and the rectory, and the cemetery as well. And you weren't going to be able to raise the kind of money I needed on bake sales and raffles and bingo.

"So I was stumped. The only hope I really had was if I could find at least some money, just a little money, so I could go with my hat in my hand to the bank and see if I could take out another loan. Pretty small chance of that. We had all we could do just to carry the debt we already had. As often as not we were a month or two behind as it was, struggling to meet just the interest payments. But it was the only prospect I had.

"So I went to some of the people in the parish who still had a few dollars to their names, and there weren't very many by then. Most working pretty hard just to keep themselves and their families within hailing distance of middle class. As it was we were having hard sledding. But I started in again. Went to some of the merchants and local businessmen who weren't Catholics themselves, but knew it was in their own best interests to stay on the Catholics' good side if they expected to stay in business very long in Norwich. And people like the Kilduffs, for example, Catholics themselves, whose whole business then was the Catholics.

"Well, they all helped me as much as they could, which wasn't really very much when you came right down to it, but I was grateful to all of them anyway. And then I went to the Ryans, which meant, of course, going to Billy. I'd saved Billy for last, hoping if I went to him with four or five thousand dollars in pledges and contributions from people whom he'd know for sure weren't as well off as he was, he might be shamed into making up the rest and maybe then I wouldn't have to make my humble visit to the bank.

"But I knew it wouldn't be easy. Billy might've been doing pretty well, as his father had before him, but he took after Bucko in more than one respect: he was damned close with a dollar when it came to giving to charities. Took good care of his family, saw to it that the kiddoes were always well dressed— well, Fannie took care of that, of course, but Billy paid the bills. Sent them to good schools—Colin and John went to Priory as soon as they were ready for junior high, and he sent Marie to Sacred Heart Academy for a year after high school before she went off to college. Patrick, I think Patrick had two years at

Priory before he went to college—Patrick, I always had the impression he was a late bloomer.

"So although this was somewhat before his real estate office became the going concern-it did later, Billy'd inherited a good bit of change when his father died, and he sold off the liquor business. And while I didn't place a whole lot of stock in the stories that you always'd heard about what Billy'd been up to in his state job, I knew very well that if he chose to he could easily match what I'd already gotten from others. And never miss it. So I hoped that if I could maybe get Fannie to soften him up a little, let him know how hard I'd been working, and what real sacrifices others far less fortunate had made, then when I finally got around to bracing him for what really should have been no more than his fair share, he'd see his way clear to writing out a good-sized check to the parish.

"Well, he did no such thing. 'I know what you're up to here, Frank,' he said, 'so you needn't beat around the bush or try to soft-soap me with all that blarney you've been feeding to Fannie. You can come into my kitchen every day for the rest of your days, if you want to, for your nice little chats with my wife, and if you don't mind all the talk that causes around this town, well, I guess I don't either. But my guess is you think you can talk me into giving you two or three thousand dollars'—actually I'd been hoping for five—'and I can tell you right now I won't do it. You can talk from now 'til Doomsday, but the most you're going to get out of me is five hundred bucks. That's it. You can take it or leave it.'

"Well, I was very disappointed, of course. I tried to tell him how so many other people in the town'd dug down deep in their pockets, pockets nowhere near as deep as his were, to promise me that much. In a couple cases, even more.

" 'That's their business,' he said. 'This is mine we're discussing here, and I've made up my mind. Lot of damned foolishness

anyway, if you ask me. Plenty of things the people in this town
need and can't afford before they should deny themselves just
so you can go around bragging about eight or nine thousand
dollars' worth of bells.'

"So that was it. There was no budging him, and he'd been
my last hope. So I had to go back to the people I'd talked to
earlier and tell them to keep their money, or give it back to
them if they'd already handed it to me. They were almost as
disappointed as I was. A couple of them even told me to keep
the money, put it toward the other repairs, or just put it aside
for a year or more until maybe the local economy started to pick
up again. *They* were consoling *me.*"

I asked the monsignor if he'd let it be known around town
who'd torpedoed the bells. That was the last thing I wanted to
have out as common knowledge—people in small towns have
memories just as long as rich, philanthropic liberals when it
comes to preserving legends about the local miser, whom they
envy, maybe even longer—especially when the miser's said to
have stolen part of his riches by abusing their government's
authority. That kind of stuff would sink Billy if some "helpful"
character witness took it into his head to launch it into the
trial.

The monsignor denied he had identified Billy as the skin-
flint who'd denied his parish her bells. "But people didn't have
much trouble guessing who it was, and guessing right, too. It
may not be known, but it's suspected."

"But some years later, I understand," I said, "Billy did make
some kind of a donation to new bells."

The monsignor scowled. "He did, yes, but not to me. Not
'til after I retired, and Father Shaw had taken over."

So the monsignor was not completely happy with Billy; it
didn't matter. Those bells were still about the only thing I had,
at that point, to decorate Billy as a man of charitable inclina-
tions. Martin's sulkiness didn't matter. I was not letting it or

him get away from me that readily. "Do you know what changed his mind?" I said.

The scowl was replaced with what he probably meant to be an expression of kindliness. "I really don't," he said. "Maybe he read A *Christmas Carol* and had his own visitations."

That was not the explanation, but I'd expected something like it. Father Shaw had already told me all about Billy's carillon, predicting the monsignor would leave out certain details. "He does that whenever the whole story would mean he couldn't take all the credit for something good that happened. Gets a mite forgetful.

"We haven't got any real bells up in that steeple. It's an Irish ghetto-blaster. The wonders of modern technology. A sound system any rock group would kill to get, sealed against the bird poop and the weather. All that's actually up there are four bodacious speaker boxes. God only knows what marvels are in them—I sure don't. The circuitry and the controls are safely down in the vestry. No more ropes, no more pulleys, no more rotting beams and beseeching the Almighty not to let the things fall down and kill some devout Christian soul. Or even an infidel, as far as that goes.

"When Billy stiffed the monsignor, he had to settle for a tape system, one of those scratchy old eight-track relics that were all the rage, oh, must be twenty years ago. It was pretty painful to listen to. The tapes were always breaking or unspooling, had to keep replacing them, it seemed like, every six weeks or so.

"I had a maiden aunt, made her living up in Holden giving music lessons. Piano, mostly, but she was a fairly accomplished musician. She could also play the organ—she retired as the church organist up there when I was assigned here so she could drive down to hear me celebrate the Mass—the saxophone, clarinet, flute and even some fiddle. Just wasn't quite good enough to get a full-time job with an orchestra.

"That tape system almost made her nuts. Said it was almost enough to make her go back to her old parish. So one day, after it did a particularly hideous number on 'Ave, Maria,' sounded like somebody tormenting ten cats, she told me she was going to leave me her life savings to get a new carillon. A real one. Well, by the time she died she'd been sick a long time, and she'd never had that much anyway. So not much savings were left, and her house and her assets'd gone first. The whole amount wasn't enough.

"But then the old apparatus just plain quit. Right after I took charge here, and I had to do something. So I ran into Billy on the street one day, and told him the whole sorrowful story. Wiring all shot, corroded. Speakers worn out, seven grand for a new one, at least. And all Aunt Margaret had left me was a little over two thousand.

" 'Tell you what,' Billy said to me, 'I know a man who sells that stuff. Now and then he sells it, at least. I'll get in touch with him, give you a call, and we'll both go and see him.'

"I guess this guy owed Billy a favor," Shaw said "*But*, Billy said also: 'I'll pay the difference. I'll pay it on two conditions.'

" 'And what are those?' I said. "Billy did have that reputation for being a sharp man when it came to playing an angle. People have been known to try to make 'donations' that are really loans, deduct 'the gift' from their taxes, and then get the money back, or most of it, under the table.

" 'The first one,' Billy said, was that I could tell no one who paid for most of the rig. 'Just tell 'em your aunt left some money. Except,' Billy said, 'for the tax men, of course. I'm planning to deduct this item.' "

" 'Can't blame you for that,' I said. 'I would do that myself. What's the second one?' Figuring this'd be the zinger.

"Billy's second condition," Shaw said, "was that on the day of his funeral, the bells should play 'Too-ra, Loo-ra, Loo-ra.' "

"He told me he'd asked the monsignor for that," Shaw told

me. "The monsignor had made him a promise. 'But I don't trust him myself,' Billy said. 'He's got a mean streak in him, and besides, he's mad at me. He wouldn't dare to doublecross me while I'm still around, but when I'm dead he'll go for revenge.'

" 'This would be because you turned him down the last time on the bells,' I said.

" 'Uh huh,' Billy said, 'I figured he'd tell people that. Well, I didn't turn him down flat. I wouldn't give what he wanted. I just said I had a pretty good idea how much he had in mind, I said I'd either give him five hundred, take it or leave it, knowing it wasn't enough, or else I'd match whatever he kicked in. "But I don't have money, Billy," he says, whining the way people who're just plain cheap always do when you've got them trapped. "You know that, surely. I'm just a poor parish priest."

" ' "Yeah," I said,' Billy said, ' "a poor parish priest with a house on the beach in Florida. Who gets a new, top-of-the-line Buick every three years and gets his suits made to order in Boston. You've got some money, Francis. Get it up." But no sir, he just wouldn't do it. And that's why he got no new bells.' "

"You'll testify to this?" I said to Shaw.

"If Billy says it's okay," Shaw said. "You don't look like the tax man to me, and I did give my word to the man."

"Believe me," I said, "Billy will. We need all the help we can get. How much did he give you, anyway?"

"It came to about thirty-five hundred dollars, I think," Shaw said. "It was quite a lot for one song. That he won't even be able to hear. I can look it up, if you want."

"Oh, no need to do that," I said. "Billy'll remember it down to the dime. He's got a great head for numbers. That's how he got into this mess."

TWELVE

As the Ides of March approached I'd begun to understand old Julius Caesar was not the only man who should have been wary of mudtime. I was bushed. The only decent meals I could recall having in about six weeks were the veal I'd had with Teddy at Tessio's and the roast beef I'd had with the Kilduffs. Day after day—Sundays, holidays, and holy days of obligation—I'd been at my desk or on the road, maintaining body temperature and metabolic function on cheeseburgers and potato chips that could have chassis-lubed two '35 LaSalles.

I couldn't plead surprise. Like Caesar, I'd been warned. A long time ago—at the time I probably had six or seven years in practice, met most of the regulars inside the bar enclosure, lost to some but beaten most and had some reason to think I was hitting my rightful stride—I encountered one weekday afternoon outside the old Dini's Restaurant on Tremont Street a very capable and genial fellow whose court work I'd admired for some time. He was picking scrod out of his teeth, which was unremarkable because it was just after lunchtime and Manny was the worst news a young cod ever had, but he had a crewneck sweater on, not a suit and tie. "Manny," I said, "I haven't seen you around."

"Haven't been around, kid," he said, grinning. "Retired back two years ago."

It was time to proceed carefully: there were at least three possible explanations that crossed my mind at once, which meant there were probably at least six. He was about fifteen years shy of sixty-five (which back then I thought a fairly advanced age; I now think of it as "seasoned"), and since not even sixty-five is often observed by private practitioners as a mandatory stopping point, retirement short of it generally provokes suspicion and generates crocodile-pious pity. Whispers circulate to the effect that either "poor old fill-in-the-name" got some bad news from the oncologist and had decided that he'd better have all the fun he could, fast, or that the booze had gotten him (we didn't lose many stalwarts to drugs back then, or at least weren't aware of it if we did). Large trust funds, coupled with a certain taste for leisure, are uncommon attributes among successful trial lawyers; rich kids who become lawyers seldom gravitate to court (and those who do straggle in seldom meet much success there). And that could be ruled out in Manny's case; like most of us, he was a first-generation lawyer, and had been the financier as well as the beneficiary of his education. Any money Manny's family had had been brought in by Manny. So that left the possibility that Manny, who'd done very well indeed representing mean-looking gentlemen who'd been caught importing large amounts of dope (it was almost all dope that we heard about then, back in those innocent years), had been convincingly threatened out of practice, either by a prosecutor with a vicious glint in his eye or a dissatisfied client with a .357 Magnum in his hand. I hedged my bet. "Got rich and just quit, huh," I said. "I'd've thought you liked it too much to do that. You were too good at it, too."

He grinned some more. "Not *too* rich," he said. "Just rich enough. But that wasn't it—I just got too old."

"Too old?" I said. "You're not too old. You ate young guys like me for light snacks."

"Right," he said, "and after you've been snacking on young guys as long as I did, twenty-two whole years, you'll find out you're also too old. It comes out of your bones, kid. Not your hide. Your bones. The courtroom stuff, sure, the toe-to-toe and hand-to-hand, all of that stays fun. But that's just a part of what it takes to win cases, and the other part, the bigger one, that one isn't fun. The bedsores on your butt, from sitting at your desk? The lying clients? Stupid ones? The ones that held things back? The things that you find out you did, to your wife and kids? The time you spend, the *time you spend*, stroking people, talking to them, holding their damned hands, not so they'll maybe help the case—just so they won't ruin it. Maybe that's the worst feature: all the time you waste, time you'll never see again. You start thinking about that and it eats your belly out."

"Never happen," I said. "Never happen to me."

"You must have some poor damned DA on the run today," he said, "or at least you think you do. Well, wait'll you've been at it for as many years as I was, the novelty's worn off, and some things have gone a little wrong in your happy life. Meet me back here at this joint, in, say, twenty years. We'll have a piece of fish inside, and see if I was right."

I never did meet him. Dini's shut down maybe five years ago, but even though there were other good fish restaurants, Manny was long gone. Moved away—California, I heard. He always did like golf. But he had still been right: it comes out of your bones.

By the middle of March, when I'd spent what seemed like two years trying to make a brick wall of defense without having any straw except those electric bells, the signs were unmistakable that Billy's kin, if not Billy, were beginning to rebel. I hadn't yet come up with a defense that looked sure-thing or even reasonably dependable to me—which meant *I* was pretty uneasy—but from their point of view what was even worse, if not unforgivable, I hadn't flattered them enough. "You don't consult," Billy said. "They say you don't consult. Colin and Marie, especially. They're both lawyers. They say they know. They say you haven't talked to them because you're not making progress. Say we ought to have a meeting."

Well, it wasn't unexpected. When I arrived at McGillicuddy & Kilduff that roast-beef evening, sore-beset and weary, one of the items on my shopping list had been the closest approximation they could muster of a Ryan bestiary. Now, from what Billy said, I was going to have to call upon it.

Still, even though I had some idea of what kind of people the rest of the Ryans were, this demand for a command performance gave me still another irrelevant, and irritatingly distracting problem to confront. At best a solution would merely enable me to return to the increasingly discouraging task of finding a way to win Billy's case. At worst I might botch my own defense against Colin and Marie, which would at the very least rattle my rattled client still further. This is never a desirable possibility, especially when it might get you fired.

So I decided to give Billy a highly selective summary of my view of his case as it stood, and work up to the place his kids should have in it. I deliberately shifted into the oratorical mode; disgruntled clients pay more heed when their mouthpieces talk like real lawyers. Read: William Jennings Bryan.

"Clients in criminal cases have one or the other of two kinds of families, at least so far as I've been able to see. The first kind does not exist, for purposes of the case. They're just not around." Left out: Estranged, faraway, dead: many or few, young or old, the people who belong to the defendant have either long since written off the man who's become my client, or else been written off by him or the Dread Angel in the sky.

"The other variety resembles your family. Close knit, close by, at least publicly loyal to the embattled defendant, united publicly at least behind him and determined to bring every available asset and resource to aid his desperate struggle and eventual rescue—I say 'resembles' because the Ryans from Day One of my involvement in the case have given every indication of carrying out battle-stations service with the same ferocious will they've individually and jointly marshalled for every other event, major or minor, they've ever encountered." Omitted: To the Ryans, what are extremes to normal people are mere minimum requirements; they're like a pack of barbered Huns in tailored suits.

"They say you've been asking around town about us," Billy said. "They don't like it none, either. Marie in particular. Says it could cause her some very big problems next time she runs for office."

"My questions won't cause Marie anywhere near the problems she's already got from the existence of this case," I said. "And if we don't win it, she won't have any political problems at all, because she'll be out of the running. As you know better than I do.

"Now, I've never managed to decide which kind of family does the most good for (or the least harm to) the eventual outcome of a defendant's case." Unsaid: The hands-off kind passively does him and his lawyer the kindness of staying out of counsel's hair, and does not burden the alleged evildoer with heartfelt sighs and gazes of trust betrayed or innocent faith and trust withdrawn. But, come conviction and the probation inquiries that precede the day of sentencing, an aging, tearful mother and a stoic-but-brave father; a steadfastly faithful spouse (one probation officer I knew calls them "the tick-'n-tinners"; "I been wid Joe since we got married, and I'm wid him, troo tick-'n-tin.") can be consolations. Hardened veterans of the process don't usually appear to assign much weight to sobbing bairns who miss their daddy, tearful wives, mournful dogs or listless cats pining for the master ever since he got trotted off in handcuffs, but at least there are some voices that will utter a kind word about him, let a tear trickle down to humanize the thug, and that's something I can use to sing my song (my pals in Probation exclude from their reports all familial expressions of bitter disappointment about my incompetence, regularly cited as the complete explanation for my and every other criminal lawyer's clients' misfortunes).

"Yeah," Billy said, "but they're not saying they want to come to court. They're saying they want to talk to you. That's all."

"I'm getting to that," I said. "I just want you—and them—to understand why I'm not going to conduct this conference they have in mind.

"The most a family can do—the only good, anyway—is stay out of the lawyer's work with the client. Whatever their private reservations about it may be. Let me ask you this, Billy: Marie's a politician. Far's I know she's never tried a case in her life. Doctor John's a surgeon; think he'd allow me to perform an operation? Patrick's a general, not a bad thing to be; think he'd let me command his troops? And Colin's a judge. If he gets himself involved in this on a day-to-day basis, he's looking down the barrel of a judicial conduct inquiry; think Colin wants that? And if he did want to get involved in it on that basis, back when it all started, why the heck did he call six or seven lawyers, the last one being me, to take your case for you? If he wanted it, why didn't he keep it? Have you got an answer for that? Or for that matter, has Colin? I'd like to hear one, if you do."

"Well," Billy said, looking troubled.

"Now let me ask another one, just for you, all right? How many DPW decisions, in all the years you've been running the operation, have you put to a damned committee?"

"Well," he said, "not very many."

"None, to be exact," I said. "You're famous for it. Now do you tell the family? Or do I?"

"I've got to tell them something," he said. "They've got Fannie all upset."

"Tell them to calm her down, since they're the ones who stirred her up," I said. "And tell them as well that I've got one more interview to do before you and I, *not* you and your family, resume our preparation. Next Monday morning, you come in here, alone, around ten. It's nearly time for you to go to serious work, like me."

Left out: Time was running out on both of us. All I could do was hope our luck would soon start rolling in.

THIRTEEN

It was raining like hell the next day when I completed my field work by meeting Mark Frolio for lunch at Bill & Ernie's in Denniston. I found it easily from his directions: in the woods a few miles east of Uxbridge on Route 16. "The grey roadhouse on the right. It's the only thing around there where you can get a bite to eat. Unless you happen to be a squirrel or something." Bill and Ernie appeared to be traditionalists who believed that a gin mill with a common victualer's license ought to look like one: all dark, inside and out, the long one-story building low to the ground, grey and seedy in the dim light under the overgrown evergreens around it, the interior furnished with comfortable captain's chairs and spacious booths, tables large enough to accommodate six and no damned ferns in sight. And the victuals proved common indeed.

"They serve an honest drink," Mark said, apparently having just received his first Rob Roy. They also offered serious beers—I ordered a Grolsch and relaxed.

"Tough driving in this weather," he said. He was one of those altar boys who still looks twenty at his fortieth birthday party. "Almost as bad as snow."

"It was getting ahead of my wipers at times," I said. "Thought of pulling over on the shoulder, wait it out, and then I thought: But if I do, some eighteen-wheeler comes along, he can't see any better, and instead of meeting Frolio, I'll be having lunch with Jesus."

"Food'd most likely be better," he said. "Dunno if He'd serve any beer, though."

"This's how far from the office?" I said. "Eleven or twelve miles, maybe?"

"Little more'n that, actually," he said.

"How often you come here?" I said.

He shrugged. "Three, maybe four times a week. Depends on whether I've got some business, takes me a different direction. I know bars in every direction."

"What's your business today?" I said. "Not that I'm minding it for you."

He smiled on the right side of his mouth. "Meeting you," he said. He drank some of the scotch and vermouth.

The waitress delivered my beer. "Want some time, Mark?" she said, wiping her hands on her apron. She was a bleached ash blonde in her late thirties, not a bad figure at all, with a nice face that showed some worry lines and framed blue eyes that over the years had seen too many nice things turn out badly.

He looked at her and said: "Give us a couple of minutes, Sandy, okay?" She said: "Sure," and departed. Each of them had rescued the other with a charity fuck, or six, at the ends of days that had gone from bad to unbearable, and they would do it again anytime—I could tell from the caresses in their voices, and even though I knew neither one of them, and it certainly was none of my business, I was silently glad for them.

"None of the Ryans come here, I take it," I said.

"None of the Ryans go *any*where," he said. "Funny, bootleg-ger's grandchildren. But no, no they don't. This kind of joint, it's beneath them. So they never come here. It's the friends of the Ryans that come, and those're the ones that cause prob-lems."

"But even they, the friends," I said, "they don't come here either."

"At night they do," he said. "At night lots of them do. Pretty hard, though, find a place where some of them aren't. There's so many, you know? They're all over."

"So where do you go at night?" I said.

He nodded. "You've really been busy, haven't you?"

" 'Just doin' my job, sir,' as Joe Friday used to say," I said. "You probably don't remember him though."

" 'Dragnet'?" he said. "Sure I remember it. Big family favor-ite in my house."

Okay, so far so good. At least he wasn't still in his twenties.

"Depends on the situation, where I go nights," he said. "Not where I go—I always go home. Which home do I go to? That depends."

The waitress returned. "You want menus, Mark?"

"I don't need one," he said. "Mister Kennedy might like to see one, but I'll tell him right now: Don't order the luncheon special. I'd recommend a burger myself."

"Whatever he's having," I said to her.

"And another Rob Roy," he said.

"Beer for me," I said.

"Which home're you going to these days?" I said.

"Nights," he said absently as the waitress returned with the second round. "Which home am I going to these nights. Days I go to the office. Try to keep that operation afloat. But nights, the apartment. Got a one-bedroom up in Grafton. Nice little place. Overlooking a pond. The tennis courts, the pool, a health club—not that I use any of 'em. But you can't beat the rent. It's a condo complex. Half empty. They're hoping I'll bring in some customers, so they're letting me use one unit for the upkeep."

"Brought any customers in?" I said.

He shrugged. "Four, so far," he said. "Market's tight. Interest rate's sky high. People're scared."

"Any of them buy?" I said.

"Like we used to say in the Air Force," he said, "no kills, two probables."

"You were in the Air Force," I said.

"Yeah," he said. "But this wasn't aerial dogfights we talked about. We were all in Procurement. This was picking up women in bars near the base. In most cases the pick-ups were dogfights themselves, but hey, we were no bargains either. And we *were* in Procurement, right?" He chuckled. "Story of my life," he said. "Get out of the Air Force. Meet Marie in law school. Get married. Of course. One dogfight into another."

"I should've told the waitress I wanted mine medium rare," I said, starting my second beer.

"Wouldn't make any difference," he said. "My theory's the cook is on piece work. The longer each piece takes to cook, the more money he gets to take home. Everything comes out well done. Charcoal briquettes. But in a way that's good. Kills the taste of the meat. Really cheap meat they serve here. Large portions, but very fatty."

That at least would be familiar. "I realize I've put you in kind of an awkward position," I said.

"No you haven't," he said. "I put myself in the awkward position. It's a common mistake. Lots of guys do it. Wasn't anything you did."

"I didn't mean your marriage," I said. "For what it's worth, I made that one myself. I meant: asking to see you. To talk about Billy."

"I don't mind talking about Billy," he said. "I kinda like Billy, what I know of him. I don't think Billy's all that fond of me, but it's certainly nothing personal."

"Then why meet me out in the woods, Goldilocks, for lunch with the three goddamned bears?" I said. "Isn't this so no one sees us?"

"No," he said, "it's so no one sees *me*. I've got a drinking problem, you see." He picked up his glass and drained it. "Okay, guess I do, but it's mine. It doesn't belong to the Ryans. I do. It doesn't. Simple as that. My problem and I get along fine. It's *their* problem with *my* problem that's *the* problem. It's like I've joined a temperance group, when 'family' occasions come up. All by myself. They all have their drinks, get pleasantly mulled and watch me. So I don't like it when their snoop network counts my drinks other places, and then reports back to them. Because then I get all kinds of grief. So I figure: okay, I'll drink in the woods. So far the owls haven't talked."

The waitress brought the burgers. They did look like something you'd dump kerosene on, and light off to grill some nice burgers. I bit into mine and said: "You're a shrewd judge of chow, Mark. Every bit as good as you said."

He nodded. "But full of calories," he said. "Chock-a-block full of the calories. You could take a team of Huskies from Anchorage to Nome on four boxes full of these, one for you and three for the dogs. You and your dogs might have a small problem, some years from now, down the line. 'Bypass should do it. You'll be okay.' But still, they keep life in the body."

"The reason I asked about Billy," I said, "is that this case presents some real problems."

He snorted before he chawed another hunk off his sandwich. Chewing, he said: "I'll say. Serious prison time. That is, if you can't get him off."

"That's begun to look hard to do," I said. I was hungry enough to continue eating. I talked while I chewed my food too.

It would've been hard to have one of those things for lunch without chewing for the rest of the day, unless you carried floss with you. "He's a politician," I said. "A powerful politician, and when one of that breed gets himself indicted . . ."

"He's not so powerful," Frolio said. He swallowed and took a potato chip. He washed that down with the rest of his Rob Roy and raised the glass with his left hand. Then he set it back down on the table.

"He isn't?" I said. "Now that's some news. Everyone else seems to think so."

"I know one state cop that doesn't," Frolio said. "Cost me almost two hundred bucks to meet him. Billy means nothing to him."

"How did all this come about?" I said.

"Oh, the usual," he said. He chomped down on the burger again, leaving about one mouthful. The guy must've had the teeth and digestive juices of an alligator.

The waitress appeared with another Rob Roy. She set it down and looked inquiringly at me. "I'm all set," I said.

"I was blowing down One-twenty-two one morning. I'm late. And so what do I get behind? A school bus. That road's a two-lane, maximum forty, double-yellow-no-passing, and already I'm running late. Pull over and stop, and pick up a kid. Start up, go a mile, and then stop again. I'm going nuts. This's one of the times Marie'd put me out. I'm living in the apartment. And our daughter, Megan, is in the school play—in Norwich, naturally—and my alarm clock didn't go off. I'm getting crazier and crazier, pounding the wheel and all, but I haven't completely lost my mind yet. I know you can't pass a stopped school bus. Besides, I might kill some kid. So after about, I dunno, six or eight miles, the bus gets going. I pass. Over the double-yellow. On a curve. Coming up on the crest of a hill.

"I've got a nice car," he said. He had some Rob Roy. "It's no goddamned Mercedes, or anything like that—the agency wouldn't support it. After what Patrick did to it, we're lucky we've still got the lights on. And I have to have a four-door, all right? For when I take customers out. But Pontiac makes a Turbo Grand Am sedan that'll run with the bigger dogs, and that car is what I have got.

"So the bus starts up, and I floor the damned thing. It comes on the boost, and I go whipping around up the hill. And right at the top is a large-size state cop, working his radar gun.

"I do believe," Frolio said, "I do believe that state cop had a radio in his car. Because there was another state cop at the bottom of the hill, and he was out in the road. Holding up his right hand like he was at a Hitler rally. Then he kind of brought it down and pointed it to his left, the right shoulder. I thought this might mean he would like me to pull over. I am sensible. I thought it might be wise to do it. From what I hear, those guys carry guns. So I pulled over.

"He was very nice," Frolio said. "He asked me if he could see my license and registration, which I was only too happy to give to him, and after he looked at those he told me that the speed limit on the stretch where I'd also gone over the double-yellow—he didn't leave that out—was forty, and I'd been snap-shot at sixty-eight. Naturally I gave him a lot of guff. 'Yessir,' I said.

"He asked me where I was going in such a hurry," Frolio said. "I told him I am married to State Representative Marie Ryan Frolio, which I legally was and legally am, at least to this point, and that I was on my way to Norwich to see our daughter, the granddaughter of William F. Ryan of Norwich, Commissioner of the Department of Public Works, in the third-grade play at Saint Matthew's School. And that I was already late.

"Cut no ice with him at all," Frolio said. "He nodded his head and he wrote me up for sixty-eight in a forty-stretch, and crossing over the double-yellow, and I missed the play. The whole play. All of it. Marie was very pleased, and her father was, too. And so was Fannie, I guess, although she never does have much to say, one way or the other. Marie and her father said I should've told the cop who they were. I said I did that, and he didn't give a shit. They were pleased with that too.

"A little time went by, and I got a thing from the district court that said I had a choice. I could either pony up by mail, or I could come in and say why I shouldn't have to pony up.

"So I still wasn't happy. I'd gotten the ticket, and I'd missed the play, but when it comes to screwing up, well, I don't settle for less than big-time. I told my dear wife about the letter that I got, and she told me to go in and tell the judge who I was. Or who they are. And I said I didn't think I really wanted to do that, because the cop hadn't been impressed by that information and I didn't think the judge'd be, either, and then we had a really good fight. I think I may've said that if I went into that courthouse and told them about her and Billy there, I'd probably get charged with manslaughter, and what I already had was enough. She called me some bad name or other.

"I went back to the apartment, and the next day in the office I wrote out a check and paid the fine. And when she went over the checks the next month—she doesn't do squat in that business, except she still goes over the checks every month, being a Ryan and money involved—she found it and we had a rematch. See? Stupid. I didn't know enough to get a money order at the bank. So that was the third fight we had over that goddamned school play, which I think was about Our Blessed Mother or something. Most of them seem to be."

I apologized for laughing. "I know it's not funny," I said.

"Of course it's funny," he said. "It's funny to somebody else. But I didn't tell it to you for laughs. I told it because I don't think Billy Ryan's anywhere near as high powered as Billy and his family think. I've heard a lot of people when they see him coming say: 'Here comes the snowplow man.' And then they laugh. The DPW is nothing but a bunch of Billy's cronies, and everybody knows it. Including the state cops. And since he got indicted, well, now it's open season. Now *I'm* even getting it: 'Oh yeah, here's Ryan's ghinny son. He's got a lot of money, most of which is ours. Let him pick up the check.' "

"Sorry to hear it," I said, and I meant it.

"Not as sorry as I've been to hear it," he said. "Now look, Mister Kennedy, all right? I know you've got a job to do. And I hope he gets off. But I can't testify for him. I don't know him well enough. To Billy and his family, I'm just Marie's wop. They fought against the marriage, and they lost. Just like I did. Wished I'd been on their side. But she was proving something to them, and I was her way to do that. Marie can be determined. Very single-minded girl. It all looked good at the time.

"So now I'm caught. But so is she. I'm too old to go out now and get a real law job. And she can't throw me out of the office, like she throws me out of the house, because if I go, that office collapses. And the Ryans don't want that. It's not much of a life, and I wouldn't recommend it, a young couple starting out, but it's the only one I've got, and I have to live with it. So I'd appreciate it if what I tell you does not get back to them. And since I'm talking to you in this place, the only way it will get back is if you take it back."

I said I wouldn't do that.

"You're sure," he said. "I hope you are. I'm depending on it. I make that bunch mad enough and they will get rid of me. And then I will be eating nuts, just like the squirrels do."

I assured him I wouldn't tell.

"Mister Kennedy," he said, "now I shouldn't tell you this. But like I said, I'm the family dago, and when this thing first came up, the thing you're working on, they decided I would fix it. I'd take care of it."

"How would you do that?" I said.

"Jack Bonaventre, right?" he said. "AG's chief witness, right? Soon as they found that out, well, they knew what to do. Bonaventre's an Italian name, or at least they think it is. So they decided I would get in touch with Bonaventre, and get him to change his story."

Subornation of perjury. Obstruction of justice. Certain doom in other words, for my endangered client, when Mike Dunn smelled it out and put a wire on Bonnie, as Mike Dunn surely would. "Oh my dear sweet Jesus," I said.

"I said: 'I can't do that,' I said. 'I don't know the guy. Why'd he listen to me?' "

"Just who was this, said this," I said. "Who asked you to do this thing? Was it just your wife?" It seemed to have become suddenly very cold and damp in the bar; I had a clammy feeling.

"Well," he said, "she was in the room of course. It was Megan's birthday, party at Billy's house. All parties are at Billy's house. Never at our own houses, anybody in the family. All Christmases, all Thanksgivings: Billy's, Billy's, Billy's. His own kids and their wives and husband, we're his satellites. And all the kids're hollering in the other room, and all these grown-ups except me are having their cocktails. Me being the drunk and all. I had ginger ale. Boy, did I get crocked when I got back to the apartment that night. But all of them were there, except the business-wrecker Pat, of course. God help this country if we go to war with him in charge. Pat couldn't run a damned flea circus for you if you spotted him a junk-yard dog."

"Was Billy there?" I said.

"Oh yeah," Frolio said. "Billy was right there. Billy was the one that asked me. It was his idea. Fannie, Marie, all the others, they were just *around*. The way it always is at Billy's when the boss is home—everybody else just happens to be there. Billy runs the meetings."

"What did he say?" I said. "As close as you remember?"

"Aw hell," Frolio said, "I don't remember, exactly. We didn't have a whole lot to do in Air Force Procurement when I was there. So I followed the Watergate thing pretty close. Some of it stuck in my mind, I guess. Like, for example, 'obstruction of justice.' Uh uh, not for me. If they can get a president for it, it's definitely not in my line."

Actually he was overlooking not only subornation but something more: tampering with a witness, even if he won't lie for you, is also frowned upon. But Mark'd made the right decision, and the bacon had not been lost. Not by him, then, anyway. Maybe I could scare the hell out of Billy before they found some jamoke who would actually try it, and blow me right out of the water. I felt a little warmer.

"Well," I said, "thank God for that. At least someone in the clan hasn't lost his mind in this."

"Yeah," Frolio said, "assuming I'm in the clan, or ever was, far as that goes. But the rest of them? Well, lemme put it this way: Billy didn't give up on the idea just because I said I didn't know Bonaventre. Which I don't. Billy's still convinced that someone can get to him and shut him up. Or at least make him do a lot of serious thinking before he testifies."

"Like who?" I said. The clamminess was coming back. It was worse than before.

"Someone who knows Carlo," Frolio said. "Carlo Donato?"

"Oh, shit," I said.

"That's why Billy asked me first," Frolio said. "Like I said, I'm the family's pet ghinny. Not good for much, maybe, but 'you know those Italians. The ones that aren't actually related still all know each other.' "

"Do you know Carlo?" I said.

"I know who he is," Frolio said. "I'd recognize him on the street. I wouldn't go up to him and ruin his shoeshine, if that's what you mean. But I've never met the guy, no, and I don't want to be introduced." He reflected. "Thing that surprises me, I guess, is that Billy doesn't himself. Billy knows everydamnedbody."

Yes, I thought, Billy does. And if Billy couldn't get his black-sheep son-in-law to do his dirty work, he'd been on the lookout for another handyman. Billy's done a lot of things, for a lot of years, that he's gotten clean away with. And one of the ways he's kept his skirts clean is by using straws and intermediaries to set up his deals. His prints are never on them. Or haven't been, till now.

"I don't mean anything, you know, insulting, when I say this," Frolio said, "but since I've told you what I have already, well, if you let it slip to them, that we had this little chat, I'm dead meat anyway. So I might as well tell you the rest."

"I told you," I said. "Lips're sealed. This's confidential. Everything you say to me. That we even met at all."

"Okay," he said, "I hope so. Or I hope I hope so, at least. Maybe what I'm really doing's hoping you *will* tell. And get me thrown out of a situation I don't have the guts to quit."

He exhaled noisily and drained the third Rob Roy. He held up the glass.

"I've got to be going pretty soon here," I said as the waitress approached with his refill. "I've got some other people I have to see today."

"You do, maybe," he said. "I don't." He cupped the fresh glass in his hands and rotated it on the table. He frowned. "I'd be careful, I was you," he said. "I don't know you. Never saw you before. Most likely won't again. But I know them, and if I were you, I'd watch my ass in this thing."

He looked up and gazed directly at me. "They don't trust you, Mister Kennedy," he said. "They don't trust you at *all*. I get most of it from Marie, naturally, when I go to pick up the kids. She thinks you're incompetent. So when I'm late, as sometimes I am, sweet-talking a promising buyer, it's not just that

I'm late and the kids've been worried. I did it on purpose, just to make her feel worse, when her father's headed for jail. 'His lawyer's no good. Just a damned down-and-outer, washed-up old boozer. A has-been.' That's what she says."

"Her father hired me," I said. "On her brother's say-so."

"That's what I said to her," Frolio said. "I said: 'Jeez, Marie, why'd you hire the guy then, you don't think he's any good. That he can't handle the job.'

" 'We didn't have any choice,' she says. 'Dad's made too many powerful enemies. They're jealous. They *want* to see him convicted. So they can get *their* hands on the DPW, and run it to make their *friends* rich. So all the top lawyers, the word went out: don't take the Ryan case on. "It's taken too long to catch up with this guy. Now we've got him where we want him, and we don't want it to end the wrong way. So all of you: turn it down, all right? One of you guys might get him off."

" 'And they know, the good lawyers, they know what'd happen if one of them took him and won it. He'd be ostracized. For the rest of his life. Shut off on the Hill forever. Colin called all over town, even called a couple hotshots in New York. Nothing doing. Not even for a quarter of a million dollars—even then no one would take it. John said maybe we should even double *that*, and Colin said it wouldn't do any good, even if we went to a million. "Dad's case is just too hot. They're worried about their own futures. We'll just have to settle for someone around here. Someone with nothing to lose. And then hope for the best on appeal."

Good. It's always a relief to know exactly where you stand. Like the marine general in Korea, with the Chinese troops on all sides: They're not getting away from us this time. That warm knowledge you're wanted, and needed, and also working cheap: it really can make you feel good.

"Well," I said, getting up, "you may not believe this, but I do appreciate your confidence. And I'll respect it, too."

"What're you gonna do now?" he said, lifting the glass toward his mouth.

"Go to the men's room," I said. "So far I've been lucky. Never gotten bad news in a men's room."

I left thirty bucks on the table. Figured that I might as well take the kid to lunch, and overtip the nice lady; I was probably on my way to piss blood.

FOURTEEN

Billy's arrival at my office the following Monday was punctual, but it was not happy. It was clear there'd been another family meeting over the weekend, this one about my refusal to appear before the tribunal at the Ryan castle. Had it not been for what Frolio had told me the preceding Friday, I would have assumed that the remarks passed about me had been even more scornful than those of the previous gathering. As it was, I didn't see how they could've been, or how that gang of amateur saboteurs could possibly have dreamed up any scheme more dangerous than the one they'd proposed to Mark.

The consensus had obviously been that Billy should appear as I had directed him, but once seated in my office, chair the meeting himself: Ryan's Rules of Order.

He crossed his legs. "Colin's worried about Keats," he said.

"So'm I," I said. "I always worry about judges."

"Even ones you know?" Billy said. "You went to law school with this guy, you and Colin."

"Billy," I said, "when I'm in front of Colin, I worry about him. A judge on the bench on a case you're trying is not a friend of yours, no matter how long you've known him or how many beers you've had with him, or whether you used to be sidekicks when you both tried cases. Doesn't matter in the slightest. Once he gets that dress on, he's not your pal anymore until the case's over. It always worries me, in fact, if he's one of my buddies outside the court, maybe he'll throw his back out doing favors for the other guy to show he's not favoring me."

"Is Keats going to do that, you think?" he said.

"If I knew what a judge was going to do in a given case before the thing went to trial," I said, "very few of my cases would go to trial. I'd blow out the ones I was going to lose, and I'd tell the prosecutor 'No deal' when I knew I was going to win. If you find a lawyer who tells you he knows what the judge will do when the case comes to trial, you've either got a liar or a fool on your hands, and if I were you I'd be worried."

"So Colin's right, then," Billy said. "He says he's never trusted Keats, not even in law school. Says Keats'd wait until you got up and left the library to go the bathroom, and then steal the book you were studying so you'd flunk the test and make him look good."

"He would," I said. "But so would everybody else, including me and Colin. But not to make you flunk: to survive, ourselves. If there was a case assigned that wasn't in the textbook for the course, anywhere from ten to sixty people in that course would be competing for the volume of decisions that contained it. Generally there were two or three of them in the library. Sometimes only one. You got that volume and you sat on it until you had that case down pat, and then you sat on it some more just so your classmates wouldn't have as good a crack at it as you had. And they'd sit where they could watch you until your bowels or your bladder made you leave that book. When you came back, it was gone. But that was within the rules, and Andy played by them. The really vicious people would get the case and read it, and then misshelve the volume so nobody else could find it without an hour's hunt. Those were the traitors among us.

"No, what Colin was saying is that there's some reason he doesn't know, and I don't know either, why Judge Keats said right at the start that he plans to dispose of your case."

"That's not regular?" Ryan said.

"It's not *ir*regular," I said, "but it's not usual, either. The judges move around the superior court from county to county to county. A couple months here, a couple months there, a couple months spent somewhere else. The general idea is this stops buddy stuff on either side of the case. The judge who's here this month maybe knows you, maybe hates you, maybe loves you, but the one who comes in next may not."

"I never had any complaint with Andy," Billy said, looking thoughtful. "He worked for me a while, and he was a young man with a lot of talent, and I knew he wanted to become a judge. Or something permanent. Besides . . . well, he made me nervous. I was always wondering whether the reason that he worked so hard was that he had his eye on my job. Waiting for me to slip so he could grab it. So when I spotted Tierney on the rise, I told Andy he should give some thought to joining up with him. Grateful governors can do things for their lawyers that other people can't."

"So can the lawyers for the governors," I said, "if they have a good reason. Colin is a judge today because of Andy Keats."

That stopped him. He'd known all along what the history of that deal was, but he'd never really been convinced that anyone else did. "Yeah," was all he said at first. Then he said: "They don't even like each other."

"They may not like each other *now*," I said, "but that means nothing. Judges're just like everybody else in every other line of work: some of them can't stand each other. Some of them act as though they should be exchanging vows. But that's got nothing

to do with it. You, of all people, should know that. It was a
marriage of convenience. Tierney wanted to leave Andy secure
in a judgeship before he went off to Washington to join the
Mondale administration, typical John Tierney miscalculation,
and Tierney couldn't do that because of all the fights he'd been
having with you. You would've torpedoed the nomination, any
nomination. And you could've done it, too, with all the clout
you had. Not to bother Andy—to goose the governor."

Billy thought about that. "Most likely," he said.

"Andy knew that," I said. "Knowing things like that was
Andy's job. So you had a luncheon meeting set up with the
governor one day at Pier Four, and the governor didn't show up.
Because he didn't want to. You were giving him too much heat.
Lunch with you he didn't need. He sent Andy in his place."

"I remember that lunch," Billy said. "I shot my mouth off."

"You sure did," I said.

Tommy Grogan had told me the story. It's been over thirty
years since Andy Keats and I sat beside each other every day in
property, criminal law, civil procedure and whatever other mandatory courses I didn't like much then and since without regret
have long forgotten (the selective memory at work, mercifully
blocking out information and events that did not work out well
—for a while, a few years back, I more or less lost track of
myself, and it showed. "Ah yes," Grogan in high spirits yelled
one night when I shambled into The Last Hurrah at the very
bottom of my fortunes, "and here comes old Jerry Kennedy,
forgotten but not gone"). It was an accident of alphabet;
"Keats" came before "Kennedy," so he sat to my right and I sat
to his left and we were mutually civil. But neutral or hostile your
feelings toward them, ever after you keep track of your law
school classmates.

Still, wary neutrality at best between me and Andy was the
extent of it back then. Andy was not "a warm person," and I
guess I wasn't either. Civility was about as much as any one of

us could manage in those cutthroat days and punishing nights that used to be the tattoo pinched into your resisting flesh by the first year of law school. Most of the males sat staring down the barrel of certain military induction if they flunked out. The few-in-those-days females were correctly and scornfully certain that the males resented their dilettantish presence, and the professors were openly disdainful of those unprepared for class. Each of us was acutely aware that we were competing for grades (because the graduates with the best grades, and only those, would get access to the top-paying jobs), and anyway, the deans had assured all of us on our first day that the person in the next seat would not graduate. The wonder of it's not that we didn't make many friends until at least the second year, but that we didn't kill each other with our bare hands.

And there was still another barrier between me and Andy. It was nothing new then, and it's nothing new today. Andy's clothes were newer and better, and during the spring and Christmas recesses he and his new wife, at the expense of his parents, acquired flattering tans at Round Hill in Jamaica. Tommy Grogan took the trolley to school, and I hoofed it up Com Ave., because Mack needed the car and we both needed her job. But Andy parked his British-racing-green Jaguar XKE roadster on St. Thomas More Drive, where we all could see it from the windows, and when the triple windshield wipers went berserk on one of his skiing trips to Vermont—because he didn't get out and flip them off the frozen glass before turning them on, as the owner's manual directed—and destroyed each other, most of us were all not-quite-secretly glad.

Nevertheless, for all the malice, there was never any doubt in my mind of Andy's intelligence. He was smart then, and hardworking, and he remains both today. That's how he became a judge, and why he's been good at it. He's not one of my favorites—my favorites were the ones I could bamboozle now and then, when the defense was a little bit thin; sad to say, all of them've died or retired—but he's good; I have to give him that. He was good enough to be a judge, without any question, but then, lots of people are. The difference between those lawyers who are good enough to judge and do become judges, and those who are good enough (and want to; not everyone does) but don't, is that the judges were not only good at the law, but good enough at other things to get the black robe too.

"It was beautiful," Grogan said. "It was the kind of thing you hear about happening, after it's happened, of course, and then you hear about it, and it just takes your breath away. Andy Keats is as cute as three ferrets, and just as mean.

"John Tierney was in so much political trouble even he had to notice it. If he ran again, he was doomed. But he was an honorable guy who really wanted to take care of his people while he still could, and still Andy kept telling him: 'Yeah, yeah, I want it. But I want it perfect. There're people out there who'd like to shoot both of us, and some of them're marksmen. You appoint me, I want hostages around me, nice and big and fat. Somebody wants to take me out, they'll have to hit their friends with the first volley.' That's another thing you had to give Tierney credit for being; he couldn't sing the first verse of 'The Star-Spangled Banner' and get all the words right, but he knew enough to get someone who could, and then listen to him; Andy knew all the lyrics by heart."

"You had a road project," I said to Billy. "The governor wasn't in the right mood to push it through for you. The *Commoner* was giving him hell every day, and when Andy showed up for lunch in his place, you decided to kick him around."

"I remember it," Billy said.

"John'd just filled some judgeships," Grogan had told me. "Been in the paper that morning. Nothing especially startling, unless you happened to be someone who'd wanted one and didn't get it—you got seats on the bench that're empty? Better put some asses in them. Looks funny, people come to court and there's no judge sitting there."

"It was a little more than that," Billy said. "One of them was the town counsel in Seekonk, or one of those damned hick towns down there, and that son of a buck'd singlehandedly blocked a project of mine that I wanted."

"You didn't phrase it that way," I said. "You told Andy the new judges were typical picks, couple blacks and some women and so forth. Then you got warmed up, and said Tierney'd rather kowtow to minorities'n take care of his own people. 'Harvard commies,' you said. 'Damned agitators. Turn the public schools into damned experiments. What the hell ever happened to white people? We're the ones who built this country, and now we're supposed to be apologizing to all the goddamned "Native Americans" and the blacks and the spics for being good enough to do what they couldn't do, and begging them, *begging them*, to take what *we* built for *our* children. You're turning us into the niggers. We don't exist anymore.' "

"I guess I did," he said.

"And that's how you made Andy a judge, Billy," I said. "He told a friend of mine right after: that was when he knew he had you. ' "Good Irish boys," ' you said. ' "Girls, too, if that's what he wants, more women on the bench. Good young Catholics. Good lawyers, too. Do they all have to be coons and Jew girls? Every single one of them? Man like my son Colin, why, he's a damned good lawyer, and he wouldn't stand a chance of getting on the bench. Because he's a white man. And on top of that, he's my son. That'll be the day in hell they'll have to turn the heat up. When John Tierney does a thing for Billy Ryan's kid." ' "

"Sometimes you say things," Billy said.

"Oh," Grogan had said, "Billy had the wind up him. 'I couldn't believe it,' Andy said. 'I had him right in my pocket.

"My goodness, Billy," I said, "would Colin like to be a judge? Is that what you're telling me?" "Well, sure," he said, "I'm sure he would. Doggone it, wouldn't every lawyer? I thought the only reason lawyers went to law school was that there aren't any judge schools. You have to go to law school first. But only so that later on, you can get a judgeship. And then give up honest work." ' "

"I guess I did," Billy said. "I guess I did say that."

" 'Well, Billy,' Andy tells me," Grogan said, " 'I certainly hope you're right. Because if Colin wants a judgeship, this is real good news for us. Have you got any idea how pleased the governor'll be to hear that Colin Ryan wants to climb up on the bench? Have you got any idea how desperate we are for men of Colin's experience, his reputation? We'd appoint a hundred Colins if we could find that many who'd take a cut in pay just to serve the public interest.' "

"Well," Billy said, "but he was qualified."

"Qualified?" I said. "He was perfect. Public defender out of law school. Then assistant DA. But the DA wouldn't retire so Colin could get his job. So he quit and did private practice."

"He didn't make any money, though," Billy said.

"I know the feeling," I said. I knew it a lot better than Colin did, because Colin didn't know what not making any money really is. Colin thought not making *much* money was not making any money. But I knew that not making any money was making *no* money. I'd had that feeling on several occasions when some DA'd dangled the hourly wage, steady pay, guaranteed, in front of my nose during a parched season in the old cash flow. What Colin thought was too-small beer had sometimes looked awful good to me. Yeah, I'm a whore. We're all whores. But I'm an honest whore. A couple small cases would come in while I was agonizing, producing barely enough money to fill the gas tank, put food on the table, and give Gretchen a little walking-around cash, and then a five-thousand-buck one'd

stroll in through the door, and I'd call the DA and say: "No."
And the DA would say: "Jerry, Jerry, you're a good kid. I like
you. That's why the offer. But you've got to get rid of this
emotional thing you seem to have for the underdogs, you know?
Father Flanagan was wrong. There is such a thing as a bad boy.
Prosecution's an honorable trade." I'd thank him for his good
advice and assure him I had never entertained any contrary
opinion. Damned right I would. I had to cut deals with those
offices. Last thing I wanted was those boys getting mad at me,
thinking I thought I was too good for them.

"That was the way Don Frears ran his office. You brought it
in, you got the cash. Others got hourly wage. John Tierney told
Andy to call Don Frears out in Worcester and ask him if it was
all right to appoint Colin to the bench, and Don said it was fine
by him, and that's how it all happened. Eleven judges in the
same day. Two superior, and the rest I forget. Colin and Andy to
superior. Man likes to do a good turn for a classmate now and
then."

"He beat me," Billy said. "I admit that."

"You did more'n admit it," I said. "You went to Colin's
swearing-in on one day, and the next day you went to Andy's.
That was class, Mister Ryan."

"I try to do the right thing," he said. "Is he gonna, now?"

"I don't know," I said. "Well, I do know, but the answer
doesn't help us. Andy's got a lot of pride, a high opinion of
himself, and he'd need a wheelbarrow if he wanted to carry all
his grudges around at once. But part of his pride is that he
thinks of himself as an honorable man, and he always does what
he thinks an honorable man ought to do in the circumstances.

"The problem is that Andy can come at circumstances from
odd angles, so that what he decides is the right thing to do may
not look like the right thing at all to you or me. May look like
just the opposite. I've tried cases before him where I knew we
absolutely agreed that the evidence was conclusive. But where I

thought it conclusively made a laughingstock out of the prosecutor's case, Andy thought it made a joke out of my defense. No malice at all in this; that was what he honestly thought. Still he tried to be fair when he charged the jury—*tried*, I said, to be fair. Fortunately for me, and even more so for my clients, some of the juries agreed with me, not with Andy, and so some of my guys walked free. But it was kind of scary until those jurors came back."

"So," Billy said, "how do we find out?"

"Find out what?" I said.

"Find out what he's going to do in my case, of course," Billy said.

"We don't," I said. "In the first place, there isn't any way. In the second place, if we tried to find a way, he'd hear about it and get pissed off, and do mean things to you. And in the third place, if there were a way, and we could get inside his head without him finding out, all we'd find out'd be that Andy probably doesn't know himself yet what he's going to do. No, our time's important here. We have to spend it on important things, on digging into things that'll help me represent you."

"Like what?" Billy said.

"Like your whole life," I said. "Dirty socks and all. Now I'm gonna start to rummage through your hamper." He did not look pleased. "I know, I know," I said, "but you can bet Mike Dunn has. Mike Dunn's done it already. Better I do it so I know what he's got than I don't and he springs it on us.

"So let's start with Jack Bonnie. Why him? Why did you hook up with Bonnie?"

FIFTEEN

"I think Jack was only about eighteen when I first heard of him," Billy said. "Philly Laverty took it in his head it was time he moved up from the house to the senate, and Jack was his campaign manager."

"That's pretty young, eighteen," I said.

"Isn't, really," Billy said. "Phil was only about twenty-five, -six himself. You meet a lot of kids that age, hanging 'round the State House, running errands and then offices, 'fore they're twenty-one. The ones with the bug catch it early. It gets in their blood.

"Phil lost. But Phil was a sharp boy himself, and the two of them learned something, you bet. Couple years later Phil ran again for the house. It'd been redistricted, and the guy he hadda beat was Blacko Boyle. Blacko'd held that seat since before I started going up there. Blacko came with the building, just like they say about me now, at the department.

"Well, the two of them, Philly and Jack, knocked old Blacko right into the middle of the next week. Big upset. Made all the papers. Talk of the town. All of a sudden Phil's very hot property, and being a nice guy, he's all over town telling people Jack

Bonnie did it. Planned it all. So Jack gets some notice himself. What's he, about twenty then?

"Two years later, Jack runs himself. The adjoining district. He loses, but he lays the groundwork again, and two years later he wins. Understand something here: Jack is a very good politician. He's smart, and he doesn't go to bed early—he gets *up* early.

"All the time, he's learning. Learned very early not to talk outta the side of his mouth. When it came to handling the smart guys that wanted to trap him, he may've been a rookie rep, but he didn't act like one.

"So I spotted him. This kid was a comer. And, well, it wasn't anything different with Bonnie that I didn't do with fifty other reps, you know? Over the course of the years. Heck, maybe a hundred reps. Who knows? I've been there a long time. They come and they go, and everybody wants different things. They all want *some*thing, the ones on the way up. Your aristocratic Yankees—well, in the first place you don't see that many anymore. When they run for office it's for something to do. And when they win, which is not very often, they don't know what to do with it. But the hungry kids that come in, they're the ones who'll do business. Jack was one of them. He was a player. You could see it in a minute."

"How?" I said.

"Well, in the usual way," Billy said. "He was the usual type of young fireball: politics was his whole life, the only thing he ever did. And, well, I get along with that kind of guy, most of them. Always have. I've had to. It's part of my business." He paused. "Used to be part of my business.

"I can tell what's on their mind. What's bothering them. Doesn't mean I mind their business for them. I just know what's on their mind. It's a natural thing to do."

"What's generally on their minds?" I said.

"Generally, money," Billy said.

" 'Money,' " I said, the way Monsignor Martin probably would have uttered *sex*, more a hiss than anything else.

"Sure," Billy said equably. "Politics doesn't pay that well, especially when you're starting out. And usually the kid who's got that in mind, running for something, I mean, he will think: 'Well, I better get the old college degree there, and a law degree wouldn't hurt.' So he's hustling day and night, campaigning every two years, himself or someone else, and he's going to school night and day, trying to make ends meet."

"Can't he borrow the money he needs for school and so forth?" I said. "I know I could, back around the turn of the century. My parents gave me most of it, but what they really couldn't spare, I know I could borrow. HELP loans—Higher Education Loan Plan. Go right down to the bank and sign the paper there, and they give you the money. Not much fun when you come out and they're staring you right in the face, but better that'n not getting all the schooling that you want."

"Well, sure," Billy said. "Of course he can do that. And they do. But then there's the costs of campaigning. I assume I don't need to tell you. Even a rep's race costs a bundle. Philly Laverty told me he spent almost eighty thousand going after Blacko. And, keep in mind, while he's going after Blacko, Philly makes no salary. Ringing doorbells doesn't pay that good. So when you're out of office—which everybody is at least once in his career, when he starts out—and you're trying to get in, all the money's going out, and you've got nothing coming in." He paused and snorted. "Now they made it illegal for the candidate to live off his campaign donations. If they catch him, it's bad news. Dreamers. Well anyway, it was the same sort of thing with Jack when he ran himself. I don't mean eighty thousand, but still a lot of dough. And you can't get that from banks."

"From contributors?" I said.

"If you've got a lot of rich friends," Billy said. "Very few poor kids have a lot of rich friends. And very few kids that're running, first or second time, find a whole lot of people standing around, waiting to hand them campaign cash. Maybe later, they win a few times, start to pile up some seniority, get some power in the place, *then* there will be people who will want to help them out, and have the cash to do it. But not in the beginning. Then you're on your own."

"So where do you get it," I said.

"From people, of course," Billy said. "From regular people you know."

"Private citizens, you mean," I said.

"Sure," Billy said. "A young guy like Jack coming up, he's finished school, he's probably got himself a wife and family—used to be unless he did he was not a real good bet for office. People kind of wondered about bachelors, 'less if they still lived with their widowed mothers, but sometimes even then. Now I guess it doesn't matter much, all the fairies all over the place, admitting they're queers and still winning—which I for one don't understand. But the normal kid, like Jack was, he's going to have a fair number of bank loans already. And, like I say, campaigning's always been dear.

"Well now," Billy said, as though teaching basic arithmetic to a particularly slow child, "where's the money going to come from? Jack Bonnie's family didn't have any. He was hocked to the hilt before he declared, with nothing to pledge except hope. Bankers aren't in the habit of lending on hope. Not political hopes, anyway. Hard to repossess hope. So it's a perfectly natural thing. He goes around and sounds out people that he knows, and he gets a few backers together. It's not like it's a lot that he's asking for. Five, ten at most."

"Thousand," I said.

" 'Thousand'?" Billy said.

"Yeah," I said. "Five, ten, *thousand*, dollars. Each. This rookie candidate that nobody knows, who can't do anything for anybody, borrows five or ten thousand dollars apiece from friends of his that he knows, because he wasn't born rich."

Billy nodded, looking puzzled.

"Right," I said. "Let me ask you something: Where did this young man from a modest background meet the kind of people who have that kind of money to loan? And how did he become such good friends with them, that they decided to loan it to him? On a longshot political campaign. I've met a few people in my time who were pretty well fixed, and I became fairly friendly with them. But it never would've occurred to me to ask them to loan large sums of money to me. So I could run for an office that'd never pay me enough to pay them back. And you can be damned sure that if it had occurred to me to ask, it would not have occurred to them to give it to me. Rich people don't get rich, or stay rich for generations, by betting on the come. By risking the whole ranch on drawing to an inside straight. By making that kind of investment. They buy AT and T stock. Private light companies. Ford. GM. Boeing. Stuff like that."

"I already told you," Billy said. "They get into politics, and they meet some people who loan money to campaigns. Your cheap friends might not, but they do. And they meet those people, and then when it comes time that they decide to run themselves, they go around and see those people that they met, and they get some loans. That's the way it's always been done. Long's I remember, at least, and I remember quite a long time."

"All right," I said. "Assuming that, then: were there any of that type of personal loans in the debts that Jack Bonnie had when you invited him into the Colchester deal?"

"Sure," Billy said. "Of course there were. He owed Carlo some money, for example. You'd better pay Carlo back soon as some dough comes along, if *you* want to keep going along. And six or eight others. I don't know who, but he was religious about them." He laughed the way an old coyote would laugh before eating a freshly killed sheep. "Nothing like fear for that old-time religion. God looks mighty good, next to Carlo."

"Besides the Mafia," I said, "who else?" Fully formed in my head was a line of questioning on cross-examination of Jack Bonnie that would discredit him in a jiffy: *So, Mister Bonnie, you're telling us your first campaign was financed in part by the Mob. Isn't that what you're telling us, sir, when you admit that Carlo Donato loaned you some of the money? Or were you under the impression that a man named repeatedly by federal and state prosecutors, and before the United States Senate, as the kingpin of organized crime in Worcester, the whole of the Blackstone Valley, was really Santa Claus? Tell me, sir, and tell this court and jury: why was the Mafia so nice to you? Did the wise guys expect something from you, if you got elected? Or were you first and foremost a member yourself, who happened to have been designated by the other gangsters to hold office, and advance their political interests? Snivel up good and loud, please, now, so the jury can hear all your pathetic lies* (well no, I couldn't go quite that far, not in the courts of Massachusetts—you can only do that sort of thing in the fictional courts on TV).

The problem, of course, was that I wouldn't dare to use that lovely little rocket. Billy couldn't very well deny he knew Jack Bonnie, and the instant I replaced the brush in the roofing-tar bucket after smearing it all over old Jack, Mike Dunn or Dermot Barry would take it out again and put a coat on Billy thick enough to make him waterproof in a downpour. The adverse witness's guilt by association's fine, if your client doesn't happen to be vulnerable to the accusation of being himself an associate.

"Heck, I don't know who else," Billy said. "People he knew around town. People who thought he had promise."

"Were you one of those people?" I said.

"Absolutely not," he said. "I never really knew Jack 'til long after he first got elected. Heard his name, sure, but that was all.

The first time I ever laid eyes on Jack Bonaventre was the day he stood up in the house with everybody else to get sworn in. And I didn't speak to him then. He was one of a crowd, far as I knew. Just the usual crop of new members. I admit I intended to get to know them, but he was just one of the bunch."

I believe that my pulse, having risen to over 120 a minute, dropped down to near normal at once. My stomach, prepared to churn, began to calm down. I didn't say: "Whew." I just nodded.

"You've got to understand my position in this," Billy said, "the position that I was in. I liked a lot of the new men I met. Very nice boys, nice young men. And I wished every one of them the best in the world. You always hope that for people. But my God, you can't go around the whole commonwealth before every election, picking sure winners to back. You'd go broke, deaf and blind in a week. You just have to wait 'til they do get elected, and get themselves sorted out. See who's a comer, who's not. And *then*, that's when you move in. You cultivate those guys. Those are the guys that you back."

"And Jack Bonnie was a comer, in your estimation," I said.

"Later on he was, sure," he said. "After he made Public Works. Or was in line for it, maybe. Either way, that's when I tabbed him. I saw that, I saw it coming: Jack Bonnie was going to get power. You realize how long I've been banging around up there on the Hill?"

I certainly did. Right after he hired me I knew I'd have to give him the hardest advice he'd ever had: he had to retire as commissioner. I might as well have hit him with a blackjack. Up to that point he'd thought the charges had been the worst news he'd ever received. But this pretty clearly was worse. He couldn't utter a word.

"I know it, Billy, I know it. It's going to be awful hard for you, and I hate like the devil to tell you. But it's really your only choice. We have to face up to the facts here. It's possible you'll get convicted. And if you stay in office, and we do lose this case, you'll forfeit all your pension rights. What, thirty-five years of hard-earned dollars that'll keep your wife safe and secure, and you too, in your old age?" I saw no need to mention the likelihood that what had stuck to his fingers along the way would've kept them both in style for the whole length of their days. "The insurance, the health care and so forth?" I said. "It's too much of a gamble, Billy. You've got to cover your flank here."

"That job's been my life," the old man said that day. By then there were tears in his eyes, and the words came out of a choke. "I've had that job all of my life." But a week later, he did it.

"I didn't blow into this town," Billy said, the day that we talked about Jack's loans, "on the trolley that morning. By the time Jack got in I'd been at it for years. I knew what I was doing. What had to be done, and how to go about it, and I was right most of the time." He raised his eyebrows and sighed. "Well, where Jack was concerned, I was wrong. Everyone makes a mistake."

"Billy," I said, "did you make any of the loans to Jack Bonnie that he told you he was paying back out of the loanshark vig?"

"Well," he said, "I loaned him the twenty there when he ran for his fourth term and he had some opposition. Some goo-goo selectman from someplace or other was going to 'ree-*form*' the state government. And I fronted Jack twenty. I did that."

"And after he made his score on the road through Colchester," I said, "and put it out on the street, and you had your pleasant discussion with him about how he was paying back all of *his* loans, did your loan of twenty, by any chance, figure in the conversation?"

"Well, naturally," Billy said. "It was my money, for God's sake. He owed it to me, didn't he? When he was running against that blowhard, and he was in line for the committee if he could just get himself reelected, he come to me and said could I help him out. And I said I could, and I did. I needed Jack to get where he was going. Put a lot of work into that boy.

"But after he was elected, and he'd made a few bucks—was making more of them, too, while we sat in his office and talked —and he told me he's buying the house on the Cape, and maybe the boat and so forth, naturally I said to him: 'Hey, Jackie-boy, what about me? You forgetting who helped you get this? I know I'm not Carlo, I'm a nice guy, but I deserve my money back too.' And he said: 'No, I'm not forgetting. I'll start paying you off next month.' "

"And did he?" I said.

"Of course," Billy said. "Until they got him in the hole he's in now, so he has to forget his friends or he goes to jail, Jack Bonnie was an all-right kid. No: 'Whaddaya talkin' 'bout?' 'Oh, slipped my mind.' No, he was all right 'til they got him. But now the poor kid's got no choice.

"I tell you, I know what Jack is doing to me, and what that's doing to my family, and I don't like it. Not one bit. But I don't hate the kid for it, all right? All the years I've been in that place, I've seen lots of guys in his position. So I know why he's doing it. It's not that he wants to hurt me. He *has* to do it.

"It's very simple. If he doesn't get up there and make up some story about me that'll let Mike Dunn put me in jail, well then, they'll put Jack in jail. They're not particular. And you can say: 'Well, but he's a coward then. He's trading his friend to save his own skin.' And you're right. He is doing that. But I understand. Put me in his position, and what would I do? I don't know. Well, I do know. I wouldn't do it. But I'm an old man. I don't have a young family, which I know he doesn't live with anymore, divorced his nice wife and so forth, but still he does have three kids. Old men like me can have principles. But that's all that's going on here."

"Billy," I said, "you're telling me, or Mike Dunn and the

grand jury are, that Jack Bonnie made sixty thousand dollars off a deal that you arranged, and that he voted for, and that he put it on the street to make loans at extortionate rates, and from the profits he made sharking it he gave you twenty grand."

"That he owed me," Billy said. "That he owed me fair and square. That was *my* money he paid me. Money that belonged to me. I didn't make him a present of that twenty thousand, you know, for a birthday party or something. It was a plain business deal."

"When did you make that deal with Jack?" I said.

"I dunno," Billy said. "Three, maybe five years before that. Like I said, the election before he went on Public Works. Because a guy on it was retiring, and Jack had a promise he would get on the committee if he got reelected. But first he had to beat this minister, whatever he was, and he needed some money for his campaign, and he told me, and I loaned it to him. Fair and square."

"Where'd you get the money?" I said.

Billy was used to disrespect and heckling, as many of his embittered former assistants would gladly testify (and Dunn and Barry would just as gladly call them to do that, if I got careless or clumsy enough at trial to open up some question that made their vengeful recollections relevant). But he was used to dishing out the disrespectful heckling, not to taking it. To suffer it at the hands of the man to whom external forces had compelled him to entrust his entire future, at considerable expense and to his considerable resentment, was not something he enjoyed. He was becoming noticeably annoyed.

I could sympathize with his reaction. Billy did not understand. He was not, after all, a criminal lawyer. He had no notion how a transaction he deemed perfectly commonplace, probably one of dozens of pieces of ordinary and customary acts of doing business, could wound him if the prosecution popped it on us when we went to trial. He hadn't failed to mention it in order to deceive me; it had never occurred to him that the Bonnie loan might be important. Therefore he didn't see how its revelation could be a potentially explosive event in the courtroom if I didn't know about it in time to defuse it. Before Barry and Dunn set it off. He thought I was trying to humiliate him, and he was en route to getting damned mad.

"Well," Billy said, "where'd I get it? It was mine, like I just told you, didn't I? That's where I got it. I had it and I got it and I gave it to him."

"Not that kind of 'where,' " I said. "*Physically.* I'm not asking you how you first came by the money." Chiefly because I suspected that was something I didn't really want to know. "What I'm asking you is: where did you go and get that twenty thousand dollars on the day you loaned it to Jack? You didn't just happen to have it on you, and Jack asks, and you say 'Oh, sure, Jack, I just happen to have, lemme see here, I think I got about twenty thou in my pocket here.' Where did you get that money? Was it in cash or a check?"

"Well," he said, "it was cash. Hundred-dollar bills. Just like the money you got. The money that I paid to you. For this case. Hundred-dollar bills. I had them."

"Where, Billy, *where?*" I said. "Under the mattress? In a coffee can buried in the yard? In a tin box under a loose floorboard at the back of your bedroom closet? Where did you have this cash stashed?"

"I didn't have it 'stashed,' " he said, now fully angry at me. I was going to get a concerned phone call from Colin that night when I got home to Green Harbor, urging me to remember that Dad was not a young man, and needed to be handled gently— one more thing to look forward to.

"It was in my safe-deposit box," Billy said. "At the bank. At the Norwich Trust. I've had that box for years. It's where I put things that I need to keep. Important papers. My insurance, my will, other valuable papers and so forth. My father taught me that much. You need cash on hand, from time to time, in the business he was in. And in my business, too. And keep in mind, I went through the Depression, banks going under all over the place. Never know when you're gonna need cash. Fast. Like when Colin told me what you had to have—I had to have cash for *that*, didn't I? And a good thing for me that I did, I guess. That I had spot cash on hand."

Yes indeed. He'd paid me a fee that still rankled him, and for thanks he was getting hectored. There's an old saw about the defense lawyer whose success at getting his clients set free was the result of judicial belief that anyone who'd paid counsel's enormous fees had already been punished enough. But I let Billy's crack pass. I had more important things to worry about, such as what would happen if Dunn and Barry got wind of that box, and the important papers it contained. If they ever managed to get probable cause for a warrant to break that box open, I'd bet my Keogh retirement fund that what they'd find would be a great many small papers indeed, all depicting United States presidents or kiteflyers, and then things would really get hairy.

Well, good morning, Mister Kennedy. IRS. Intelligence Division? We believe you represent William Ryan, William F. Ryan, is that correct? We'd like to talk to your client. Any objections, sir?

"So you're telling me, Billy," I said, "that Jack told you he needed some money, and you went to the bank and got it out of your safety-deposit box, and brought it to the state house—was it the state house, Billy? Did you give him that dough at the state house?"

"Sure," Billy said. "That's where he worked. That's naturally where I'd bring it. It was probably the next day. And I went in his office and said: 'Here.' And he said: 'Thanks. I won't forget this, you know.' And I said: 'You bet you won't.' And he put it into his pocket. I don't remember if that's exactly what happened, or the exact day I took it in, but that was the way it usually happened, and there was nothing unusual about this time."

"All by yourself," I said.

"All by myself," he said.

"Nobody with you," I said.

"Nobody with me," he said.

Of course not. You don't invite spectators when you're passing out bribe money. Or at very least, unlawfully making political contributions, illegally solicited in the first place, on state property.

"And nobody with you when you opened the box at the bank," I said.

"At the bank?" he said. "No, there wasn't anyone. Well, I mean, Striker Monahan went with me to the cage, to open the cage there, and he hadda use his key along with mine so we could get the box out of the vault. But then I took it into one of those little rooms they've got there, where you can go through your stuff by yourself, no one looking over your shoulder. And I went in the room and I opened the box and I took out the money and counted it, and I put the money into my pocket and closed up the box and called Striker. And we went back in the vault and put the box back, and then we went out of the cage. And that was all. That was all there was to it."

"No cancelled check from you to the bank," I said.

"Nope," he said, "it was cash."

"No withdrawal slip from a bank account," I said.

"No," he said, "like I said: I had the cash in the box in the vault. Went and got it and took it to Jack."

"No cancelled check that you wrote to Jack," I said. My God, this was plain terrifying.

"I told you," he said. "Didn't write any check."

"And when Jack paid it back," I said, rubbing my hands on my pants to get rid of the dampness, wishing I had my nice, warm, ratty, old grey cardigan (that Mack and Heather were both after me for years to throw away, bombarding me with cashmere and Shetland wools for Christmas, all to no avail and their consequent frustration) that I wear watching TV when there's a draft in my "winterized" house at Green Harbor— which there always is from Labor Day to Memorial Day. I felt the same chilliness that afternoon in my office. "When Jack paid you back, did he pay you in cash?"

"Yeah, it was cash," Billy said. "I loaned him in cash; he paid me in cash. Naturally, he paid me cash. I put it back in the bank."

"Anyone else around when he paid off the loan?" I said. "Anyone see him pay you, Billy, even just one installment?"

"Nope," Billy said. "And it wasn't installments. That's what I expected from what he said, he'd start paying me off 'next month.' But he had it all for me the next month. I took it and that was that. Finished."

"And when you 'put it back in the bank,'" I said, "you mean you put it back into the box."

"Right," he said. He crossed his legs. "Matter of fact, some of what you got, that twenty might've been in it. What're you getting so upset about here? What's all this damned business about?"

I wanted to say it was about him going to jail, which suddenly appeared to be no longer a mere threatening and dire possibility but a dead certainty, awaiting only selection of a jury and doleful presentation of a procession of dreary witnesses who would back Jack Bonnie to the hilt, while leaving me powerlessly stymied to destroy him, followed by a short deliberation by the jury, announcement of a date for sentencing, imposition of sentence, stay of sentence on notice of appeal, briefs and arguments on appeal, affirmance of the judgment of the guilt of William Ryan, and execution of sentence by incarceration. For a term of, my best guess was, five-to-seven to be served. With some luck at MCI Concord, not Cedar Junction, given the convict's advanced years—maybe even MCI West Boylston, if Judge Keats felt uncharacteristically merciful that day; more convenient for the prisoner's elderly wife and friends, middle-aged children and bloody damned herd of grandchildren to visit the old desperado.

"It's about," I said, now sweating instead of shivering, "it's about how all of a sudden I'm beginning to think I should've picked a less nerve-wracking line of work. Like, say, catcher on the javelin team."

SIXTEEN

So someone, either Mike Dunn or Dermot Barry, had planted a land mine in the case. I'd been through the grand jury transcripts like a burrowing animal. I'd compared the testimony they contained word for word with the statements the witnesses had previously given to the cops and the prosecutors. I'd made careful notes and cross-referenced them. That transaction wasn't there. There wasn't so much as a hint in either collection of Billy's thoughtful loan of twenty thousand dollars to Jack Bonnie. There wasn't the slightest clue that Bonnie'd paid it back, that he'd done so out of his share of the Colchester land-deal profits, or that he'd waited until those profits had gone to work for him on the street in the loanshark racket (Billy told me he seemed to recall Bonnie telling him once that his weekly take came to seven thousand dollars, a nice annuity if you're not too jumpy about breaking the law, or people's legs). So that left two possibilities.

The first was that Dunn and Barry didn't know about the loan and the repayment. This seemed pretty unlikely. Dunn in his federal disguise had been a prosecutor as methodical and dogged as the private posse that tracked Butch Cassidy and the

Sundance Kid down into Central America. Bent on digging out every scrap of data they could find about Billy Ryan and his games when they hammered Jack Bonnie, they never would have overlooked the question of how Jack disbursed his loot. They'd had him interviewed by the best state cops they had; they'd reinterviewed him themselves; they'd made it very clear to him that unless he gave them the full skin of Billy Ryan he was going to the taxidermist himself. They'd trotted him in before the grand jury for two consecutive days of detailed questioning, commencing each session, morning and afternoon, with a reminder that he was still under oath and a refresher review of the perjury statute. They'd done everything to him except administer a barium enema and a proctoscopy. What he did with the proceeds of his scheme with Billy Ryan would never have escaped their notice; they would have wondered from the outset who else he might help them get, and even though he hadn't bagged another villain, so far as I could see, they would have done their damnedest to determine if he could. And that would have uncovered the loan.

So they did know. One or both of them had deliberately refrained from asking Jack about the loan while Jack was talking on the record. This was a new wrinkle for Mike Dunn, holding back something defensively explosive in the hope of mousetrapping the opposition. From what I knew of Dunn, he had a good brain indeed, and a fierce appetite for work, but his was a linear mind. His style of making a case was to begin at the beginning, plod on through the middle, and emerge at the end. The grand jury transcripts he produced in federal court were blueprints of the cases that he planned to try. He did that on purpose. He believed that a carefully documented investigation tended to intimidate defense lawyers, and thus defendants, into throwing in the sponge and pleading guilty. That was the book on him; that's how he described his approach; and it worked. The only time Mike Dunn's cases went to trial was when the target was a

fellow like Lou Schwartz, who had to shoot the works. Yes, I'd
hoped to win Lou's case. But I didn't expect to, not after I
reviewed what Dunn had on him. It was formidable. He antici-
pated all my moves. Closed every possible escape hatch. The
son of a bitch may have been a humorless bastard in a perfectly
stuffed shirt, but he was good at his job.

This ploy was different. It was cute. I figured Barry for it.
There wasn't much of a book on him. He'd been a junior partner in a big white-shoe Boston firm until he joined up with
Mike Dunn's campaign and changed his ambition from rich
partner to high-court judge, or so the betting was, but he'd
spent his private-practice time mostly in SEC law. Securities
lawyers tend to be crafty. They're always thinking up convoluted
ways to maneuver the adversary into doing their dirty work for
them, so they get the result they want without risking their own
reputations. Cute ploys don't always work—I've used a few myself, and most of them have not—but when they do they're
dynamite, and this one had that potential. No matter how many
times the spectators have seen the rabbit come out of the hat,
they remain impressed by the magician's elegant sleight of
hand.

The theory of the well-planned trial ploy is that the oppo-
nent doesn't know about a piece of information that you'd love
to introduce in evidence at trial but when you aren't completely
confident you can get away with it. The defense has more lati-
tude than the prosecution when it comes to that, but there are
limits even for us. The $20,000 loan could create a problem for
the commonwealth on appeal, if they got it introduced over my
objection, which I would surely make. It was pretty remote from
the land deal. Therefore I would argue it had been introduced
purely for its prejudicial impact. Someone, probably Barry, had
therefore decided to see if I'd stumble over it and let them run
away with it. In real estate sales, Mack told me, it's "Location,

location, location." In trial law it's strategy, strategy, strategy. Let me give you an example.

I had a client named Donald. He was a banker who had appeared to have had everything going for him. He was tall, broad shouldered, with a winning smile and an easy manner. He wore good clothes and grooming as though he'd never noticed either of them. He had a wife, at least in name, three fine-looking kids, a comfortable Georgian twelve-room house, perfectly situated on a two-acre wooded lot bordered by a gentle brook, a financially rewarding job as executive vice president of a prosperous if small suburban bank, and an Ivy League resume that would have made him a sure-bet hire almost anywhere in the Northeast, if his president and board of directors for some inexplicable reason had chosen to make him feel discontented. He came in and introduced himself to me only after he had acquired a major problem to go with all those blessings.

The deposits of the bank were insured, as most are, by the Federal Deposit Insurance Corporation. The FDIC was understaffed in those days, running up to three years behind conducting its regular examinations and coping with shorthandedness by concentrating its auditors on banks believed to have problems. His was not one of them, so nearly nine years had passed since their previous visit when they popped in one day and took out their reading glasses. What they found must've made them nearly drop those glasses. It appeared that the long-term deposit and trust accounts were short around half a million dollars. They called in the FBI. Together the FDIC boys and the FBI lads found that things were even worse; by the time they were finished, and the FDIC was engaged in merging Donald's bank with another one they knew to be in good shape, the total missing was over $800,000, not much by today's billion-dollar savings and loan predators, but still not exactly small change, either.

The auditors believed Donald had taken it, starting off small, a grand here, a grand there, gradually gaining assurance, greed and recklessness, working his way up to around eighty or a hundred thousand a year. The federal grand jury agreed—reasonably enough, since he had done exactly that—and indicted him, bringing us together.

Now there aren't many criminal cases that are realistically possible to consider as potentially complete victories, even if the client's not a pol, as Billy Ryan was. A triumph for me, and therefore for my client, is a deal with the prosecutor that puts the defendant on the street, instead of yielding him a year in the jug, or two years of being very watchful in the showers instead of five—that sort of bargain.

But there are two kinds of criminal cases where you can't even hope for that much: prosecutions based on wiretaps, in which the jury gets to listen to your guy hatching his plots—and then bragging afterwards about how smart he's been carrying them out—and cases based on bad paper that your guy filled out himself. You know you're going to have to try the things, either kind, because the Mob guys usually have long records and're going anyway, and the guys with the white collars who have no records whatsoever will be ruined if they plead. Therefore they have to take a shot. But you don't expect to win. So when you ask your client in a case like that to suggest anything that might maybe convince a jury that it wasn't his fault, or it was his fault but he shouldn't be convicted of it because he's basically a very nice guy and a bit of a victim himself, what you're doing is looking for straws to grasp.

Donald crossed his legs and took a deep breath, and said the explanation for his defalcations was his distraction by his wife's numerous infidelities. I found that preposterous but nonetheless intriguing. Back then I was still under the misapprehension that I would never experience distress for such a reason, let alone wreck my career over it, so I suppose my stated reason for wishing to see her, alone—it was, after all, a novel excuse in mitigation of the crime of looting a bank, but since I didn't have anything else to offer a court, I was in no position to be picky—wasn't the whole truth. There was a certain prurience involved as well.

She came in a few days later, looking in her tailored blue wool suit and white blouse with a bow at the throat, every inch an alumna of the Katherine Gibbs School, most likely employed the first four years of her two decades out of school as secretary to a dynamic senior partner in a major Boston law firm who had unsuspectingly described her to his unsuspecting wife and anyone else who would listen as "indispensable"—until she got lucky and married one of the firm's hot, rich clients—a guy like my new one. She wore white stockings and black pumps—I learned that word from Mack, describing the lady to her the night she'd come in—and she sat with not only her knees together but her ankles together as well. I supposed her to be crowding forty. I took the brusque approach, figuring that was the best way to conceal my embarrassment.

"Your husband's in serious trouble," I said.

She was polite enough not to call me a pure fool for supposing she hadn't seen a paper or TV for the past three weeks and therefore hadn't been aware of that sad fact. "I know," she said.

She had a nice voice. Not one of those sultry instruments that promises gardens of smutty earthly delights; just a real, nice voice. "I don't know quite how to put this," I said, "but I didn't see any way to get him out of it—I still don't. So I asked him what got into him to swipe all that money and put his whole life in jeopardy. And he said as far as he was concerned, that was why he'd started doing it in the first place. Because his whole life was already in jeopardy, and he had this desperate hope that maybe if he had more money, and then lots and lots more money, maybe that would fix his life, and afterwards he'd figure out how to get the money back."

"I think that's about right," she said, quite composed, entirely calm.

"Look," I said, "what he told me was that the reason he started taking the money, and then doing all the things he did to cover up his thefts—all of which they're going to prove; they've surely got the evidence, and it's not going to disappear —is that he found out you were running around on him, and he thought maybe if he wined you and dined you and made you a rich lady instead of one just very well to do, you'd maybe cut it out."

"I think that's true," she said. "Don found out what I was doing—it wasn't the first one, either; just the first one he found out about—and it just about destroyed him. I've never seen him so upset. I've never seen *any*one so upset. And he confronted me with it. He asked me if I was seeing one of the other members at the club, a man he played golf with, in fact. And what could I say? I couldn't deny it—it was true. It'd only been going on for a while, a month, maybe six weeks, and by then— as I say, he wasn't my first, not by any means—I'd learned how to be pretty sneaky. But I think I must've been his *first*, his first girlfriend since he'd been married. And he got careless, and drunk, and started bragging one night after a bar association dinner. Well, not bragging, exactly, but he said something that nobody had much trouble figuring out meant he was having a fling. He didn't give my name, but it didn't take long for someone to add two and two, see who it almost had to be, and within a week or so after that it was all over town. And sooner or later somebody who didn't have much of his own business to worry about decided Don ought to know.

"He was in tears," she said. "Don was. He did the whole routine with me. First was it something about him. He'd been neglecting me, or maybe I wasn't having a good enough time in bed with him, this other guy was doing things I'd always wanted Don to do but he hadn't thought of himself. Which if he hadn't been so upset he would've known couldn't've been the reason, because we'd always had a wonderful time in bed, and we had them often, too. At least four times a week. And I said: 'No, no, Don, it's nothing like that.' Well, was it the children, maybe the kids were getting on my nerves. And it wasn't that either, of course. And: no, I wasn't ashamed of him; yes, I still loved him; no, it wasn't because he'd been working too hard, or smelled bad, or was stupid—it wasn't any of those things."

"Well," I said, having at the time no inkling of how bitterly instructive the answer would be to me some day, "forgive me, but what was it, then?"

She shrugged. She might've been getting ready to say No, she didn't care for any more coffee right then. "I like men," she said. "I've always liked men. I like looking at them with their clothes on, and imagining what they'd look like with them off, and I like what they've got that I don't. To put into me when we're in bed. And before you start spinning all kinds of theories, no, I wasn't abused as a child, and yes, my parents did love me, and I didn't come from a broken home, or any of those kinds of things. I just like men the way some men—most men except Don, I think sometimes; isn't it strange that an unfaithful woman, like I am, winds up and chooses a faithful man to get married to? When there're so *many*—and believe me, I know—men who're absolute dogs, screwing all over the place? I suppose, well, I *know*, what I thought, maybe hoped, was that if I picked Don, if I married Don, then I'd stop running around." She sighed. It was a sigh of puzzlement, not regret. "But I didn't," she said.

"You didn't," I said stupidly.

"Oh, for the first couple years, yes, I did," she said. "For the first couple years, I behaved. I was a very good little girl. But we were busy then. First getting the house, then decorating—Don left all that to me, spoiled me rotten, wanted me to have what I liked. *Things*, I mean; furniture, oriental rugs, appliances. He didn't know then what I *really* liked—I doubt he would've approved any more than he did when he finally found out. And then the first pregnancy. Maybe it was closer to three years, I don't know. But I didn't fool around at first, when we were first married.

"Then, after Amy was born, and I got my figure back, well, I guess it was partly that I wanted to find out if I was still attractive to men. That's the usual explanation, isn't it? As though most of them wouldn't jump into bed with Margaret Thatcher if they'd had a couple pops and she winked at them.

"Well, I was," she said modestly. "Still attractive to men. But that was just an excuse, and I knew it, and after a while I just stopped pretending and went back to being what I'd always been. A woman who likes men the same way so many men like women. All of 'em. Every single one. Most of the married ones, too. Gimme, gimme, gimme. One time when I was with a man, and we'd finished, nothing special, but not bad, I asked him, just out of curiosity, how many women he'd had, and—he was buttoning his shirt in a hurry because he had to get back to his office, had a patient coming in—he just sort of grinned at me and said: 'Hell, *I* don't know. Why, you going to ask me to rate you? You were the best, my sweet.'

"Well, that wasn't what I'd been going to ask him at all. Because the next thing he would've asked me was to tell him how good he was. And like I said: nothing special. 'Oh nothing,' I said. 'Just wondering, I guess.'

"He got the funniest look on his face. Like I'd insulted him. 'Oh really,' he said, 'well, let me ask you this: how many men've you fucked in your time?' I guess I was just feeling good, nice and lazy—relaxed, like I usually am, afterwards. 'Hell, *I* don't know,' I said, and rolled over a took a nice nap."

She snickered. "After that I had to get a new gynecologist. Don couldn't understand it. 'I thought you liked him,' he kept saying. 'I thought you liked Frank a lot. He's taken good care of you, through two pregnancies—why go and make a change now?' I didn't tell him, of course. He didn't find out till much later. Not about the doctor—about me."

You have to understand that I grew up in a Catholic family, in a Catholic environment, in Catholic schools, surrounded by Catholics, all through the fifties and sixties. As did my former wife, the former Joan McManus. All of us, male, female, neuter alike, knew (because we'd been instructed, had it hammered into us) that such women as Don's wife were (a) "tramps," and (b) not Catholics—or not for long anyway. All of the males therefore hoped desperately to meet at least one of them each weekend, but knew very well that the places where we spent our weekends and vacations harbored no such wanton hussies. Or thought they didn't, at least; I was sure they didn't.

Almost thirty years later I discovered that the "nice girl" I'd married had become one. My former wife was a late bloomer, I guess, but then: what did I know? And I knew also the "Witness for the Prosecution" gambit, in which the desperate defendant and his kinfolk or pals get together to cobble up some pack of lies so astonishing they gain credibility with jurors unable to imagine the bald-faced gall to tell such stories under oath. I had real reservations about this bold woman's veracity. Which is not a comforting situation for the trial lawyer who remembers that by the mere act of calling his witness he represents to the court his own belief in the truthfulness of the evidence to be offered. This lady required further testing.

I cleared my throat. "When he found out," I said, "when Don finally did find out, when would that've been?"

"Just about the time when they said, on the news, that he'd started taking the money," she said. The woman was uncannily serene. She might as well've been commenting on a flower arrangement, or ordering groceries or something. "He wouldn't, he just wouldn't believe me, when I said it had nothing to do with him, that it was just the way that I was. And that I was sorry, and I wouldn't do it again. Which wasn't all true. I *was* sorry. But I knew that sooner or later, I *would*. Do it again. I'm like a reformed drunk: one drink's all it takes; the next ones're easy.

"And I'm off. The drunk off the wagon, me off with my clothes. Ever since I was twelve or thirteen, I've really liked looking at men. Men with their clothes on, men with their clothes off, imagining them naked and then seeing them naked, seeing what they've got, and having them put it inside of me. Maybe some day I'll be old and get tired." She pondered. "Then again, maybe I won't.

"Anyway," she said, "when he told me he was hiring this nice widow that we knew to come in and take care of the kids, and we were going to Paris and Venice, well, naturally I said: 'That's great.' Because I'd always wanted to see those places, and I never had. But I knew why he was doing it. He was trying to, well, to buy me, to get me so distracted with first class in airplanes, and the best hotels, and dinners and shows, and gondola rides, that I'd never set eyes on another man again without thinking: 'Oh no, can't risk that, all that shopping and all the good times.'

"Well," she said, "I didn't mess around while we were on the trip, even though I was tempted a few times. But not very much. I like to know something about the men I hang out with, and I didn't about those Europeans. And even I couldn't've gone that far, far enough to do that, cheat on him on our second honeymoon. Then for a while, after we got back, I didn't mess around either. But it wasn't because he'd met my price, you know? It wasn't that I'd reformed. It was just because I didn't happen to see anyone that interested me in that way."

She shook her head. "Our summer place's down in Yarmouth," she said. "I suppose we won't be seeing that place any more summers. Well, that won't bother me too much, though

—nothing but bores down there then, and people I didn't know. Like I say, I never screw a man I haven't known for a while. Well, not very often at least. That's too risky even for me. Might pick up some guy who gets rough, or maybe's got a disease.

"But after Labor Day, when we got back, maybe three weeks or so later, this guy that we met at a banking convention—you want to talk 'boring,' try a bankers' conference sometime. God. Anyway, he called me up at home and said: 'Well?' And I said: 'Why not?' And back to the races I went. I must say he was pretty good. For a banker. More'n lived up to his promise."

"And this went on for eight years, you say?" I said.

"Uh huh," she said. "That's what the news said, at least, about how long Don'd been taking money, and that's more or less what I remember. I got the presents, the jewelry, the fur coats, the trips—all of that good stuff, you know? Like Don was paying the lease on a car, and all these other guys drove it."

"Didn't you ever think that was kind of, well, mean?" I said. "I mean, knowing what he *thought* he was doing, doing it to keep you. And really, look at what's happened to him. And most of it he spent on you. Did you think that was fair, to let him do that and then cheat? Wouldn't it've been better, as things've turned out, to've divorced him and just broken his heart?"

"Look, Mister Kennedy," she said, her voice turning metallic but remaining soft, "let's get something straight here, all right? Until the shit hit the fan here I had no idea Don was stealing the money, all right? *No, damned, idea.* If I'd've dreamed, if I'd thought for one instant, that he was ruining everything for himself and the kids just so I'd keep my pants on, I would've said to him right off: 'Now look, Donsie. You've had some bad luck in your life. You fell in love with a person who thinks there's a difference between marriage and sex, and you're never gonna talk me out of it, no matter what you do. So don't go making your bad luck worse. Put the money back. Sell the house, the cars, the whole bit, and put the money back, and divorce me with no contest. I won't hinder you at all. But don't for God's sake go to jail. That makes no sense at all.'

"I know what I am, Mister Kennedy," she said. "I know what the men in the locker rooms call women who look at them the same way that they look at us. 'Easy lay.' 'Good for it.' 'Sure thing.' Well, that's all right. It's not what I think. I'm okay with myself. I think I'm taking advantage of them. I think I'm a fairly smart lady. I don't think that's what *you* think I am, but that doesn't matter, either. If I'd ever thought this guy was going to get into trouble like this, trying to do the impossible, I would've run away with the circus or something, and tried out the animal trainer."

There seemed to be no reason not to admit she baffled me. She obviously knew it. "I have to say," I said, "I don't know how to handle all this." I thought I'd been around a lot—one of my first regulars was Captain Midnight, a major-league pimp—and I guess I thought I was shockproof. But at least I could see a motive for what he did, and his ladies did, and what the customers paid them for doing. Strictly business. But what she'd been telling me—except for the sex itself, which maybe is enough, but she said she could get that at home—it seemed like motiveless behavior. And I'm not used to that. "Why do it, then?" I said. "*Cui bono*'s what we say in the law. Who benefits?"

"Well," she said, as I might discuss the advantages and disadvantages of latex versus oil-based housepaint, "there're the orgasms, of course. But there you're right—they don't last very long, and neither do the affairs I have with the men I get them from. But there's also peace of mind."

" 'Peace of mind,' " I said.

"Yeah," she said, very patient with her backward pupil, "it's like a craving with me or something. Friends of mine who've quit smoking? They can't stand to smell fresh cigarette smoke.

Drives them batty. Well, sex has that involved too. It's pheromones."

I didn't know what those were. "Pheromones," she explained. "It's not only a person's moves, or what he says, that lets me know he's ready, and really ready for me: it's like I can smell it. And I guess the men I've been with, I guess they could smell it too, when I've been hot to trot, and with them. Why do you think women wear perfume, they make all that musk stuff for men? Sex. It's a proven fact, Mister Kennedy. They've shown it with monkeys. Like dogs smelling fear. Like people, people that don't need any bread, stopping in their tracks and going into bakeries because the bakeries always blow the baking-bread smell out the front onto the sidewalk. That kind of thing. I have this appetite, and I can smell when some man I meet has the appetite too. So we satisfy each other, and that's all there is to it."

"You'll testify to this?" I said. "You'll get up in open court and tell the judge and jury that your husband embezzled all that cash because you can smell sex?"

"Sure," she said. "If you think it'll help. Why shouldn't I say it in court? It's something that happens to be true."

Well, that did it. Either she and her husband were telling the truth, in which event I had no choice about putting her on the stand, the pity for Donald being that was just about the only shot I had of getting him NG-ed, or else they'd collaborated on a last-ditch, fantasy ploy which guaranteed she'd come out of the adventure notorious on the front pages of every supermarket screamer tabloid in the country, maybe even in the world, no matter how well things might turn out for her husband. Cool courage in adversity does tend to charm its observer, even if all it amounts to is brazen but bulletproof perjury.

Beautiful. I don't like diminished-capacity defense ("I'm not saying my client's not guilty because he's completely nuts, Mister Foreman and ladies and gentlemen of the jury. I'm just saying he got so distraught he did something completely out of character, and ought to be forgiven, told to go and sin no more"). It seldom works very well, because it sounds to the jurors like you're not saying the guy's batty and should be excused; all you're saying is that he was temporarily goofy, and ought to be absolved—"Uh huh," they think to themselves, "another tricky, fast-talking lawyer out to blow smoke at us here."

And I was going to use that strategy—strategy was all it was —in a case of high six-figure embezzlement, committed and skillfully covered up over a period of eight years or more, not exactly your ordinary and impulsive first-offense-for-shoplifting matter. I was going to tell twelve perfectly rational, hard-working men and women that my client was a pussy-whipped wimp who hadn't been able to help himself and horsewhip the wench, while all but admitting that he *had* been able at the same time to help himself to almost a million bucks. Every last one of those jurors was going to start thinking right off about how they'd feel if their bankers stole their deposits. Their security for their old age. To bribe a harlot wife. Because that was all I had.

So when we went to trial I used it, startling the devil out of the government. The prosecutors were flabbergasted. My strategy worked. But it didn't work the way Donald and his wife had probably hoped—unless you count the many headlines that it brought, and the titillation it afforded talk-show addicts every day for weeks—because it only worked for a while. The prosecutors, caught flatfooted, regrouped overnight, and argued just as I would've that any man so addled by his wife's infidelity never could've done what he'd done and hidden it so long. Still, Donald and his shameless wife kept that jury out two full days and so horrified the judge, as conventional a fellow as I was in those days, that when the prosecutor asked that Don get ten-to-fifteen to be served, the judge said: "No. I don't know what sort of thing I'd do in the situation he was in, and I doubt you do either." Donald got five-to-seven, thirty-nine months to parole, instead of probably double that, so there was some small profit to the humiliation.

Of course, while he was making furniture down at Danbury, the doxie divorced him on the indisputable, statutory grounds that he'd become a convicted felon, got custody of the kids, and moved to Seattle. Life sucks, and then you die.

SEVENTEEN

As I'd expected, I got a call from Colin the night that Billy first disclosed to me the actual extent of his financial dealings with Jack Bonnie. Just what I needed. It was around 11:15. Colin, in that same soft voice, devoid of undignified passion, that he uses to send people away for long stretches in the penitentiary, reprimanded me for gross mistreatment of his father.

"We're all very concerned here, Jerry," he said in sad reproach. "Mother doesn't know, of course, and Patrick isn't here, but John as a physician fears this sort of added pressure, from Dad's own attorney, may have most adverse effects upon his health. You probably know that there's research to show that too much stress, even for a young man, can lead to serious health problems. Not just heart disease, although God knows that's bad enough, but even cancer, they now think. And Dad, tough as he is, and courageous, is no longer a young man, you know."

At the time no one had seen fit to tell me Billy already had a case of Big Casino. To this day I'm not sure why they held that back. Maybe it was a hole card, to be sprung at sentencing, a sympathy bargaining chip. Or then again, they might have thought that a new lawyer, later on, could use it at a hearing to revise and revoke, to piss all over my work. That night all I could think of was that now *I* was getting mad.

I endeavored to restrain myself. "Colin," I said, "believe me, I appreciate your concern. And if there were a way for me to defend your father well, as strenuously and as aggressively as I possibly can, or if I knew another way to represent a man who's in legal trouble as bad as his is, believe me, I would do it that way. But with all due respect to you, Colin, with your knowledge of the law, and to John with his medical experience, I don't think either one of you, or your father, either, quite understands how serious a problem this is."

"Marie's also very upset," he said, proceeding as though I had not responded at all, but had silently acceded to his opening complaint. "She says all you seem to be doing here's going around town and gossiping with people that our family's known for years. She holds political office, Jerry. When you encourage people like the Kilduffs to scrutinize our history, they pretend to know a lot of things they don't. But after they've related them to you, they get so they believe them themselves, and repeat what they've said to others. There was more than enough nasty talk around this town about us and this case as it was. Now, I know this was not your intention when you did it, Jerry, but the fact is that your coming out here just stirs more of it up. And it hurts, Jerry, it hurts. This could do Marie a lot of damage, Jerry. It could even inspire someone to challenge her in the primary, run a smear campaign. And that's precisely the sort of thing we don't need to have heaped on us now."

I had had a long day. It already had featured some extremely unwelcome news, and I was in no need of a late-night call from someone who proposed to treat me as a spitballing sophomore and send me to the principal's office. It was no longer a matter of exercising self-restraint; it wouldn't work anyway. Not that I could have managed it; I was damned mad, and the best I'd be able to do for Colin was to try to keep my voice down.

"Colin," I said, "bear with me now. I have several points to make here, and I want you to hear them all."

"Jerry . . . ," he said, a velvet cozy on the mace. He was warning me to take my chiding penitently, and promise to mend my disobedient ways.

"No, Colin," I said, being used to judicial displeasure, having provoked so much of it, "you called me, remember. I assume you didn't do it in order to deliver a soliloquy. Or, God save the mark, to tell your father's lawyer how he's going to try his case. Because if either one of those is your reason, Colin, I will hang up right now, and I will go to bed. *And*, if you tell me that your reason was the second one, tomorrow I will march my well-rested body up to the clerk's office in Suffolk Superior and file a motion, neatly typed, for leave to withdraw as counsel for defendant Ryan in *Commonwealth* v. *Ryan*. In that motion I will cite irreconcilable differences between myself and your father that make it impossible for me to represent him further. And Andy Keats won't like it. He will grumble some. But he will grant that motion, Colin, just as you would grant it: because he'll have no choice. As we both know very well."

Colin did not say anything. "Then, Colin," I said, "I will go back to my office and instruct my secretary to add up the hours I have put in on this case, multiply that by one hundred, deduct that amount in dollars from the retainer your dad's paid—less than one-half of my usual hourly rate, Colin, in case you were wondering; I'm even giving you a rate here—and write a check on my account for the remainder of the fee. Made out to William F. Ryan."

Well, $225 *was* my usual tariff then; my problem was that for a good many months I hadn't been able to find many folks willing to pay it. But there was no need to bring all that up.

"And then, Colin," I said, "you, and Representative Marie, and Doctor John, and even General Patrick, should he care to get involved this time, as well as your embattled dad, can put your walking shoes back on and hunt up another lawyer. But you'd better be quick about it, and you'd better find one more pliant than I am. And you'd better hope he's greased lightning when it comes to preparing a case. Because I've been at this for about two months now, and I know how to go about it, and I'm still not ready for trial. In fact, I'm not even as close to being ready as I thought I was when I got out of bed this morning, because this afternoon I found out my client's been holding out on me, and I've got more case to prepare than I thought I had. Which discovery, Colin, did not please me.

"Because you see, Colin, Andy, after he grants my motion and your new cat's paw signs on, is not about to grant *his* motion to set a new trial date, say sometime in July. For one thing, he doesn't want to, because that's when he sits in Barnstable" (read: out on his nice boat). "And if Andy did want to, Andy wouldn't do it. Mike Dunn would scream bloody murder, and Andy would back down."

"Now, Jerry," Colin said, "there's no reason to get all worked up here. I only wanted to call your attention to some of the things that concern us. We don't want Dad getting ill, and Marie does have some stake in this. But there's no need for you to get so upset."

"Well," I said, "I disagree with you there. I think that there's every reason for me to be upset. I was upset anyway, after today, when I found out that something had been kept from me. And, I might add, I'm beginning to think all those guys who turned this case down may've been smarter than I am. Or maybe knew something I didn't. Which upsets me even more." The hell with my charitable interpretation of Billy's reticence about the loan. I still thought it was the correct explanation, but I learned something from my failure to unlock the musket locker promptly when Mack's mutiny got underway; that mistake I will not repeat.

"You know just as well as I do, Colin," I said, "that there's nothing more disastrous for a trial lawyer than ignorance of his own case. And I don't mean just the law. Time and time again, I've been present in your courtroom when you've eloquently chewed out some hapless bastard who thought his ass was third base and didn't know the facts. 'Most lawyers know the law,' you say. 'The good ones know the facts.' And the guy just shrivels up. Well, no judge's ever done that to me, and no judge ever will. That you can take to the bank.

"I don't care whom I upset, not when I'm getting ready. And that includes the client, the client's family, and especially Marie. I haven't finished getting ready. I'm busting my chops on this thing, and I've had one hell of a setback today. A setback caused by my own client. So you tell Marie, and Doctor John, too, that I'm on the warpath now.

"If I can't find something to neutralize the testimony Mike Dunn's got, your father's sunk. I have to put him on the stand. I have to have at least available two good, solid witnesses to follow him and say nice things about what a great guy he is. Because after Dunn and Barry get through with him on cross, Benedict Arnold's going to look like Francis of Assisi, and I'll have to rehab him for that jury.

"If getting those witnesses also means that Marie gets a primary fight she didn't expect and isn't that eager to face, well, frankly I couldn't care less. I'm not Marie's campaign treasurer or manager, and whoever those people are, they've got at least until June to worry about what happens in the September primary. I'm Billy Ryan's lawyer. He goes to trial in a month."

"I understand," Colin said.

"I hope you do, Colin," I said. "I sincerely hope you do."

EIGHTEEN

Another one of The Rules in the practice of criminal law (yes, I know, there seem to be a lot of them, but that's to be expected; if we're going to have The Rule of Law, we must have the Law of Rules—otherwise there's likely to be blood on the floor and hair on the walls when we get through a brisk tussle of practicing the law) is that you represent your client, *and that's all.* You do not adopt him. The two of you do not become fast friends. The only thing worse than an ingrate is a former client who literally can't thank you enough for the acquittal you obtained for him. If you're too old now to change occupations, but you'd like to see for yourself whether what I am saying is true, try feeding a stray cat some cold winter night, and letting it sleep in your breezeway. Keep that up for a couple days and you'll have a new cat; you will never get rid of the animal.

I have represented Teddy Franklin for almost thirty years. I have done so frequently. The police have been convinced for three decades that Teddy steals Cadillacs; from time to sporadic time they have gone to remarkable efforts to catch him at it and put him in jail. This has made him a dependable source of legal fees. But in exchange I have returned dependable and effective legal service, and each of us considers that a fair bargain.

Teddy was a young man, when he first came to me. He had no serious convictions then. He has no serious convictions now. The only conviction is a fine of $175 which he paid to the clerk of the Stoughton District Court on the day he was convicted of punching a Framingham cop named Earl Glennon—the sergeant, engaged in a stolen-car investigation, had roused Teddy's intemperate ire by driving about twenty miles southeast of Framingham to stake out Teddy's house in Sharon in the daytime. But that's it. Teddy has a record out to here, but it's just arrests. No other convictions. No time in the can, except that spent when he's been first jugged to wait for me and the bondsman.

I do not by any means claim full credit for this. It's much easier to mount a successful defense for a client who knew what he was doing when he did what caught the cops' attention than it is to keep a bumbling idiot out of the slammer. My job, as I tried with less success for years to make Mack understand, is not to ascertain whether my client did what he's charged with doing, but to make the cops prove it, beyond a reasonable doubt. Except for the afternoon when Teddy burst from his house in Sharon Heights and whacked Sergeant Glennon in the chops, cutting Glennon's lip with his signet ring, and got arrested for it, the cops have had truly extraordinary difficulty meeting that standard with Teddy.

Whatever Billy Ryan's other shortcomings may have been, and they were certainly a great many, Billy had it right: there's a shortage of friends in some lines of work, and mine is one of them. Trial lawyers get to know a lot of people pretty well, but few of them for very long. Friends require time. Weldon Cooper was about the only one I had. Coop was good at gaining confidence, an art he'd acquired in his years with the bureau, but that was not the only factor in creation of my trust of him. He made a believer of me by trusting me first. I never missed Coop more than I did in the last two weeks before Billy Ryan went to trial. As much as his death some two years before had bothered me, I'd never truly realized until then how much I'd depended on him to help me work out my thoughts.

The dependency all started with the house in the Caribbean that Coop never got, although neither of us, I think, understood that at the time. Coop never got it because his son, Peter, fell under the spell of a pusher who offered him free samples of some magic-carpet powder. Peter accepted, ingested, enjoyed, and pretty soon the pusher had a new and eager customer. Then the dealer had an assistant dealer. The kid crashed and burned, of course, so that Coop and his wife, Karen, had to sacrifice the savings they had built up for that island home—not to mention college for Peter—on a series of camps, schools, hostels and what-all, each of which positively, absolutely guaranteed to wean Peter from his addiction and teach him some manners as well.

I rode through that ordeal at Coop's side as Peter proved equal to each challenge, conning credulous keepers into letting him out, escaping the custody of incredulous warders under cover of darkness. There was one cold night when I collected Peter on a street corner on the South Shore, shivering his buns off in clothes that he had stolen for his latest trip over the wall; I had a vagrant but tantalizing thought that I might serve my friend Coop better by letting the little shit freeze, but that was not what I'd told Coop I'd do, so I picked Peter up and brought him in. And I did what I could after that episode to help Coop see it through. It wasn't much, I'm sorry to say; while the death certificate recites a massive heart attack caused his death, I think I can guess what in large part brought about the cardiac event.

So anyway, long before my personal struggle began, I'd watched Coop struggle against the forces that beset him in the later middle years, years that he'd justifiably looked forward to as the reward of the dedicated labors of his youth and early middle years. "I was a damned good special agent, you know," he told me wonderingly once over lunch, and I believed every syllable. But he'd inadvertently committed some oversights at home during those exhilarating years with the FBI, and he didn't hold those back, either.

"Karen's always been protected," he said. "Her father protected her, and she grew up and went to college. Then she got out, and I came along, and her father liked me a lot. He thought I'd protect her too, just like he had, and he was getting tuckered out, so he approved me.

"And I did," Coop said. I think we were having knockwurst and German potato salad that afternoon at Jake Wirth's, and furthermore, I think it was my turn to pay. But that was all right, if I did—Coop and I did not split checks; we went tap for tap.

"I've got three years on her," he said. "That was my advantage in our courting days. Do kids still court nowadays? Or do they just whip off their knickers and jump into the sack?"

"They just whip off their knickers," I said, having even then some rather disapproving notions of what Heather had been doing—or at least not refusing quite as vehemently as I would have liked to do what the boys plainly wanted her to do.

"That's what I thought," he said. "But anyway, in those days, well, all the cards were mine. I was established. I had a steady job, and with the government, to boot. FBI was special to civilians in those days. We were the first line of defense against the communist menace, and people actually admired us. You buggers nowadays hold us up to scorn and ridicule, but when I said: 'Cooper, FBI,' that carried weight, my friend. Karen's other boyfriends were all kids, as, of course, she was herself. They didn't stand a chance.

"Now don't get me wrong here, Jerry. I loved Karen when I

first saw her, and I love Karen today. But Karen's background, Karen's life, Karen's whole experience, they haven't made her tough. She doesn't have street smarts. And this thing with Peter, Jesus. I think it's killing her."

I thought it was more likely to kill him, and events sadly proved me right, but I didn't say that. I regret that, even though I'm sure it would have made no difference if I'd given him a speech. But at least I could've tried.

Karen had never held a job. Karen stayed at home. And as Peter proceeded further and further down the toilet, she proceeded further and further down the drain of some indeterminate depression for which she would seek no treatment, and which Coop could not reverse. So he had two weights on him: first the kid and then his wife; while I was dismayed and grieved when he fell off the exercycle, I can't say I was surprised.

Just lonesome. I'd returned Coop's entrustment of his worries by confiding some of mine. He was the one who told me I could not survive much longer, wondering what Mack was up to, and who with. "Oh, good," I said, most likely munching goulash on his tab, "so what do I do instead?"

He let me have it right between the eyes. "Put a tail on her."

I am seldom speechless. I can almost always chew. I lost command of both functions. I just sat and stared.

"You'd tell a client to do that, client in the shape and situation that you're in," he said. "You'd tell him: 'Hey, you've got to stop this, all this doubting and worrying. It's getting in the way of things. It's screwing up your life. May be you're just a damned fool. Maybe she's really just working. You have her tailed, you find that out: she's working too late. That simple. As chances are, she is. She had a model, you know—she is married to the guy.'

"The PI reports. He tells you this. You sit down and think it over. This is a relief, what the eye has told you, but you still have a situation to correct. So, all right, you can handle it.

You've handled a lot worse. You go home, get dinner ready. Everything all set. She comes in, she's whipped like you are, after a long day. You eat, you have a glass of wine, you talk about the day. Then after dinner you sit down. You say to her: 'Now look. We're losing track here of our lives. What we wanted them to be. We've built a good life for ourselves, and now we're blowing it. We've got to work out some agenda where we put each other first.'"

"That's the best-case outcome," I said, my voice still somewhat clogged.

"I know it," he said, sawing away at the meat.

"There's another possibility," I said.

"I know that, too," he said. He left his knife and fork on the plate and steepled his fingers. "If you put a tail on her, and he comes back, worst case, I tell you, Jerry, you will still be, you'll be better off. For God's sake, man, don't do what I did. Don't let things go by. They don't get better, my friend. They don't improve at all. What looks to you like trouble today probably is trouble. I wish I could tell you: 'It's not. You'll be okay.' But if you just glance at it and say 'Oh oh, got to think about that soon,' and go off to work, you'll find next month or next year that you've got a holocaust. If she *is* fooling around, it's better you should know. Not highly complimentary, no, but better'n stomach acid. Then you can do something. Sort things out in your mind. Get your life in order. Stop running in place and get moving on it. Before her life pulls you down."

As I said, I'd been using Bad-eye Mulvey for years. I say that (*de mortuis, nihil nisi bonum est*) as a compliment, Bad-eye having gone to the Great Squadroom in the Sky earlier this year. He was thorough, and that made him good, even if he did most likely think improvisation belonged on the complete list of sexual perversions. But if he had clear instructions, he would follow them to Greenland. And then come back, on time.

Bad-eye was greatly troubled. I called him in and told him

the client suspected the wife of carrying on an adulterous liai-son. "You know, Mister Kennedy," he said, his lazy eye focused somewhere over my left shoulder, "this is not my real preference of a good assignment."

It was not that Bad-eye by any means condoned adultery. Bad-eye had much less patience for straying spouses, homosexu-als, women who had abortions or practiced birth control, or persons bent on divorcing, than he had for robbers, murderers and car thieves. He more or less expected the violent and ac-quisitive to commit wicked acts, but "those other things," as he called them, were shocking, shameful *sins*. Because they were performed by men and women who should have set examples for the community. Good examples, not bad ones. He had no wish to foil them in their sexual escapades. He simply didn't want to get involved in their misdeeds, even as an observer.

"I realize that, Bad-eye," I said, "but it's necessary."

"Well, Mister Kennedy," he said, "if you're sure, then I will." He took out his pen and his pad. "What is the name of the suspect?"

Bad-eye always called the subject "the suspect." Old habits die hard, if at all, and his didn't die until he did.

"Joan McManus Kennedy," I said.

The blood left his face. He dropped his pen on the pad; both items fell on the floor. *"Mister Kennedy,"* he said, in the sort of hushed voice he would've used to murmur responses at the Stations of the Cross.

"I know, Bad-eye, I know," I said. "I know this is a hard thing for you. Believe me, it's harder for me."

He strove to regain control of himself. "I've known you, sir, for a good many years. A good family man, and provider. I'd've never believed such a thing. That such a thing even was pos-sible."

"Bad-eye," I said, "I don't wish to believe it myself. And that's why I'm imposing on you. It may very well be I'm imagining things. Running away with myself. But you understand, I must know for sure. I need to be easy in my mind."

He nodded. "Oh, I know, Mister Kennedy," he said. "A man must know where he stands. Especially in his home life."

"So if you'd undertake this, I'd be obliged." I gave him Southarbor's address. I described her Mercedes, model, color and plate. I told him there was no need to door-to-door her, tail her from our house, or pick her up out on the road. "What I have in mind is for you to be there, around when they all break for lunch. Follow them to that, follow her back, and then stay around until closing. See where she goes, and if anyone's with her, and when you get that down, knock off."

"How many days, Mister Kennedy?" he said, the misery wet in both eyes, good and bad.

"We'll start with five," I said. "Pick her up Monday. Report back to me the week after. We'll see if more work is required. And by the way, unless you thought otherwise, usual rates and expenses."

"Of course, Mister Kennedy," he said, snapping the pad shut and standing to stow it, along with the pen from the drugstore. "I'll be on the case as of Monday."

God was good to Bad-eye, at least. By Wednesday night he had enough to satisfy him, which was always enough to convince anyone. Bad-eye called me Thursday morning. "I was praying I'd made a mistake and followed the wrong woman," he said. Monday lunchtime had been uneventful. But Monday night she had gone to Roy's house, out on the beach down at Westport. Bad-eye had had his camera with him, the long lens and the film that sees black cats in coalbins, and he took some memorable portraits. She got there, as Roy did, around 7:30, after they had drinks and dinner. She came out of the house at 9:48, rearranging her clothes—Bad-eye snapped off a few more frames—and headed back up the road to Braintree. Bad-eye's prayers had not been answered. The next night Bad-eye still had his camera, and she kept the poor old man out most of the night—she didn't come home until three. On Wednesday Bad-eye went into the restaurant and unlimbered his Minox camera. Much kissy-facey and feelies and so forth.

"It was disgusting, Mister Kennedy," he said, "and I mean to cause you no pain." Indeed, he didn't. He had developed those pictures, so he had to know what the prints showed. But he was not about to tell me that Mack and Roy liked to do it with the lights on, and get each other naked first with the shades up—I had to learn that from the pictures.

"The pain, Bad-eye, I will not deny," I said. "But you're not the one causing it."

"I think I am finished," he said pleadingly. "I see no further purpose in this."

"Nor I," I said. "Send me the pictures. Send me your bill. I'll settle with you by return mail."

"I will do that, sir, and may I say this? I'm sorry indeed for your trouble."

The pictures, with the negatives, arrived the next day, Express Mail and certified. Bad-eye wanted the disgusting images, all of them, out of his good Catholic home. There was no bill in the parcel, and no bill ever arrived. I suppose Bad-eye, knowing what'd had happened to Judas Iscariot after he got his payoff, did not care to risk the remorseful onset of an overpowering urge to hang himself with a halter, or be buried in a potter's field.

To a degree, I followed Bad-eye's lead. "I got Bad-eye's report, and the pictures," I said. I told Coop about the surveillance over lunch, his buy, but I didn't show him the pictures. Nor did he ever so much hint that I should. Odd: the cuckold shielding the slut's right to privacy in her acts of his betrayal, while the cuckold's best friend deliberately ignores the horns on his head. Delicacy has a strange sense of the fitness of things.

"Bad news, huh?" Coop said.

"Well," I said, "yeah, but not exactly unexpected bad news. Generically bad news."

"What're you gonna do about it?" he said. Lasagna that day, I think, with the house red, in the darkness of Tessio's joint.

"Well," I said, "so far the only progress I've made has been negative. I know what I'm not gonna do. I'm not gonna slap a big wet kiss on her lips, or buy her a diamond necklace. Or even give her a round of applause for best interpretive dance. But that's about as far as I've gotten. Sure, I've thought it over, haven't thought of much else, but I don't see too many prospects.

"Last night," I said, "I left the office at seven, wasn't getting much done anyway, no point in sitting and staring into space. I thought about a slow dinner at Locke's—the condemned man ate a hearty, and so forth. Then I intended to go home and hit the sack early, fake sleep if I had to when she got to bed. But I settled for a salad and a small bowl of bisque. The condemned man didn't feel hearty. Not much of an appetite, I guess. Not much fun celebrating alone. Even when what you're celebrating's the prospect of being alone. Went home without much knowing what the hell I would do. Make it up as I went along, I guess.

"Well, I didn't have to worry. She must've pulled an all-nighter this time, or pretty close to one at least. I was so exhausted I must've gone to sleep five minutes after I hit the feathers. The last thing I recall seeing was the weather tease"—I did a local TV panel show on legal matters for a while and no pay some years ago, seeking to capitalize on a public brouhaha I'd had with a boneheaded judge by at least getting some free advertising, but it didn't bring in much business, so I quit. "The set was still on when I woke up at two-twenty with a strong urge to dispose of some used beer. So I shut it off and got back into bed, and went right back to old Morpheus there."

"Like you'd been pole-axed," Coop said.

"Or hit with a maul," I said, "yeah."

"That's happened to me, time to time," Coop said. "When I've had a big problem to deal with, you know, I can't seem to sleep, save myself. Just thinking and thinking, and then thinking some more. Up most of the night with the thinking. Not that it does any good; it's all circular, like a wheel. Regardless of whether I worked out that day, or had half a fifth after dinner. Peter's done that to me many times.

"But when I've had an enormous problem, like the one I'm afraid I've got with Karen now, I could drink ten pots of coffee at midnight and sleep like a stone until morning. Peter drove me about nuts, until he finally went too far. Once it was obvious to me I couldn't change a thing, well, then it didn't make much sense to lose sleep over him. But until then, toss and turn. Still, since I kissed him good-bye, well, that leaves me Karen in this world. All the family I've got left. If she cracks up, what do I do?

"The answer's 'Nothing, pal, because there's nothing to do. Might as well get your rest.' Strain on your mind does that to you when it gets so heavy a piano wire'd snap. There's a switch, I think, inside our heads, a circuit box or something. When it reaches 'overload' it breaks the circuit for us. And I, for one, thank God.

"But you know what it means when it blows," he said, leaving about enough of the house red in his glass to ensure that if the waitress happened to knock it over, reaching for our dirty dishes, stains would be limited to a few small red droplets on the tablecloth.

"No, I don't," I said. "I'm new at this. Tell me what it means."

"Tells you that you've already made up your mind," Coop said, reconsidering the glass. "You know what? I think we should order up another carafe of this ghinny paint thinner. This looks to me like a situation that requires a two-carafe lunch."

"Fine by me," I said. "I'm not getting much money-making work done at my office while I'm sitting here gabbing with you, but then there's not much work like that to do in my office right now, and even if there were, I couldn't do it."

"Right," Coop said, and signalled.

"So, how have I made up my mind?" I said.

"Well," Coop said, resting his elbows on the table, "in the first place, you're not exactly the lab-rat-in-the-maze on this one. This here's a two-elevator decision. One is Up, the other's Down, and you're either too far up to walk down, or too far down to climb up. So you gotta choose one. Either one you pick, when the door opens, Mack'll be in the car."

"How do I know which one's the right one?" I said.

"Simple," he said, as the waitress replaced the empty carafe with a full one, "both of them are the right one. Either one's the right choice. The one thing you can't do now is stay suspended between heaven and earth by the horns growing out of your head and the grass growing under your feet. It's time to shit or get off the pot. You can say: 'Nope, I won't stand for this —I'm gonna divorce the bitch.' Or you can say: 'I love her too much to let her go, even if she is putting out somewhere else.' That's it. You either keep her or you ditch her. Which is better? Better for you. That's the only question left."

"Well," I said, "still moving in reverse here, I guess, another negative. I can't stand to have my wife out fucking other men. I don't even know if I could stand it, if I did think I could stand it." I stopped. "That doesn't make sense."

"It makes sense," he said, pouring wine for each of us. "It makes very good sense. What you're saying is that you know damned well if you decided to ride this out until she either stops entertaining the troops or you just can't wait any longer, you couldn't stick by that decision. It'd eat your belly out, and pretty soon you'd explode."

"That's about it," I said.

"Well," he said, "that's what I said, right? That you've already made your decision. You punch the Down button, and when the car comes—and it comes fast, because these're your private elevators and you're all alone in the place—Mack's on it. You get in, the door closes, you ride down to the street, and then you kick her out, and that's it."

"It's that simple," I said.

"Simple, yeah," Coop said. "But I didn't say it's going to be easy."

I didn't say anything.

"Still, it seems to me," Coop said, "that that's what your choice is. You pick the Up car, you're signing up to do something that you already said you know you can't do. And *I* knew you couldn't do it before you said so out loud. Look, this is real life, got that? You oughta consider yourself lucky. At least your problem's clearcut. There's some kind of end in sight to it.

"Look at me with Karen. The ceremony says 'in sickness and in health.' Karen's sick. I'm stuck. I can't run out on her now. I gave my word, goddamnit. I've got to bitter-end it. But you've got a loophole in your case, and you could sail the QE-Two through it. Because the ceremony—I assume you papists include this clause, at least—also says, unless I'm mistaken: 'forsaking all others.' From what you tell me, Mack ain't been forsaking, and you've got the pictures to prove it."

"Breach of contract," I said.

"Right on the button," Coop said. "I was never on what you'd call intimate terms with the Uniform Commercial Code, but if memory serves, the minute the innocent party spots even so much as an anticipatory breach, and you've sure got a lot more'n that, that party's got the right to make efforts to cure, and mitigate damages. Right?"

"I defer to your superior command of the subject," I said.

"Well, that's what you've got to do, my friend," Coop said. "Mitigate damages here. To yourself. She'll be all right, regardless of what you do. But you won't be all right. Kiss her off."

"Easy for you to say," I said.

"I know," Cooper said, "believe me, I know. But now try to think about all that you know, all the stuff I've told you. That little shit Peter, and so forth. You know more about me than my wife does. It's better for me it's that way. If I piss you off, you'll say: 'You dirty rat' and tell me where I can head in. So I'll think: 'Well, Jesus, maybe I'm wrong. This guy's got my interests at heart. I'd better give this some more thought.' And things will proceed in a rational manner. Always the best way, I think.

"What you won't do is sulk at me, give me the silence, refuse to cook dinner, or screw. You couldn't sulk if your life depended on it, and silence is also beyond you. You've got a hair-trigger mouth. I wouldn't want to eat any dinner you could cook, and as for the other thing, well, cute as you are, I've always preferred women myself. Besides, you're too fat and too far out of shape. You should get more exercise. I may've mentioned that to you."

I didn't feel especially cheerful, but he had me laughing.

"If I think you're behaving like a horse's ass," Coop said, "and we both know you will, 'fore this thing's over, because everybody does, I'll tell you what I think in no uncertain terms. And you'll take it for what it's worth. Won't make it easy for you, anymore'n writing Peter off was for me, but few of the things we have to do at our age ever seem to be. I'm around, okay, pal? I'm not smart but I'm loyal and brave."

We finished the second carafe. The next morning I called my classmate Roger Kidd from my office. I told him the facts in the case. "Well," Roger said, "this could be messy, unless it's discreetly handled."

"That is precisely the client's concern," I said.

Roger drawled out his Yes to infinity.

"As I understand it," I said, "there's someone in your shop whose specialty's that kind of discretion."

"Well," Roger said, "yes." Taking a long time; Roger thinks about what Roger says. "That would be Dodge, Dodge Bailey. Very experienced man."

"That's what I thought," I said. "Now, what I have in mind here . . ."

"Jerry," Roger said, "would you by any chance be the client here?" They make lingerie for sexy ladies from fabric of the same texture Roger's voice had then. Roger had finished his thinking. Roger always thinks before he speaks, but Roger's very smart; he doesn't need much time.

"Yes, I am," I said.

"I was afraid of that," Roger said. "Well, I'm sorry, Jerry, but we have a firm rule." Meaning: a rule that is firm in the firm. "We only handle such unpleasant matters when the misfortunes strike existing clients. We don't take them on from outside. It's a service we offer because we must, familiar as we are with their histories. Otherwise we'd farm them out." Yes. And desirous, I thought, as you also are, of making sure that the firm's client gets the winner's share of the probate estate, and the firm retains the winner's still-lucrative business—and keeping the details of that business safe from vulgar prying eyes.

"You're not a client of this firm," he said. "And you never have been." Nor would I ever have money enough, especially after going through a divorce, a client whose personal fortune would ever equal his troubles. "So, as much as we all respect you, I'm afraid we must decline to take your case."

"Thank you, Roger," I said as drily as I could. "I do appreciate your help."

"But I can recommend a man," Roger said smoothly. "We've referred several probate matters to him when for one reason or another we felt we shouldn't get involved, and he's always proven most reliable and . . ."

I cut in on Roger's discourse. "Sort of the probate version of a Jerry Kennedy, reliable in the disposal of distasteful criminal garbage, Rodge?" I said. " 'We'll call you, but don't call us'? *'Please,* do go 'round to the servants' entrance'?"

"Now Jerry," Roger said.

"As I said, Roger," I said, "I do appreciate your help. I'll find my lawyer myself."

So Coop had to conduct another therapy session, but he knew a snarling shark who did only divorce work, name of Terry Collins. "Tough as nails and mean as hell," Coop said. "Represented several bureau friends of mine, had this kind of trouble. Priced reasonable, too. Office rents in Randolph aren't as high as they are here. You'll like Terry right off."

I met him and I did. He told me he would be my lawyer, not my friend. "You need a friend to talk to," he said, "you call Coop, all right?" But since I was a friend of Coop's, he'd do the best he could when it came to billing me. And I give the man his due: 16K is not small change, but he earned every dime.

The trouble was that long before the time came to pay him, I had lost my friend. Coop had died eight months before, and when I whacked the party wall, as I still do sometimes, out of force of habit, all I got was a hollow sound: Coop's old space was vacant.

It was sometime during that first year, I'm not sure exactly when, that I discovered an exception to the Law of Rules. I didn't violate the one that forbids adoption of clients. I just let Teddy adopt me. That was how Teddy acquired so much knowledge of my business. Even learned counsel needs to have one friend.

NINETEEN

The year that Billy went to trial, we started on the second Wednesday in April—just before tax time; more cheer—and April wasn't ready. April looked more like March, or maybe February, cold and raw and slippery, a slattern of a month, and the people who showed up for jury duty were as dour and gloomy as the weather, as though they'd gotten Opening Day tickets to Fenway Park in their Christmas stockings, looked forward to the afternoon with pleasure all the winter, and then had driven a long way to the ballpark to find snow on the field and chill in their seats, and learn that the game was postponed. But the commonwealth was ready, and I hadn't been able to think of any reason why I wasn't, and so with my client grimly convinced that nothing I was likely to do was going to save him, and no real hope in my own heart except Micawber's frail confidence that something would turn up, I said the defense was ready and we went to work.

Now and then you get a break. The sunlight makes it through the clouds; somebody gives you an opening; the world spins and the most ordinary things you do every day suddenly turn out to have been inspired. We'd been through the usual tedium that attends fraud and corruption trials, day after day of document after document and expert after expert, all to prove how much a lot of low, wet land had appreciated in value once Billy Ryan rammed the road through, but finally we were down to how come, the commonwealth alleged, Billy'd rammed the road through. I was not prospering. How the hell do you cross-examine a document in a devastating fashion? If you know a way, call me. Collect.

John Bonaventre was on the stand. On direct he had harpooned my man, and I honestly believed I had as much chance of destroying him on cross as I would've had dismantling the Tobin Bridge—I still call it the "Mystic River Bridge," but I'm one of the older parties—with my bare hands.

"You never got it, did you," Teddy Franklin said on the morning of the funeral. "You just never got it." I didn't know what he meant.

"Mister Bonaventre," I said, "you are otherwise known as Jack Bonnie."

"From time to time," he said.

"Have you ever told a lie?" I said.

"From time to time," he said.

"Whenever it's seemed useful?" I said.

"Generally," he said.

"Has it seemed useful today?" I said.

"Once or twice," he said.

If I live forever I will never know for certain what in blazes makes an adverse witness, coconspirator in a criminal case— read: "fink," or "rat"—grin at you and come coco. I think it all depends, maybe on what day it is. Then again, as Teddy said, there was something I didn't know at the time, and if Teddy's right, I just didn't get it. But that day I suspected it was the same impulse that makes an old reprobate lurch into the confessional and admit to a life of riotous dissipation; even though he isn't truly sorry for his sins, and his dejection is at most just a camouflage for bragging, in his own sweet way he really does want some kind of forgiveness. Maybe not the absolution that the liturgy discusses, but some kind of grudging concession that he's still maybe not a thoroughly bad fellow for all of his bad acting, and has some hope of readmission into the lodge of worthy men. He isn't likely to get it, of course, but you don't tell him that when he rolls over.

I'm now less certain I was right. I'm a lot less certain, in fact. But I do know that when it happens, no matter what the reason, the best thing you can do is snap a leash on him, quick, and see where he wants to lead you. It could be some hidey-hole you never dreamed of, where your client's treasure—his personal freedom—is buried away in a pot. "Did Bill Ryan ever promise that he'd give you money if you helped him buy some land?" I said.

"Nope," he said. Crafty lad, Jack Bonnie was. He hadn't mentioned any such exchange under questioning by Mike Dunn's trial man, Asst. Atty. Gen. Dermot Barry, either, before the grand jury or that day. In answer to Barry's question, solemnly put from under reading glasses perched mid-nose for the purpose of increasing *gravitas*—hotshot prosecutors ramrodding heavy cases while still in their early thirties hunger for the weight of years they won't like when they get it—Bonnie had said only that Billy'd told him "we would make some money if we got that land tied up."

Barry made a halfhearted gesture of objection, sectioning his six-three body out of his chair, but Judge Keats equally as half-heartedly saved him the needless wear and tear on his larynx: "I know, I know, Mister Barry: the witness didn't suggest that, on direct examination. But this is cross and I am generous. Mister Kennedy's entitled to explore the transactions you allege as fully as he needs to—or as fully as I think he needs to, at least. I will let him have it."

"Did Bill Ryan ever tell you that he wanted to buy some

land because he planned to build a road through it and he expected to make a lot of money when he did?"

"Nope," he said. Jack, of course, couldn't be sure *why* I was asking him about events and conversations that he'd never claimed to have witnessed or conducted. Most likely he surmised I was doing it to trap him, make him claim to have said something that he'd never said under oath, something that would contradict a statement that he *had* made under oath. Tricky mouthpieces have been known to try that, chiefly because occasionally it works. But it only works if you're dealing with a witness who is arrogant, surly, stupid, nervous, or a combination of all three distractions, and Jack Bonnie suffered from none of those conditions. He had good posture on that stand, shoulders back, legs crossed, red fleshy face relaxed and open to a smile, grey polyester blazer and red tie comfortably arranged, voice firm, eyes clear and rested (Jack at forty-three had evidently not yet reached the plateau of age after which the recuperative powers decline and a night of heavy drinking and too little rest debit-memo the next day's bodily composure; Billy'd told me with disgust that sometimes he'd tolerated Jack "for the same reason I hadda deal with all the rest of those no-goods and bums that hang out in booze joints all night: he had the votes I needed. But I suppose he hadda do it for the same reason. Jack needed votes himself").

Beyond the fact that I couldn't think of anything else to do, offhand, and hadn't thought of anything before the trial began, I wasn't too sure why I was doing it myself, except that I had to do something.

"Did you buy some options on property in Colchester because you expected to make a lot of money on them when Bill Ryan put a road through there?"

"Yep," Bonnie said. There was an undertone of caution in that forthright answer. Barry had coached him well. The prosecutor's gratitude for an unafraid, fairly smart, stool pigeon with aplomb is always tempered by his fear that his trained bear will get cocky when he gets up on the stand, and start fencing with the defense. My guess was that Barry'd been particularly spooked by the prospect of that happening with Bonnie. Jack, after all, had been a pol behind the scenes probably from his ninth birthday on, at least from his eighteenth, going for coffee, tacking up signs, door-to-dooring the flyers, holding up placards over commuter routes mornings when he should've been in school. Barry must've dutch-uncled Jack well past the point of exhaustion.

"What prompted you to do that?" I said. Yeah, yeah, I know: I must've been absent the day the professor admonished the class about asking a question to which you don't know the answer. Well, hogwash. Professors go to court about as often as the Easter Bunny does. When they give advice about trying cases, all they're doing's coloring eggs. You start making your living by going to trial, you discover America much more rapidly than Queen Isabella's brave sailor. You do what you have to do.

"Lucky guess," he said. "I knew the guy a long time. When Billy Ryan started scouting up some territory, he was getting ready to do something, and it was almost always a road. So if you had any brains you went and bought land there, and you made some money. It wasn't complicated. Nothing good ever is."

In my line of work, that is known as a reasonable doubt, and when you get one you sit down and shut up. Life is about reasonable doubts; the pity is there's so many of them. Still, I'm sure everybody in that courtroom, at least all the experienced people, expected me to seize that sugar plum and sit down. They didn't know about the loan, Dermot Barry's land mine. I had more work to do, bomb-squad duty, and I was damned scared I'd have to do it on recross. I was right.

"You must've gone to a lot of these things, Jerry," Teddy Franklin said to me on the morning of Billy's funeral.

"Thousands of 'em," I said. "Well, maybe only hundreds. More in recent years, of course. I'm getting to that age. Hell, I reached it some time back. You're in your twenties, what you go to mostly is weddings. Your friends' weddings, when they marry women who don't like you. Then your own wedding, when your friends come despite the fact that your new wife dislikes them. Most of them, at least. That's the twenties. That's how you can tell. The only funerals you go to're the unexpected ones, where some parent of a friend of yours bought the ranch ahead of time, barely turned sixty.

"You think about it," I said, "there really isn't any need to keep track of the decades. In your thirties you don't do much of anything along this line. Any churching you do's either automatic, or else all that stuff you got, back when you were a kid, all about eternal fire and everlasting damnation, that's still working on you.

"Then the forties come around, and you begin to notice one day that all of a sudden you seem to be going to an awful lot of wakes. Most of them're the parents of your friends. But there's a few in there, maybe only one or two, maybe five or half a dozen if you tracked with a fast crowd, of guys a little older, that you met professionally. Guys in their fifties. Booze got some, smokes another, maybe a car crash killed one. The dead parents you can take. When you're in your forties, doesn't seem like a real threat, personal to you, when some guy close to eighty has the old brain wave go flat. But the guys only ten years or so older, they get your attention. Especially if you ran with them a couple times yourself. Those wakes aren't much fun. Can't phone in your part, like with the other ones.

"Then comes these fifties," I said. "This's when the parents start stacking up like cordwood. This'd be one of them, if I hadn't gotten to know Billy myself, defending him, you know? Colin and I were good friends in law school. First year moot-court team and that stuff. I always liked Colin, for all his unction. So I would've come, just for him.

"What the hell," I said, "I've done it for enough other people, I didn't know as well. There was one stretch, back last spring, when I had eight wakes in six weeks, three of them in one. Seemed like every time I started a case, I was asking the judge to recess early so I could hit a wake in the western part of the state.

" 'Mister Kennedy,' Judge Horace Gammon said to me one day, he was sitting down the Cape, 'do you know any live people? People on the ground? Or are all the people that you know under it? It's downright depressing, having you here, mentioning all these dead people. I'm beginning to wonder if it's not dangerous to know you. It seems to lead to death.'

"Twice I had to ask for mornings, so I could go to funerals, and I wasn't stalling, either—these were funerals of people that belonged to my close friends. One of them was closer. Mack's father died, down in Florida. Fortunately I wasn't on trial that week, so I could just drop everything and fly down."

"You went?" Teddy said. "After all of that, all that stuff you went through with her, you still flew down there?"

"I know," I said. "That's what Gretchen said. 'Now lemme get this straight, Jerry,' she said. 'First you give the dame a break. You don't say 'adultery,' you say 'irreconcilable breakdown.' Is she happy? No, she's not. She still reams you out for every penny she can get. And then to make it interesting, she drags it out forever. So now her father's dead? Big deal. Let her handle it.' But I couldn't do that, goddamnit. We did have some good years, and besides, I liked the guy. I liked the guy himself, and I liked his wife there, too. So I felt I hadda go. And I went."

"And it made you feel better," Teddy said. "Jesus Christ. Saint Jeremiah rides again, a saint in a grey suit."

"It didn't make me feel better," I said. "It made me feel worse. In the first place, the whole place's depressing. Central Florida there, Lake Worth. The geography's depressing. What's not flat is under water, and any time a thing looks pretty it's because some human built it and for some reason or other it didn't turn out ugly like he planned. Or else it's plastic-pretty, like Cypress Gardens, and it takes a regiment of minimum-wage workers to keep it that way, and it's fake, and you get there from Orlando, got to drive past Disney World.

"And then Heather was there when I got there, with Charlie. They left the kids with his mother, out in Colorado. And that made it seem like I was the interloper. The damned fifth wheel, you know?"

"Well," Teddy said, "was the new boyfriend there? 'Cause if he was, you were."

"No," I said. "I dunno. I guess Mack figures *I* may be sufficiently sophisticated to deal with the facts as they are, but maybe she doesn't think her mother is, quite yet. Not while she's still getting used to being a widow, at least. Besides, you're a little behind in the news. The new boyfriend's now history. He's the old new boyfriend. The new new boyfriend's her current passion, and he wasn't there at all.

"No, it was just that they, Mack and Heather and old Charlie, they were all bunked in at the house with her mother, and here I am in the Holiday Inn, looking at orange bedspreads. Mack's not my wife any more, and that I at least understand. But even though Heather's married, all right? Even though Heather's got two kids, isn't she still my own daughter? Don't I have at least some connection with Charlie that I hardly know? Even though what I know I don't like?

"So how come they're all off in a house and I'm looking at orange bedspreads? I felt like Willy Loman, for Christ sake. I felt like I was on the road, peddling Lydia Pinkham's Vegetable Compound. Father John's Medicine."

"You should've stayed home and sent her a card," Teddy said. "You and me, Jerry, we're too old to be taking this crap. Especially when we don't have to. When we go and we just volunteer."

"I know," I said.

"There's enough of this stuff that you have to get through, all right? There's a certain amount of it that there's no duckin', and you just got to keep your head down while it's coming in and not stick it up 'till it's over. Dorothy's brother. Now there was a kid that you could see it coming. If that kid'd lived to a nice ripe old age, I'd say God wasn't minding the store. 'Somebody's not paying attention.'

"You know what Tony used to do? Tony used to talk his way onto junkets. Out to Vegas, you know? And they would say to him: 'Tony, this ain't gonna work. You don't pay your markers, all right? You know it's not personal. But those guys out there, they don't like when you do this, and then they make us pay up. And *we* don't like it. Because then we haffta come and chase you.'

"And then he would say: 'No, no, no credit this time out. And then he would show them this big horse-choker roll, which he only had because he didn't pay somebody else like he should've, and he conned some poor jerk outta the roll so he could go and do that before they had the dogs on him, and the junket boys, they would say: 'Okay, okay,' and let him sign up again. And then Tony'd go and pay off the guy that he hadda pay off alla the time with the roll, because that was what the roll was for, and why the guy loaned it to him. And so when he went onna junket, naturally he wouldn't have no money, and he wouldn't tell the guys, and they would let him onna plane because they still thought he did. Because after all, they seen it, right? And Tony would do it again.

"I don't know how many times he did that. The no-good bastard should've been dead, three behind the left ear there, ten, a dozen times, and they never even busted his knees. I tell my wife Dottie one time, I say: 'This kid should be dead. All the things that he has done, this kid should be dead.

" 'But he isn't dead, is he. No, he's not dead. He's jumping the hookers all over the place, and getting in scrapes with the bouncers, and still he looks like a million in gold, and people like us bail him out.' And she says: 'Well, everyone likes him, all right? And Tony knows this. Tony knows everyone likes him.' No wonder he thinks he can't die.

"Well, one morning he wakes up and he is dead," Teddy said. "Forty-seven years old. Everything gave out at once, it looks like. The heart, the lungs, the liver and kidneys—everything let go at once. All of it. Whammo. And Tony is dead. Never one ache, never one pain, never one call to the doctor. *And everybody's hysterical.*

" '*What?*' I say. 'What is this crap? You're feeling sorry for him? What's to feel sorry? He did what he liked. Not a full day's work in his life. Lived off of other guys. Sweet-talked his girlfriends, stole what he needed. Got loans and didn't pay back.' I figure he had, well, I *know* he had, ten thousand dollars of mine, he got 'fore I shut him off. And I know my wife, well, she lied to me. She said she was with me, which she was when she said it, but then he come around again, afterwards, and I didn't happen to be there. Like you know he didn't check first to see. Right. And then she wasn't, anymore. With me, I mean, and Tony had more of our money. He left with a check. Another check of hers. She forgot what she told me. Just slipped her fuckin' mind, once he started talkin.' Charm? The birds right outta the trees. When Tony talked, angels sang. And he did, and I know she was slipping him money.

" 'I'm sorry,' I say, 'I can't cry for Tony. The truth of it is, when my time comes, I bet I will envy the bastard.' Boy, did that get me in the shit."

"Well," I said, I thought, slyly, "why didn't you just give Carlo a call and have somebody take Tony out?"

Teddy's generally been at least a jump and a half ahead of me. "Carlo didn't have no reason to do nothing to Tony," he said. "Tony was my problem. Carlo has to have a reason to do something for a man."

TWENTY

When Heather was about four years old, back around what now seems to have been the turn of the century, Santa one Christmas brought her a Messy Bessie doll, apparently devised to give young children an inkling of the sanitation problems they'd presented before they mended their ways and succumbed to toilet training. I find that I recall such foolish things now, in moments of idleness or very high pressure, and remember the days when I was more than just a trial lawyer.

Like most marvels of modern technology, Messy Bessie was a better concept than she was a product. She wasn't actually designed to be messy, of course; her performances for her owner were more a matter of what the accountants call "liquidity" than solid waste, but apparently the minerals in the waters of Braintree clogged her valves or something, and Bessie started to get stopped up. The satisfying stream dwindled gradually down to a feeble trickle. After a few short weeks of increasingly unsatisfactory micturition, the built-up residues in her system shut off Bessie's spigot entirely. When you shook her she sounded like the tide coming in.

Heather was inconsolable. Her favorite doll couldn't pee.

When the problem was called tearfully to my attention, I failed to improve matters. I suggested that Bessie be given a couple beers, that home remedy generally serving efficaciously to clear my own drains, and was rewarded with a wifely scowl. Then one insightful day, Mack prescribed an industrial-strength dose of Efferdent for Bessie, having learned from an elderly client that the stuff not only cleaned false teeth but tea-stained mugs, and we learned to our joy that the foaming denture cleanser removes mineral deposits from doll plumbing as expeditiously as it dissolves berry stains on dentures and fake pearls baked in pies. I never said Mack was not a good and resourceful mother. My regrets are directed solely to the proficiency she later demonstrated as an adulteress consorting with her colleagues at work.

Anyway, when Judge Keats invited me to speak to the issue of the $20,000 loan, I knew how Messy Bessie must have felt when she contracted fluid build-up. A couple of beers seemed out of the question, and I had no Efferdent handy. "Yes, Your Honor," I said, "the matter of the loan."

Not knowing whether I had cottoned on to his little stratagem of leaving that landmine in my path, and preferring to let me blow it up in my own face if possible, Barry hadn't touched on the matter of the loan when he had Bonnie on direct. Holding my breath, I'd done my best to stay away from it on cross, while at the same time laying the groundwork to blow it up in Barry's face if he opened it on redirect.

There were two reasons. The first was the obvious one. If I didn't get anywhere near it on cross, somehow danced around it, Barry would do his best to explode it on redirect. The chances were pretty good he'd succeed. There was no way I could conduct Bonnie's cross without impliedly raising the entire history of dealings between Jack and Billy. That would cripple, if not moot, any objection I might make to Barry's redirect on the loan; he would placidly observe that I'd "opened it up on cross," and Judge Keats would side with him. Unlimited scope of cross-examination looks like an awful good deal to the novice defense lawyer, until he discovers for the first time what a nimble prosecutor can do with the topics he's raised. No exaggeration: I have seen defendants go away—none of mine, praise God—on the basis of evidence that the government could not have introduced with the aid of a front-end loader, but for the unwitting assistance of a naive defense counsel who'd "opened it up on cross."

I have to digress again here. The floors numbered on the pushbuttons in the wood-panelled elevators and listed for court business in the cavernous, echoing lobbies of the Old and New Courthouse at Pemberton Square (the Old and the New are joined at the hip; we do things that way in Boston) do not correspond to the floors on which the real court business is done.

The floors above those listed, connected to the courtrooms below them by a staircase enclosed to waist level by wrought-iron railings painted grey and to ceiling level by chain-link fence, are where the fates are sealed, and where the fated in custody wait to see whether they will be set free. They seldom are. The staircases lead to rooms where juries deliberate the destinies of defendants in custody who await their days in court in cells—the chainlink additions to the staircases were installed after some defendants impulsively preferred the prospect of freedom at the bottom of a ten- or twelve-story drop down the stairwell to what awaited them at the hands of some vengeful judge shortly to be armed with a jury verdict authorizing him to lock them up forever. Or in times gone by: to lock them up for a relatively brief period, to be terminated by three jolts of electricity.

When the jury in Billy's case filed out of the box and across the courtroom en route to that staircase after lunch on the second Tuesday in May of that year, I watched them depart with my hands clasped in the Dürer position of prayer, but over my nose. I did not think prayer was Billy's only hope—he didn't think he had even so much as that. I was satisfied that with Jack Bonnie's cynical assistance I had raised considerably more than a scintilla of a reasonable doubt, a very substantial one, in fact, and being no virgin at the argument of cases, I knew I had driven home the points I'd made as clearly as anyone could have.

Still I was bothered by the same concern that had led Billy to conclude he was doomed, and thus to forbid any of his family or friends from making more of a show of support by appearing behind him after they escorted him into the first day of trial. After the jury had been sworn (I used only two peremptory challenges, one against a woman married to a lawyer whose hatred I'd incurred years before by taking a civil case he'd cavalierly refused to settle—"a ridiculous, frivolous claim"—and ramming it right up his ass to the tune of two hundred and twenty grand; it was not difficult for me to surmise what their pillow talk had been, after he'd learned who defended; the other against a Lutheran minister who smelled of righteous bigotry to me; Barry'd only used one, against a sweet little old retired Sister of St. Joseph, too charitable for his taste) and the clerk had intoned his *Dies Irae* message—"To this the defendant has said that he is not guilty . . ." but of course we don't believe that for a minute, do we, friends?—Billy had banished all kith and kin, leaving him sitting erect and expressionless beside me at the defense table (I had managed to wangle at least that small concession out of Andy Keats, so Billy didn't have to sit in the dock) like an old hawk with his pinions clipped so that he could no longer fly.

"I don't want them to see this happen to me," he said grimly, the fifth or sixth time that we talked. "If I could stop them from finding out, after it happens, well then, I would do that. But I can't, and I know I can't. So they'll just have to get used to it, get used to it best way they can, when I get taken to jail."

"Billy," I said, "you can't go into it in this frame of mind. Jurors smell resignation like dogs smell fear. If they get a sniff of something that tells them you think you're guilty, what poor magic I can work won't matter. If they see you hangdog, they'll say: 'Hang that dog.' And then you're a goner, my friend."

"Jerry," he said, "tell me something, all right? I've been around a long time. Many years. I've seen a lot of good men, and a lot of cheap crooks as well, get into the kind of fix that I'm in now, and damned few of them ever got out. I'm a politician, Jerry, and I'm accused of stealing money. You tell that to the man on the street, and he'll grin in your face and say: 'What else is new? They're all of them crooks, every last one.' If I was a black man, up on a murder case, or maybe some sex fiend or something, well then I might think I had a chance, at least, to get a fair trial. But I know this state. This is Massachusetts. And everyone thinks we're all crooks. Tell me the name of the last guy you know of, got off on a bribery case. Doesn't happen. 'He didn't do this, he did something else. Put him away on this one.' "

It was hard to argue with him. The Ryan family's insistence on the priority of college educations had begun with him and Fannie, neither of whom had one. Their parents saw no need of such refinements, Buck Ryan having been a prosperous and contented saloon-keeper in Norwich until the nuisance of prohibition for drinkers created a golden opportunity for what would be called today *entrepreneurship*, and transformed him from a restaurateur of entirely local reputation into a bootlegger of regional and considerable power, dealing and scheming regularly with many luminaries of several ethnic backgrounds to import and deliver the stuff their loyal customers used to wash the dust down their throats.

When the Noble Experiment ended, Buck was a man well

fixed, controlling two more bars in towns around Norwich—the owners had ordered his products without reckoning the extra costs of illegal importation, and bridled at meeting their just obligations until their joints got shot up, the light burst upon them, and they took him on as a partner—along with a legal distributorship in malt beverages and ardent spirits.

Buck had obtained his education as he went along, following a utilitarian curriculum of his own design, and he correctly saw no reason why Billy couldn't do the same, and prosper on his own. Billy was a natural autodidact, and he'd managed very nicely—he not only learned such subjects as surveying and perktesting on his own; he learned birds and plants and a good deal of geology, and one night at dinner at Maison Robert, he delivered a lecture on various greens used in salads that Grogan never forgot; what Grogan called "herbs," Billy called "forbs"; and when disbelieving Grogan got home and looked it up, he found Billy was right. But in the process of prospering without an education, Billy had noticed as well that the time for such improvisation was passing rapidly, and insisted his children get schooling.

He was, in other words, smart enough to see that his generation was the last that would be able to get along without the modern advantages, and that intelligence made it tough to argue a hard point with him. He was a practical man. When he had his facts right, as he did when he said that politicians were presumed guilty, not innocent—"Corruption's what they call it when finesse is what they've seen"—silence was my own best defense. It was my only option.

What bothered me especially that afternoon as the jury filed out was that the directed verdict device, supposed to be the failsafe in such instances of potential prejudice, appeared from my point of view to have malfunctioned. The generations of Englishmen and rebels who collaborated in the writing of Anglo-American law were no fools. They were well aware that juries, rendering verdicts lest the people who appointed judges get all the breaks in the courts, were not individually immune to spells of savage passion, vengefulness and ignorance, that would bias them as well.

So provision was made for the presiding judge to take the case from the jury, directing a not-guilty verdict when the evidence against the man in the dock was plainly insufficient to warrant a reasonable—and unbiased—person from finding him guilty regardless.

I had pressed that point very hard, both at the sidebar and then in open court, with the jury absent, on Judge Andrew Keats. I approached real eloquence as closely I ever have, pounding away at the insufficiency of what Dunn and Barry had offered to justify any mature, thoughtful and fairminded citizen's conclusion that Billy, *beyond a reasonable doubt*, had ever offered anything to Jack Bonnie, or anybody else, to influence any of Bonnie's official acts, induce Bonnie to commit a fraud, or omit to do anything he should've done, in order to get money.

I said, and I was clearly right, that there simply wasn't any evidence that Billy had asked Bonnie for anything for himself, or anybody else, or had received anything for himself or anyone else. I returned several times to what Bonnie had said.

"Your Honor, Jack Bonnie stressed that my client never once even mentioned to him any possibility of joint or separate profits for either of them as a result of that highway construction. Obviously you could infer, and these jurors can infer, that Jack Bonnie was telling less than the whole truth when he attributed his profit on those land options in Colchester to a lucky guess. He bought those options up as soon as he learned, in his official capacity, that my client had proposed to build a state highway through there. He thought he'd make some money, if that road went through, because he knew other people had seized similar opportunities before him, when new roads were proposed, and they had made big money. And he was right as it turned out: he did. Sixty, thousand, dollars.

"One could argue, Your Honor, that thus when Jack Bonnie cast his vote in committee, and then on the floor, supporting that state highway project, he acted in accordance not with his oath of public office, but in expectation of personal gain. And I would not dispute you, or any of the jurors who might agree with you. But that deduction you or they might make comports no illegal act by my client, William Ryan. Jack Bonnie, moved by greed, was acting for himself. Not at my client's behest. And that's what these charges allege."

"Yes," Keats said. "So, what would you have me do?"

"Take the case from the jury, Your Honor," I said. "Make a finding that the evidence against my client does not warrant his conviction. Direct the jury to return a verdict of not guilty on all counts. Prevent this group of men and women from possibly allowing a deep-seated and widespread suspicion of all state government employees to overcome their good judgment with emotion, so that they commit a grave miscarriage of justice and convict my client because of what he is and always has been, not because of anything he's been proven here to have done."

"Your Honor," Barry said in anguish, getting to his feet.

Keats sat him down with a languid wave. "Resume your seat, Mister Attorney General," he said. "You'll get your chance to be heard, if you still think that you need to exercise it." And right then, of course, I knew I had lost that round, at least. Andy Keats was going to let it go to the jury. And if I hadn't known, as I did, of course, why he was going to do that, his next question would have enlightened me. He was doing it because I'd been so clever.

"The loan, Mister Kennedy," Keats said to me, his black eyebrows crowding each other over his sudden fierce squint.

"Granting *arguendo* everything you've said so far, and assuming that it's my view of the matter as well, you haven't addressed, at least that I've heard, the matter of that rather large, loan."

Ah, yes, my dear, as W. C. Fields said, the matter of the loan. I hadn't touched it on cross, except for my questions about documents and other memoranda reflecting other business dealings between Jack and Billie, because, of course, there weren't any. But Judge Keats, on a flimsy argument by Barry that their mutual monetary history "showed a course of dealing," had allowed him on redirect to ask how Jack had disposed of his take from the 7K a week the loanshark collected in street interest on his $60,000 real estate profit. Barry was determined. If I refused to tromp on his trip wire, thus saving him problems on appeal, well, devil take it. The election would take place before a conviction could be reversed. Well, there's a big pail of cold water over the prosecutor's door when he sits down after redirect. It's called "recross."

I had not seen fit to inform Billy of the full extent of my knowledge before the trial began. I was afraid he and his conniving offspring might call an emergency coven to plot new devilments; the full-disclosure obligation runs from the client to the lawyer, not the other way around. So when I saw Jack Bonnie on the stand for the first time, knowing the commonwealth had sent two state troopers to bring him back to Boston, and had stashed him in a hotel room under twenty-four-hour guard until he came into the court, I proceeded on the assumption that if Billy had persisted in his work behind the scenes, he was certain to have failed.

Jack gave me some good exercise, and I gave him some as well. Like the Ryans in their rancorously disappointing quest for some bold advocate to represent their father, I had little choice. It was either that approach, or a forthright statement to the court that I had reason to believe my client had attempted to suborn perjury, tamper with the witness, intimidate the witness, and obstruct justice in his case. Such a declaration would have cleansed me spiritually (if vengefully), but it would also have amounted to an application for the next place on the guillotine of professional careers. Kamikaze heroism never appealed to me.

"Mister Bonaventre," I said, "your venture in Colchester was not the first of a business nature that you had undertaken with my client, I take it."

"Is that a question, counsellor?" he said. The kid had been well schooled indeed.

"Please take it as one," I said. "Was it?"

"Yes," he said.

"I call your attention to your fourth campaign, sir," I said, donning reading glasses and retreating to counsel table where I leafed through papers having no bearing whatsoever on Jack Bonnie's fourth campaign, and then, frowning, said: "When you asked William Ryan to loan you some money. Did you ask him? Did he loan it?"

It is important here to realize that while I knew from grilling Billy over a low flame until he was well done that there were no paper records, Jack had not been present, and so Jack did not know. Billy had sworn, up the front and down the back, that he had never given Jack any information whatsoever on that point. "Why would I've told him where I got the money?" Billy had said, always the practical fellow. "He wanted the money. He didn't care where I got it. Just so long as he got it. He didn't know where it came from, and he didn't know where it went to, after he paid it back."

So Jack, being too smart for his own good, could not be certain that there was not some document, somewhere, that would prove Billy had obtained that $20,000 in cash to give to him. Consequently he could not safely deny, flatly, that he had asked for and received the loan. I might have some proof that he had.

But, on the other hand, he didn't want to say he had. The prosecutors had him by the balls, and they had pliers. He wanted to please them. He had to please them, or he was going to feel pain. He did the sensible thing. He waffled. "I don't recall," he said.

Playing for time. I've done it myself. I've done it when I smell human scent on the cheese that I see temptingly poised before me. I think there's a trap under it. "Let me refresh your recollection, if I may," I said. "When you found that you had opposition from a gentleman with strong ties to the financially powerful electronics industry six years ago, long before anyone even thought of the Colchester bypass, and that opposition if successful would not only remove you from the legislature but scuttle your expectations of serving on the House Committee on Public Works, do you recall whether you had occasion to tell Billy Ryan that you needed some money to go up against the man who was challenging you?"

"I may have," he said.

"And whether, if you recall—and I can refresh your recollection on this if necessary—," I said, which, of course, I couldn't, because there were no documents, "you told Billy Ryan you needed twenty grand from him, at a minimum? In order to fend off this challenge?"

"I don't remember," he said.

"And whether," I said, "you received an affirmative answer from my client, and further whether some time later you met him in your office, and there accepted from him twenty thousand dollars in hundred-dollar bills, for use in your campaign, and put it in your pocket and said: 'I won't forget this'?"

"I don't recall," he said.

"So you have forgotten it," I said.

"I don't recall," he said.

"Indeed," I said. "Would it be fair to say that your memory is selective, Mister Bonaventre?" I was out from behind counsel table by then, and marching right up to the stand. When you plan to get into the witness's face rhetorically you might as well get into it physically as well. It adds drama, and jurors like that. We live in a TV generation. People expect a certain amount of theatricality in their relaxation, and those on jury duty are not behind their desks or at their lathes, so they look for a little excitement.

"Mister Kennedy," Judge Keats said wearily, indicating he wanted no histrionics.

"I'm entitled to approach the witness, am I not, Your Honor?" I said. "Is there some kind of *cordon sanitaire* around this fellow in this court? I hadn't heard about it."

"*Mister* Kennedy," Judge Keats said, coming forward in his swivel chair and glaring at me, "whatever your notion may be, I am still running this court, and you are not going to run rough-shod over its rules while I am doing that. Is that clear?"

"Perfectly clear, Your Honor," I said, "as it was before you saw fit to interrupt my line of questioning just now. Quite un-necessarily, and with no objection stated by the commonwealth. May I proceed?"

"Proceed," he said.

"Mister Bonaventre," I said, "please answer Yes or No. Did you borrow twenty thousand dollars from William F. Ryan in order to finance in part your fourth campaign for the State House of Representatives?"

"Well," he said, "I may've. . . ."

I held up my hand. "Nope," I said, "that won't do. Yes will do or No will do, but nothing in between. Did you or did you not?"

"Did I or did I not, do what?" he said.

I allowed my shoulders to slump. I grinned at the slimy rascal, hoping to God that the jury would see that I was grin-ning at a slimy ferret. "Mister Bonaventre," I said, "you know very well what I'm talking about. You know very well that I know very well that you don't go around every day borrowing twenty thousand dollars from every man you meet, and that when you do it, you remember that you did it, and when you pay it back, you remember it even better. Because you didn't like the second part as well as you liked the first part. So let's stop horsing around here, all right? Did you or did you not ask Billy Ryan to lend you twenty thousand for your fourth campaign, on the understanding that if you didn't win, he'd lose a friend in line for DPW? And that if you won, he'd have one? Yes or naked No. What's your choice?"

"I don't remember," he said.

"Okay," I said, "but you do remember, as you told Mister Barry, giving Billy Ryan twenty thousand dollars, all in cash, later on, after the Colchester bypass went through and you made a nice bundle from land sales? A bundle you farmed out in illegal small loans so it produced the twenty grand? Wasn't that to repay the campaign loan?"

"No," he said, "I don't remember that."

"That production," I said, "being your share of the proceeds of those small loans from the persons who collected them from debtors who had borrowed them from shylocks who hung out in barrooms and had put your sixty thousand dollars on the street at interest? That jog your memory at all?"

"No," he said.

"My goodness," I said, "you must be a man of wealth and fame. Let me please introduce yourself. Jumpin' Jack Flash, as I live and breathe." Heather never did learn to play her Rolling Stones tapes softly enough so I couldn't hear them when she was growing up in Braintree.

"Your *Honor*," Barry said, getting up.

"I withdraw it," I said before Keats could utter the order to do so. "So, Mister Bonaventre," I said, "inasmuch as I have been unable to refresh your recollection about this loan of twenty grand in petty cash, its extension to you or the fact that the money you gave Billy Ryan was repayment of your loan, I and this jury are entitled to expect that if, as, and when my client takes the stand, and testifies that he remembers vividly not only the making of the loan but the fact of that repayment, you will not return to this courtroom to deny that both transactions took place and you have had a vision that crept softly toward you in your sleep and reminded you of it? Yes or No."

"Well," he said.

"Yes or No," I said. "I've heard enough of 'Roses from the South' from you, Mister Bonaventre, and so, I hazard the guess, have these jurors."

"Mister *Kennedy*," Keats said.

"Please the court," I said, "may we confer at the sidebar, please?" When you have it in mind to get stern with a judge and insult opposing counsel as well, you can get away with more if you save their faces for them by not including the jury in the audience.

At the side I said: "Your Honor, this guy's been playing the waltz music in your courtroom for two days now, and you can tolerate it if you want. But I've got a client here, and his tail is in the crack, and I'm going to represent him. That's my job. This witness was put on the stand by the commonwealth. The commonwealth vouched for his veracity when it called him. I'm entitled to challenge that voucher on cross, and that's exactly what I'm doing.

"Mister Barry booby-trapped this case, and he knows he did it, but what he didn't figure on is that neither my client nor I is a booby, and we wouldn't fall into his trap. I want to know whether this bozo has a Lazarus act in mind, where he suddenly remembers that twenty grand some moonless night after my client takes the stand and describes it, and then intends to come back in here and tell this jury the repayment was a payoff. A bribe, in other words. Because if he does, I think we're entitled to have his version of the matter laid out before us now, so

when my client takes the stand, we'll be able to rebut it. As I
guarantee this court, we will. And if he doesn't plan to come
back and do that, to have him so state, on the record."

Keats sighed. "You may have it," he said. We returned to
our places.

"Thank you, Your Honor," I said. "Mister Bonaventre: Yes or
No. Did you borrow twenty grand from my client and then later
pay it back?"

"I don't know," he said.

"Thank you," I said. "No further questions, Your Honor." I
went back to my table and sat down. Sat down to wonder how
the jury had taken it, and how the judge thought the jury had
taken it. Obviously, given the outcome of my argument in support of his direction of a verdict of acquittal, he had not found
the cross-examination quite as devastating as I had hoped. But
that still left the jurors as twelve wild cards.

You never know what a jury will do. This figures, because
juries are made up of ordinary people, just like you and me, and
none of us ever knows, really, what the hell he will do. I had a
case some years ago in which the client was a twenty-six-year-
old man who'd had at least six drinks in a suburban saloon and
gone staggering out into the parking lot at two in the morning
to find two women, at least half-loaded on some kind of jungle
juice themselves, beckoning him into their Datsun 280Z. Like
the damned fool he was, he'd accepted the invitation, and they
transported him to an apartment where they shared more booze
and a gram or two of nose candy, and then, because it was a
cold night, one of them offered to drive him home, stoned and
smashed as they both were, and on the way she pulled into a
cemetery "to get her bearings."

My own view was that she had had it in mind to get his
bearings, too, but his bearings and prowess had been impaired
by all the booze and narcotics he'd enjoyed, so they had to
settle for whatever amusement he could orally provide. During

that provisioning she'd run out of cigarettes, having forgotten to bring along a book of crossword puzzles or a cheap novel, so that when she drove out of the cemetery at eight in the morning they had to stop at a convenience store for butts. Then she drove him home and gave him her telephone number; and the next day she went to the police station and charged him with rape.

At his trial I walked her through the memory of that exciting night with what I thought was loving care, and I made an impassioned argument to the jury that they must not convict a man who'd voluntarily brought so much joy into the world. They were out half an hour before returning and convicting him of the lesser-included offense of indecent assault.

The judge, taking a more tolerant view of cunnilingus than the jurors had apparently favored, gave him three years in Concord, suspended. So with that case, and some other confounding verdicts as well in mind, I was disheartened when Andy Keats made it clear that he was going to let the case against Billy Ryan go to the jury.

"Your Honor," I said, "the mendacity of the commonwealth's chief witness on the subject of that loan was transparent. And I remind the court that the prosecution did not see fit to educe evidence of that transaction on direct. Nevertheless, the commonwealth's witness remains the commonwealth's witness, and what he said on the stand is the commonwealth's burden to bear.

"I suggest to you that no reasonable person could conclude, beyond a reasonable doubt, that Jack Bonnie either never borrowed twenty thousand dollars from my client, or that he does not recall paying it back.

"I suggest to you further, Your Honor, that to allow this matter to go to the jury is to invite them to decide this matter on the basis of prejudice against a class of people: public servants. I know they get bashed all the time now, on the radio, in the papers, on TV. It's a popular sport. But this is a serious matter. Mister Ryan's spent a lifetime in the service of the commonwealth. His decades of work, his reputation, his personal integrity: all of them are endangered by the possibility that a jury, *this* jury, will nod knowingly at the uncorroborated and manifestly self-serving testimony of Jack Bonnie, and say that he is guilty of corruption.

"The case has not been proved. *The case has not been proven.* Say what you will about William Ryan's judgment, about his exercise of power or his cultivation of politicians, the only thing that has been proved about his life in this court is that he wanted to build a road that he thought would improve not only the area where he planned to build it but the prospects of travel through it; that he divulged his intentions to a member of the House Committee on Public Works, as he had to; that he oversaw the construction of the road; and that the member of the committee made some money. A good deal of money. On his own."

"That's your position, counsellor?" Keats said.

"That's my position," I said.

"Motion for directed verdict denied," Keats said. "Commonwealth?"

"No argument, Your Honor," Barry said, being sensible.

Keats nodded. "Bring the jury down," he said. "I assume you have your witnesses here, Mister Kennedy."

"Just one," I said. "He'll do for today."

TWENTY-ONE

I went to Billy's wake on the second night. I had a pretrial motion in Worcester and Norwich was on my way home, so I had a solitary early dinner over the evening paper at the counter of a diner half-full of other men eating pork chops and beans alone, far from home, while their eighteen-wheelers sat idle out in the broad parking lot, earning no profit from distance covered that hour to carry the heavy mortgages on the tractor units. I surmised that explained their brooding attitude toward food; there's nothing like being rendered powerless by circumstances to make a good man sullen.

I paid for my meal and got into my car and headed east-southeast to Norwich. Time was in the disorienting frame that night inside of Kilduff's that it always lapses into when a wake begins. Tommy Grogan and Andy Keats had made it through the first big room where the hot air of many conversations leached cloying smells from big bouquets, ignored by all the suits and dresses milling on the carpet. The two of them stood just beyond the double doorway to the viewing room at the rear, Billy Ryan's body exposed to vulgar gazes at the far end of the house, the seconds and the minutes somehow lasting longer in the rooms where corpses lie, the live folks come to see them adapting in the presence to a slightly slower speed.

Dead people are more dignified than live people, even if they were important when they were alive. Our fathers told us they were "not in any hurry" after death, so either time did not apply in rooms where corpses lay, the dead being exempt from statutes of limitations, or else the time was always ample to make sure everything was done for them, carefully and right, now that it was clear to all that it was too late. Keats shuffled forward one or two steps as those ahead of him proceeded through the receiving line; Grogan shuffled up behind him, and when the two women ahead of me and behind Grogan had completed their advance, I followed without a hitch.

That is the most important of the mourner's obligations when visiting a wake of some importance: always to perform each act, no matter how minuscule, observed or unobserved, in its proper order, and not to interfere when a predecessor or successor has completed the preliminaries and reached the stage of performing obsequies. Since I had seen Tommy's silver BMW in the parking lot, and had not seen Andy's black Buick Park Avenue, I could have deduced from their proximity in line that Andy had hitched a ride with Tommy, but that would have figured anyway: Andy was sitting in Suffolk Superior that month, and when he shut down for the afternoon he would've dropped into Tommy's office on Beacon Hill across from Bowdoin Street and joined him for a cocktail at the Parker House before setting out for Norwich.

The ritual point was that while Tommy's annual take was about five times what Andy's was, and Tommy'd done the driving, Andy was a justice of the court and Tommy wasn't, so Andy at the funeral home would have pride of precedence.

I had made it through the double doors—past the stairwell to the smoking room adjoining the restrooms in the cellar; some male caller down there was using his resonant baritone to tell a current dirty joke I'd heard, and not a bad one, either, so although I moved along again too soon to hear the punch line, I was able to supply it for myself—I did not laugh again—when the woman in line in front of me abruptly stepped away and turned back toward the stairs. Her expression betrayed no urgent distress, so I moved up just as Andy reached the outskirts of the receiving line.

I envied him. As the judge who had presided over Billy's trial, he had had at most a transient glimpse or two of the defendant's many nears-and-dears before Billy banished them at the end of the first day of the case, and therefore lacked my disadvantage of having been the reluctant second-hand recipient of their unwilling—often inadvertent—confidences during many agonizing months and meetings of bitter stress.

Inescapable discoveries that someone else, not one of them, was in charge of running things, were neither familiar nor welcome to Ryans. They had grown up habituated to smug awareness of Billy's genuine political power, and become complacently accustomed to the comfortable, arrogant assurance that nobody nowhere did nothin' to no Ryan if the Ryans were agin' it. Then as adults starting out with power derived from their name, they quite speedily got some more, at least in part by their own efforts; all this did was make them prouder. So, when they found themselves first with very little choice other than to humbly accept my services, and then to pay me a good sum for their performance, they figured they had done enough, that they had leased me for the long term if not bought me fair and square, to do their bidding for them, as they might choose to order. I'd had to explain to them, several times, either indirectly through Billy, when he relayed their concerns, or with heat and man to man, when Colin braced me on the phone, that if the trial lawyer you hired is going to let you try the case, you are definitely in the market for a (new) trial lawyer, because the spineless lackey you chose is in the wrong line of work, and can't do the job.

They didn't like it. When they had found themselves, as they repeatedly had, with reservations about my attire, approach or attitude, they invariably recalled that Colin's first-through-fourth-or-fifth choices of counsel for the patriarch had turned the case down flat. So even though they'd all come close to desperation, and were relieved to have escaped by signing me, their gratitude, though profuse, was insincere—until the jury said: "Not guilty," and that came a long time later. Then, as the preacher said, I not only had them in the church—I had them in my choir.

But that was as far as it went: it extended through the second generation of existing Ryans, that last remove of the consanguinity of thankfulness. Acquitted defendants, Billy among them, usually harbor a lively understanding of the danger averted, and the talented hard work that went into it. When they say they thank you, they mean it. Their spouses, too: they mean it, and so do any parents who have suffered the ordeals.

Adolescent grandchildren do not. They generally have to make an effort to conceal the wrathful impatience they feel when the legal travails of their damned obsolete old fossil, allowed to bore them since their infancies at will with familiar tales, bad breath and annoying medical problems, has the gall on top of that to get himself indicted, and thus distract the entire world from constant and immediate satisfaction of their whining demands and whims. The effort made by the Ryan grandchildren had been no more than generally halfhearted, and seldom convincing at all.

They would not have made any effort at all, but for Billy's four adult children. They may not have been truly convinced, deep down inside, that their whelps had shown proper respect to Gampy in his woe, but the fact that they'd succeeded against

all odds in extorting any show of concern at all from their bat-
talion of blithe brats was sufficient to warrant the expectation
that I'd, of course, flatter them as dutiful parents by remember-
ing the names of all the little wretches, and call them out in
order as I reviewed their ranks that night.

I did not recall them. The best I could do was remember
vaguely that the gangly redheads belonged to Colin and Nancy;
the little cookie in the tight black dress, whom Kilduff had met
at fifteen, was Patrick's eldest; and that one of the other four
fungible hormone-stoked geeks was the seductress's brother, the
remainder being distributed among Marie Ryan Frolio and
Mark, and Dr. John and his lovely bride, whose name escaped
me too. I envied Andy his pardonable ignorance.

Predictably, he didn't even need to plead it. Colin spotted
him from his post next to John at the front of the line, next to
his father's remains, and at once cantered softly down the file to
rescue him. Those judges take care of each other, they do. The
measures they take in each other's behalf make the old-time
Mob's showy displays of solidarity seem shabby.

"Andy," Colin said, taking Keats's right hand between both
of his soft palms and pressing it ever so gently, "so good of you
to come. Mother will be touched. Nothing means more to a
man at a time of sadness like this than to have his colleagues'
sympathy, their compassion, and to know they share his sorrow." Then as Andy commenced his solemn incantation of the
rote of formal sorrow, Colin took him by the left elbow and
whisked him from the line, leaving Tommy Grogan to deal as
best he might be able with the ostentatiously bored array of
third-generation Ryans, and me with only the one woman between me and my imminent discomfort. I reflected once more
that even though I know quite well that I don't wish to be a
judge, and wouldn't be a good one if I did (that's why I don't
wish to be one), the job does have its points, and not just the
steady wages.

Tommy began his acceptably *pro forma* "sorry-fer-yer-trouble's" to the glassy-eyed grandchildren. Since none of them had ever laid eyes on him before in their lives, had no idea who he might have been, or why he thought they cared whether they were glad or sad, and he cared less about their lives than he did the lives of birds, this was not going to take very long. I began to hope fervently that the lady preceding me had been their nanny since their births, and that she would save my bacon for me by singing out their names.

But Grogan was spared even the perfunctory discharge of established protocols. Colin, having rescued Andy and installed him in his proper company among the chiefest bereaved, glided back down the file like a benevolent apparition, and omitting only the allusion to collegiality—he substituted "old friends' sympathy"—otherwise employed exactly the same honeyed words and practiced moves to extract Tommy from the line.

Of course. Tommy had most of the state reps on Judiciary, Counties and Appropriations in his thrall, if not on his clients' payrolls. Colin Ryan had been raised properly, and was not about to disregard such a visitor, let alone one in line to become president of the American Bar Association. Tommy did not resist, and quite certain in my mind that the taste rising in my gorge was that of hot bile that would soon choke me, I shuffled forward as the woman took Grogan's former place. I regretted I had always shunned bar association meetings.

The woman fell upon the first startled adolescent Ryan—he looked to be the youngest—and put a hug on him that but for her sobbing cries would have reflected credit on an NFL line-. backer who had broken through the coverage to blindside and dismember a Pro Bowl quarterback. Both Colin, extending his right hand to grasp Grogan's left elbow, and·Tommy muttering the platitudes, were as distracted momentarily as I was by this drama, and Colin, as I stepped back a pace, spotted me and reacted like the thoroughbred he was. "And *Jerry*," he said softly, taking his grip on Tommy, moving him back toward me, "Jerry Kennedy. Steadfast as always in adversity." The bile receded without a trace as Colin took my hand, and with the practice of the decades I said: "Colin, what a sad thing. I'll miss your dad a lot. Of all the clients that I've known, and I've known a lot, he was unforgettable."

TWENTY-TWO

Colin escorted the pair of us down the line to where we were to justify his expectations that our attendance at his father's wake would touch his mother's heart, smoothly ad-libbing the patter to suit my different station—where Tommy had been one of his "old friends," come to share his sorrow, I was his "dear friend and classmate, and always his comforter." Meaning, I supposed, not to imply that he thought me stuffed with feathers, useful on a cold winter's night, but that I had eased his mind a bit when Billy appeared well on his way to the penitentiary for a spell, and no one else would take his case.

Time at the head of the line was even further out of joint. Andy when we arrived was still engaged in satisfaction of his duty to ratify Colin's eminence on the bench to Colin's siblings. But Andy had apparently caught Dr. John in a mood to demand not only that assurance—as well as the customary profession of sympathy, of course—but also firm judicial acknowledgment that the head of surgery at Assumption Hospital was professionally of eminence equivalent to that of any judge, including Andy, and therefore brother Colin. Dr. John, his widow's peak combed straight back over his long face, his blue eyes pale but challenging behind his silver glasses, his six-two frame erect under his faultless dark-blue suit, had something on his mind. He rocked back and forth as he spoke. ". . . a real emergency on our hands here in the next few years. Not that we haven't got one now. It's one thing for a man in my position, who's been at it long enough to've reached the point where I don't operate myself on all that many patients."

He allowed an expression of displeasure to cross his face. "Damned paperwork takes up most of my time. But for the young ones coming up, the ones who see the patients, and especially the people in obstetrics, plastic reconstruction, this constant harassment by lawyers has them terrified. And then, well, the insurance bills, come close to prostrating them." He raised his eyebrows. "Well," he said, "what do I tell them when they come in to see me? 'Sixty thousand dollars for malpractice coverage now? With all the debts I've got?' They're thinking about quitting, Andy, throwing in the sponge. It's a bad problem we've got, or will have, all of us, when the doctors up and quit."

"Well, of course, it is, and will be," Andy said. Andy's been around the track more times than Secretariat totalled. There's no judge on the bench now with finer stratagems for the temporary consolation of an angry partisan than Andy calls upon when he's got his mind made up and just wants to ditch the guy. "But you can't stop the lawyers from bringing those cases, Doctor, as long as the injuries happen. And you can't stop the juries awarding the damages when they're convinced that the bad result was the result of medical incompetence. You can't, as a doctor; I can't, as a judge. It's something that just can't be done."

Colin identified his next task at once, and was up to it. "John," he said, and introduced Grogan, reminding John that Tommy was a classmate from law school, "and now a leader of the bar, of national stature. Soon to be the president of the ABA. Why not tell him about your views? His thoughts carry weight among those you'd like to reach." At the same time he was easing Andy, with his full cooperation, away from his bigger brother and me up to the wing chairs, close to the foot of the casket.

Rt. Rev. Msgr. Francis Martin held the first chair, somehow managing in his black clerical suit, his dickey with red piping and his Roman collar, to occupy it as majestically as the popes in full gold-brocaded robes preside from the Throne of St. Peter in the Vatican. "They don't make domestic prelates now," Father Shaw had said to me that long-ago day before Billy went to trial. "The official thinking was that in these modern times there's no longer any need to have all these junior bishops running thither and yon all over the diocese, so they would make no more. The suspicion was that the title hadn't been awarded in recent memory on the basis of merit anyway, spiritual or material. The younger men who got it were the bishop's pets, and for the older ones it was just a nice tombstone promotion, based on how much cash they'd raised for the cardinal's fund drives. Which meant that the best priest in the world didn't have a Chinaman's chance if the parish he pastored was poor.

"But even if they did still make them," Father Shaw had said, "no matter how they worked at it, they'd never make another Martin. And praise the Lord for that."

Colin had to clear his throat to divert Monsignor Martin's imperial attention. The monsignor, interrupted in his methodical patting of Fannie Ryan's left hand on the arm of the next chair, did not bother to conceal his irritation. I doubt he ever had; he was too good at its display to resist a performance opportunity. He shifted his gaze and stared at us intruders. His full mane of white hair had been carefully shaped by a stylist to frame his face. When Mack met another good-looking woman whom she'd disliked on sight, usually a competing realtor, her diplomatic tactic for handling later mention of the name by prospective buyers was to agree that they'd met casually, "but I don't know her work at all. I do envy her bone structure, though. Her face will outlast time."

The monsignor had that good structure, and there was no softness of the flesh that covered it. His brilliant blue eyes were large and searing. "Forty years ago," Father Shaw had said to me, "heck, maybe still today, if he had the proper costume, Frank Martin could've played Field Marshal Rommel, the Desert Fox, in the movies." Shaw had laughed. "And considering his politics in real life, he could've done it without reservation."

"Father," Colin said, his choice of address showing off the Ryan intimacy with the clerically powerful, "I'd like to present Judge Andrew Keats of the superior court, one of our most brilliant jurists, and my valued colleague. Andy, this is Monsignor Frank Martín, one of Dad's oldest and dearest friends."

For a long moment, even for casket time, the monsignor said nothing. I don't know whether he remembered Andy, at first. After the ninth day of trial he'd perceived I had no intention of giving him a speaking part, and had given up attending. He used the interval to assay Keats's sincerity, bearing and demeanor, calculating not only his standing in the community but whether he deserved it. Gradually the old priest's expression changed from fierce challenge to grudging acceptance of Keats's worthiness. He extended his right hand as though to have a ring kissed.

Grogan appeared to my left. We exchanged data silently, with glances and body language. With his face—he underlined the chagrin in his eyes by extending his tongue to moisten the right side of his lips—he made plain to me his view that my evasion of Dr. John gave him an indisputable claim to his old place in line. I acceded and took half a step back.

"You were the judge at the trial," Martin said to Andy. His voice was a low rumble, something like distant thunder over the Lakes of Killarney, presenting no immediate threat to the good people of Tralee, but reminding all who heard it the danger was always there.

Keats bowed. "I was, Monsignor," he said, clasping the limp paw. "A hard time, too, that was. That was a hard time for all." Good old reliable Andy; in such company he knew the importance of being Irish, especially for one whose surname was the same as a British poet, and therefore the importance of declaring proper ancestry, with just a lilt of brogue. "And sorry for this trouble, too. I'm sorry you've lost your friend."

It worked like Lourdes water. The old eagle beamed. "And a fine job you did, Judge, as it came out. A fine job and fair one." The dishrag fingers and hand clenched around Andy's, and pumped away firmly three times.

"And Father," Colin said, clearly having ducked another calling as a maitre d', "let me just introduce Judge Keats here to Mother. . . ." The monsignor released the hand of his new-found, lifetime friend. Colin sidled Andy up to the next chair and brought Tommy up. "Father, this is attorney Thomas Grogan, one of the leaders of our bar and vice president-elect of the ABA."

Grogan extended his hand. In the time that Colin's maneuver had taken, the monsignor had completely recycled. His right hand again patted Fannie's left; all evidence of good will had vanished from his face. "You've heard of Irish Alzheimer's?" Father Shaw had said to me before Billy went to trial.

" 'You forget everything but your grudges,' " I said.

"Exactly," Shaw said. "Well, if Frank Martin ever starts to lose his grip to disease, that's the kind he'll get. And just as the Ryans will, too. They live in a world where there aren't any bygones. No bygones at all to let be. It's been over thirty years now since Frank Martin made his big miscalculation, took Cushing at his word. The cardinal hated communists? Well, Frank would hate them more. And what His Eminence could *not* say about those against Senator McCarthy—that they were all Jews, of course, 'just like Marx was in his time'—Frank could and *would* say, every chance he got. Cushing could be Edgar Bergen to Frank's Charlie McCarthy, and in New England Frank would be our own Father Coughlin. In gratitude for which, of course, the cardinal would consecrate him as a bishop somewhere.

"Well, it didn't work out. And *well* that it didn't work out. The best Frank may've been able to do was a free couple hours late Thursday nights on a sixty-watt station out here, rousing the rabble with 'Red Channels' hogwash about how Peggy Wood was a commie, and no one should 'Remember Mama.' And all of that kind of thing. Yellow snow. But it got back, as that stuff always does, and pretty soon Cushing's generous Jewish friends were making calls to Lake Street, saying: 'What is going on?' So the cardinal invited Frank in to the residence and had a talk with him. 'Yeah, Frank, what *is* going on?' And Frank's answer didn't please him—end of bishopric."

When Heather was a little girl, I read to her at night. One of her favorite characters was Peter Rabbit, so we went through his adventures many times. She's reading those stories to her two kids now, and when we chat on the phone, every two or three weeks, she tells me my grandchildren are just as delighted when Charlie tells them about Squirrel Nutkin as she was when I read about Peter. "But Peter's still my favorite, Dad. Peter's my Number One bunny." And, I assure her, I'm loyal, too: my favorite's still Benjamin Bunny, old Uncle Benjamin Bunny, who had no regard at all for imposing big cats. That was what Monsignor Martin had for vice presidents-elect of the ABA.

Tommy did not gain his seat in the general court, develop his network of elected and appointed loyalists who will almost always do as he suggests (unless compliance would certainly lead to indictment and conviction, or, almost as bad, political oblivion), or reach his present position in the ABA without being able to read people. And Tommy, having attained most of his goals before he turned fifty, has not for some years dissipated his time on the cultivation of people whom he's read as indifferent, of dubious use to him, or hostile beyond hope of conversion. Monsignor Martin, before his fall from the cardinal's grace, might have found himself subjected to a full dose of Tommy's blarney. But not afterwards. Tommy makes good use of many crafty prelates, of several denominations, as they simultaneously make of him. He'll do it again, if it helps. When the interests of the secular intersect with the sacred, as they seem to have a way of doing, here in Massachusetts, alliances disintegrate, form and re-form at a dizzying rate (some decades back, the Calvinist clergy and the Mafia, the members of each echelon carefully holding themselves aloof from the members of the other, combined in opposition to legalization of church bingo nights—preachers disliking wagering of all kinds, legal or not, and gangsters all competition—but ultimately lost, valiantly but predictably, to the massed array of Roman Catholic and Jewish clergy), no one has been more adroit than Tommy in arranging coalitions. He can butter up a promising priest faster than a famished man could grease up a Parker House roll. But Tommy, carting more Massachusetts political history in his head than the State Archives have on paper, had to know that Martin's star had been set by Cushing many years before, and could see at Billy's wake that Martin was too old to be useful to him. The monsignor's hauteur thus concerned him not at all. Martin gave him a limp fish to shake, and Tommy put a cold, dead haddock in his palm. "Mister Grogan," the monsignor said, afar off.

"Your Excellency," Grogan said as he bowed, giving the monsignor the bishop's address Martin had never won—in boxing known as a stinging jab. "When you're cutting the guy's head off," Billy Ryan said to me, after one long day of trial, "you want to do it, if you can, so he doesn't notice it 'til after he gets home. And then his wife says something to him, and he doesn't quite catch it, so he turns his head to hear her—and his head falls off. And while it rolls around on the linoleum, that head is thinking: 'Who did this to me?' And then he realizes who did it to him."

"And what do I call you, sir?" Martin said. "Your vice presidency, elect?" In boxing known as working-the-body; infighting never is pretty.

The ritual underway between Grogan and the priest was familiar to me, and so I listened instead to the conversation among Colin, Andy Keats and Fannie Ryan at the next chair over. Colin gave his recitation about Andy's prominence. She didn't seem to hear. She didn't seem to want to hear. She'd gotten frail herself since I had seen her last—understandably enough; she was eighty-five when Billy died, and for a woman who had never had an easy life, had endured a very hard one in her later years. Unexpectedly, when the danger's seemed to pass, and then it reappears, it's more difficult to bear.

She did not shift her gaze immediately when Colin produced Andy. She kept it fixed on the effigy of her dead husband.

It got stuck in my mind, too, that night, waxily and lifelessly replacing the image I'd had of the live old bastard's ax-blade face: the neck, cheeks and forehead rouged and powdered pasty rose; the pocked skin now without the deep pores and liver spots; the nostrils clean of black, curled hairs; the ever-watchful eyes closed as I'd never before seen them; and the lips a bit too red, sewn closed, against the yellowed, crooked teeth. Billy was fond of baring them, but only partially, between slightly parted lips when he thought you thought you had him balked. At dinner in the evening after the opening day of trial, when he had every right to be downcast and woebegone, I told him not to be discouraged by the prosecutor's opening. "Their rule is that if they're not sure they can prove it, they put it in the opening. And hope the jury'll remember what they said, not what got backed up on the stand. Our day'll come. When we open, whatever we're not sure of proving, I'll use in my opening."

The first cut may or may not be the deepest, but the first day of trial is traumatic. Clients react differently. Some get despondent and rehash the long-term prospects of what will occur if they fold up and plead. Some get revived by a rush of adrenaline. Billy was one of that kind. He laughed. He curled his lips back to expose his fangs. "See these? No dentist's ever touched 'em. No dentist ever will. These're all my own teeth, got that? And no one's ever knocked 'em out, but a lot of men've tried. Now, if Mike Dunn or his errand boy, that Barry character, think that they're boyos that can do it, kick my teeth out for me, well, there's been lots before them, and nobody ever did."

The day I first met Fannie, she wore a troubled look. At the time it troubled me, not because I didn't understand it, given the fix she was in—because her husband was—because he *was* in it, and so she was, too, and both of them would stay in it unless I somehow contrived to get them out. That look, that day, reminded me that she was counting on me. But it was still an expression less troubling to me than the one I saw on her that night at his wake. The first fix of his indictment had been one that she could fight. Another in a long series of battles, she behind the lines, of course, another one she hadn't bargained for, welcomed when she married him, and was not sure could be won. But at least then she could fight.

His death wasn't such a fight. At the wake she sat gazing at his body with a slight frown on her face. Obviously more than fifty years of marriage to the man who'd been in that body had been inadequate to explain to her something significant about him that had always puzzled her. Insufficient even to establish what on earth it was. I didn't know exactly what it was, and never would, but I knew the feeling.

I don't think you ever really get to know the person that you marry, no matter how long you may be married before death or some other business more pressing takes you away, alone. The day of the last hearing in *Kennedy* v. *Kennedy*, before the decree *nisi* issued, both Mack and I had to show up with our lawyers and state for the record that we'd finally agreed on the property division. It was pure formality. Then I watched her leave the courtroom in a yellow suit I'd always liked, just as attractive as always it seemed, and I could've almost wondered who the hell that pretty stranger was.

I didn't make the speech that I extemporized in my head. "That one over there, Your Honor. The woman in the wool suit with the lovely figure. The one I slept with almost twenty-five years. Had our daughter. Suffered with me without stint when I was getting started. Put up with me when I lost a case like I put up with her when she lost a sale. The one I took to London when things started to go good. The one who raised our daughter, who turned out pretty well. The one who raised the devil when her incompetent assistant started sleeping with the owners at Southarbor Realty, so that Mack couldn't fire her. The one who finally got rid of the assistant, and then promptly started sleeping with Ace and Roy herself, having become a third owner in a joint venture with them that I still think stinks of fraud, and—I guess—wishing to demonstrate that female co-owners have the same sexual poaching rights as the original male partners did. You can see I vaguely recognize her, Judge. But do you know who she is?" *Bewilderment*'s what it is.

I don't know for certain what Fannie Ryan may have said to Andy Keats. Colin concluded his spiel about Andy to her as Grogan and the monsignor completed the brief decencies observed by calculating men, silently agreeing that neither is likely to be of the slightest potential use to the other, so no further tail sniffing's needed, and it was my turn with the prelate. Colin was detained by his introduction of Grogan to "Mother," so I stepped up to the monsignor, having the same regard for monsignori that Uncle Benjamin Bunny had for cats.

TWENTY-THREE

"Are we going to the funeral home when we get there?" Teddy said.

"No," I said. "I was going to, but I thought it over and I decided against it. I was there. I was there and I signed the book. We'll just show up at the church and go in. The procession will come. The Mass will be said. Then we'll go up on the hill and see him off. That'll do it. Then I'll be finished. We'll just go on to Worcester, you and me, and see if we can do as well with the grand jury there."

"Took a long time, though, this one did," Teddy said.

"It did that," I said. "It did that."

"It's all the same to you, Counsellor," Teddy said, "I'd like it just as well if we got through a little sooner with the Worcester thing. Knowing your hourly rate and all."

"I know about overhead, Teddy," I said.

"Yeah yeah," Teddy said, "but you remember it when we talk, and you didn't with this dead guy."

"Teddy," I said, "it would blow your doors off to know what

he paid me. Just like it blew mine off when I found out by accident what I could've gotten."

"What was it you got, again?" Teddy said.

"None of your business," I said. "I earned it."

"Rotten crook," Teddy said. "Not you—him. Guys like him don't deserve a learned counsellor."

"*Deserve*'s got nothing to do with it," I said. "You know how restaurants work. You go in and you order your meal, they assume you've got money to pay for it. They don't ask for character references, and they don't care where you got the money. Law business is a little different, but not that much. You come in and ask me to work for you. I figure you picked me instead of some high-rise, white-shoe outfit because you think I'll work cheaper, and you're right. Same as the restaurants, same as hotels, same as the suits and the houses—if you've got any brains at all, you shop where you think you can afford to.

"I know this. I look at the work and I ask you for money. Not what I think you can afford, or what I think the traffic will bear —whatever I think it will cost. Plus a reasonable profit, of course. I have to eat too, you know. But I don't require references either. Where you got the money is not my concern. My concern is whether you've got it, and're willing to give it to me."

"You don't do that with me," Teddy said. "Price it out by the job. You just go along and don't even bill me until you run out of money. Then you clobber me right on the head. I don't even know what it's for."

"You're different," I said. "You and I go back a ways. Besides, I know you're good for it. And you damned well do know what it's for."

"Well, that's what I mean," Teddy said. "This guy had to've been a total skunk, you hit him up in advance."

"No, he wasn't," I said. "I had a witness who said he was the salt of the earth. Wasn't a dry eye in the house."

"Another crook, I suppose," Teddy said.

"Not at all," I said. "A member of the clergy, as I live and breathe."

"Same thing," Teddy said.

"You know, Mister Franklin," I said, "you're a hard man indeed. Without any redeeming social qualities."

"So're you, Kennedy," Teddy said.

"And for that reason, useful," I said.

"Well," he said, "I wouldn't go that far. Handy, maybe, handy." He paused. "But you shouldn't be handy for crooks."

"Why not?" I said. "If they've got the money, why shouldn't I hire myself out?"

"It's not dignified," Teddy said. "Look, what did you do for this dead crook, huh? You got him off is what you did. All you did's encourage the rest of the thieves—'I get caught, I'll hire Kennedy.'"

"I hope they do," I said. "I could use the business." I overstated that. Since the Ryan case, I've had plenty. A surfeit of business in fact. So much that I pondered hiring an assistant, and someone to help Gretchen out. But I regained my senses and did neither one; what pharaoh couldn't seem to grasp about the transience of the fat years I have engraved on my brain.

The river in Norwich was bright blue that morning. I drove along it to the triangular intersection, the left fork leading into the center, the right an oblique angle up the hill to Saint Matthew's where both curbs were already filled with parked cars, and cops were making people double-park on the wrong side.

"You know," Teddy said, "I know you told me about the case, that you were excited about it. But for some reason or other I didn't really follow it, you know? You got the guy off, right? He was acquitted?"

"Uh huh," I said. A cop was directing me to triple-park on the wrong side, thus starting a new line that would fill the whole lane. I did as he directed.

"Lemme ask you something," Teddy said. The carillon tolled. It was deafening. It was so loud it hurt my teeth. "Jesus Christ," Teddy said, between peals, "what in God's name is that?"

"It's Billy Ryan's good deed," I said. "That's his carillon. There was a fire in the church, and the bells cracked. So Billy knew a guy who sold sound systems, sometimes, and probably other things other times. And he took the pastor to see him, made up the difference in cash, and that's what you're hearing right now."

"All the crooks know each other," Teddy said.

"In my experience, they do," I said. In the rearview mirror I could see three cops on motorcycles making the sharp turn at the intersection, leading the hearse up the street, the cortege following slowly. "This guy owed Billy a favor."

"Sure he did," Teddy said. "All the crooks also owe each other. What'd your client want from the priest?"

"Teddy," I said, "if you ever gave a dime to charity, which you never have, you'd know you get nothing for it."

"How about what I paid you," Teddy said. "If that wasn't charity . . ."

"You know, Teddy," I said as the cops rolled by on their bikes and the hearse wheeled in at the curb, "you can always go to that grand jury session in Worcester alone, and take your best shot at confusing them."

"You also got a bad habit," Teddy said. "You make smart remarks to your friends."

"I do that," I said. The limos lined up behind the hearse. The bells continued to toll.

"Billy's only condition," I said, leaving out the part about the tax man, "was that on the day of his funeral, the bells should play 'Too-ra, Loo-ra, Loo-ra.'"

"What the hell is that?" Teddy said.

"It's an Irish lullabye," I said.

"Well, I wouldn't know that," Teddy said. "How the hell did you get the guy off? Do you know?"

A detachment of soldiers in ceremonial silver helmets and white-webbed Sam Browne belts formed two files behind the hearse.

"Sure I know," I said. "The usual way. You have seen it. Sheer magnificence—I was simply superb."

The jury went out, that day in the kindness of May, and they did not look happy. I didn't blame them. Nothing I had said would've made anybody happy. It certainly didn't make Dermot Barry or Mike Dunn happy, and I don't think it pleased Andy Keats a great deal, but I wasn't representing Dunn, or Barry, or Andy Keats. I was representing Billy Ryan. Him only. I try to keep my eye on the ball.

"You have something to do here today, Mister Foreman and ladies and gentlemen of the jury. It's going to be hard work, and my guess is that you won't like it. You will not understand why the devil it falls to you to do, and frankly, I don't either. But it has, and you have to do it.

"What you have to do is vindicate the judgment of our Founding Fathers. They operated on the assumption that the civilians knew what justice was, and would render it. No matter what the position or the reputation of the person accused. Some fun, huh?

"So now you have in your bare hands the fate of William Francis Ryan. As the clerk told you: to the charges lodged against him, he has said he is not guilty, and for his trial has put himself upon the country. And you are the country this time out, and you were sworn to try the issue. The clerk told you that if he was guilty you were to say so, and that if he was not guilty, you were to say so, and nothing more.

"Well, that will do nicely, thank you. You've heard, and will hear, enough talk out of me and Mister Barry, and the judge, and all the witnesses, in these past weeks, to last you the rest of your lives. Now you have to decide, on your own, without any interference from any of us, whether Mister Barry has proven, beyond a reasonable doubt, that William F. Ryan is corrupt. Not whether one of his friends made some money because he knew what Billy Ryan was going to do next. Not whether you like Billy Ryan, or would have him as a guest in your home. Just: whether Jack Bonnie made some money because Billy put him up to it to get some for himself.

"*Not:* whether Jack Bonnie made some money. He did. It's not disputed. *Not:* whether Jack Bonnie's crooked. He is. He admits it. No, the question before you is whether Billy Ryan stole money out of your pockets, as taxpayers. If you think he did, you should convict him. If you think you don't know, on the basis of the evidence you have heard and seen, beyond a reasonable doubt, then you should acquit him.

"It's that simple. It's that hard. I don't envy you. My client's been involved in Massachusetts politics since the dinosaurs departed. He's got tar all over him, and the feathers will probably come next. My client stood convicted, long before you ever saw him, guilty, dead to rights, on charges of having been a public servant all of his adult life.

"But he isn't charged with that—I hope. If he is, he is a gone goose, and I've wasted hours and days that you will never see again. I don't believe I've done that. I've read the indictment, the one you had read to you, and it says what my client did was—let's be blunt here—plain corrupt. Well, I submit to you that on the basis of the evidence that has been presented to you here, in this courtroom, that he is not guilty, beyond a reasonable doubt, of the corrupt offenses he's been charged with committing.

"Now, this is my job. This is what I do for a living. I get up on my hind legs and I holler and yell at people, and sometimes the people who pay me my fees are pleased by my efforts. Sometimes they aren't. That's okay. It goes with the territory. But every so often I get one like this, when the idea of the client going down the dumper really bothers me, and I get to wondering—not how *he's* going to live with it if that happens, but how *I* am. It's what you call a personal investment, I guess. The kind a defense lawyer's not supposed to make in a case that he's trying.

"Well, I did it. Mister Foreman and ladies and gentlemen of the jury: to these charges this defendant, my client, has said that he is not guilty, and for his trial has put himself upon *his* country, which country *you* are, and you were sworn to try the issue, and if you find this man guilty, beyond a reasonable doubt, of corrupt behavior, in doing exactly what he was supposed to do, on the basis of the testimony and the evidence you have seen introduced before you, then he was mistaken about his country.

"I hope he wasn't. I hope you will weigh what you have seen and heard and do it carefully, as you would wish twelve men and women, whom you have never met, to weigh the evidence against you. And then decide that it was not enough. Because this wasn't."

When it was over and I had gripped hands with Billy, and bade him go to the phone, I did something I had never done before, and probably will not do again. I accosted the foreman of the jury before he could leave the courtroom, and I shook his hand and said: "Thank you."

He said: "No thanks necessary, Mister Kennedy. Dunn didn't prove his case. You were absolutely right. We all agreed your client did it, but somebody had to prove it. And nobody did. Least not to us." I thanked him again. "No, no," he said.

"But no matter what anybody ever tells you, don't you ever think this is not a great country. If you start to, think of us."

"So it was Bonaventre that got him off," Teddy said. "Son of a gun." The bells tolled again.

"It was the way I handled Bonnie on cross that got Billy off," I said. "That's what I think, at least. I buckled the guy. He never did actually contradict himself, but I rattled him enough so his story looked shaky, and that's enough with a jury." I do take a certain pardonable pride in my craftsmanship, and if it isn't pardonable, I really don't give a damn.

"Yeah," Teddy said. The soldiers pulled the casket out of the hearse and covered it with a flag. Six of them grabbed the handles on the sides and started up the walk to the church. The other four, led by a young lieutenant with a blond mustache, lined up behind them. A group of officers in dress uniforms waited behind them. "This guy was a veteran too, huh? What was he, a general or something?"

"Staff sergeant," I said. "Quartermaster Corps. Yankee Division. World War Two."

"Unusual," Teddy said. "This kind of a turnout for a non-com."

"Not if one of the noncom's sons is a general," I said.

"Ahh," Teddy said, "there's always a good explanation."

"Usually," I said. "Usually." I took the key from the ignition and opened my door partway. "We'd probably better go in." The carillon tolled again.

Teddy shifted himself around in his seat and faced me. He was grinning. "You still don't know how you did it, do you," he said. "You still haven't figured it out."

"Figured what out?" I said.

"How you got the guy off," Teddy said.

"Sure I have," I said. "I made the jury see him as a human being. I made them care about what happened to him. I made them think how they would feel if somebody accused them."

"By using what Bonaventre said," Teddy said.

"Sure," I said. "That's my job. I care about my clients, and I care what happens to them."

Teddy laughed. He opened his door. "Has it ever occurred to you, Counsellor, that your clients care about you?"

We sat in the second pew from the back. We had a good view of Monsignor Martin and a number of elderly priests who met the casket on the shiny trolley in the vestibule, waited until the flag had been replaced with the white drape, embroidered with the large gold cross, and then preceded it down the aisle. We stood, as did the people in front of us, now that the show was on. I could hear Martin singing very softly.

Apparently I was not the only one. As the procession moved toward the altar, people in row after row heard the same thing I did, and when Billy Ryan's casket came to a stop before the communion rail, most of the people were singing, along with the monsignor, just as nasally and badly as he did. The old goat began to lead us, *a capella*, using his gold shepherd's crook the way a symphony conductor employs his baton, and we didn't croon any more. We sang at the tops of our lungs, most inappropriate for the kind of song it is, but highly suitable for the occasion that had summoned us. *"Hush now, don't you cry."* If there is a second verse, nobody seemed to know it. So we all sang the first one again.

Then the monsignor wheeled toward the altar and ascended, followed by his coterie of other guys in vestments, grey hair or none at all, and before it he turned as they dispersed to their chairs, shifted his crook to his left hand, raised and extended his right hand and blessed the congregation. I was stunned. *"In nomine Patris, et Filius, et Spiritus Sanctus,"* he said.

"Hey," Teddy muttered, "when they buried Tony, they buried him in English, right? What is this?"

"This ain't Tony," I muttered back. "Just shut up and enjoy it, all right?"

The monsignor didn't stop after that, either. The old bastard did the whole requiem in Latin. I remembered enough of it to be able to make some of the responses automatically, and that was a good thing, because I was distracted. I was thinking.

I was still thinking as we stood on the slope at the cemetery on the other side of the river and waited for the wind to bring us faint sounds of the graveside services. The three volleys fired by the guardsmen were ragged, the grandson who played taps fluffed the high note, and it appeared to me that Billy's box was a bit tipped on the slings that would lower him down. But that perhaps was appropriate; he might as well go crooked into the next life too.

We were back on the road to Worcester and the two-o'clock with the grand jury when I got it sorted out enough to ask Teddy a question. But I never got to do it. "All right," I said, "you started this."

He grinned again. "No I didn't," he said. "You did. I called you up one night and you were in a rotten mood. I asked you why, and you told me, you asked me if I knew this guy, Bonnie. Because he was gonna sink you. And I didn't. Which I told you. And you said: 'Oh shit,' or something, and I asked you where he came from. And you told me. From Worcester. And I said: 'I'll call you back.' "

"And you did," I said. "You said he was down in Florida with his goddamned boat, which he pretended he used to catch tuna fish, but actually used as a scout boat for drug smugglers."

"That's right," Teddy said. He settled back into the seat, rested his head against the rest, and closed his eyes.

"I guess I still don't get it," I said.

"Jerry, Jerry," Teddy said, "you're not some tourist down from Maine, seeing your first tall buildings. You told me you needed to find out some information, a guy that's from Worcester, right? And you can't find out where he is? I didn't know him. I hadda call someone. Who do you think I called?"

It took me a moment. "Carlo," I said. "My guess would be you called Carlo."

"Right," Teddy said, "I called Carlo." He was settling into that bucket seat the way Rip van Winkle settled into his leafy bower in the Catskills, getting ready to take a nice long nap. Teddy doesn't fret about grand jury appearances. They're part of his occupation.

"What did Carlo say?" I said.

"The first thing he said," Teddy said, "was 'I dunno. Who wants to know?' I told him. He said: 'This is your lawyer, guy I met, am I right?' I told him he was right. He said: 'I thought so. Get back to you.'

"And he did," Teddy said. "He got back to me. He told me where Jack Bonnie was. I called you up, and I told you. You thanked me, and I said: 'No problem.' Which as it turned out, it wasn't."

"Jack Bonnie," I said, and stopped—I had to clear my throat. "Until Jack Bonnie came up to testify, he was hard to find. And when he did come up, he had state cops all around him."

"That's what I heard," Teddy said.

"Night and day," I said. "Isolated."

Teddy yawned. "Well," he said, "Jerry, now, even you

wouldn't tell a boy's poor mother that she couldn't see her son."

"Does Carlo know Bonnie's mother?" I said.

"Well," Teddy said, "not specifically. Or he didn't, at least. Probably he doesn't now."

"But he knew somebody who knew Bonnie's mother," I said.

"Carlo knows lots of people," he said. "I told you he liked you, you know."

"Did Carlo have somebody call Bonnie's mother and tell her to deliver a message?" I said. "Like: 'Give Billy's lawyer some slack in the rope, or we'll put one around your damn neck'?"

"How the hell'd I know?" Teddy said, and yawned again. "You know me. I never ask questions. Not about your bills, or anything. The important thing is that you won the case, and now you're okay again, right?"

"I do believe so," I said.

"Good," Teddy said. "That's the most that you can hope for."

I suppose it is. It's all I'm likely to get, and much better than what I had. But these days when I go to the office, arriving by 8:10, and make my regal way through bowing groups of clients like an archbishop proceeding to the altar in a still monastery chapel, all the silent monks in place, I find that I still wonder what it *was* that I hoped for. Was it a reputation, as the Magic Man? "Bring Jerry Kennedy your problem"? "He can make the lame to see, and the deaf to walk"? "The blind to hear, the dead stink pretty, the guilty be acquitted"? I guess maybe it was. It's turned out that way, at least, although I didn't mean it to. I think I did, though, some good at least.

But I didn't win Billy Ryan's because I was good, although I still insist I am. I won Billy Ryan's case because I won some other cases first, over many years, involving stolen Cadillacs, cops and baseball bats, or maybe other things. In those cases I was good, as I was in Billy's case. But in those cases I was right. At least I thought I was. In Billy's case, I may have been, but that's probably not why I won. Quite unwittingly, I collaborated in the presentation of, well (forgive this further waffle; the old habits die hard), testimony not quite true, though not from a witness that I'd called, and for whose veracity I had therefore not vouched. A prosecutor with a gimlet eye would say I'd known the fix was in, and I'd exploited it full bore. That prosecutor would be wrong, but he would get me sent to jail. I'd have trouble defending me on that one.

But I didn't know it at the time. Not until Billy died. Yes, I kept quiet until now, to let the statute run. I had other folks to think of. Some of them had helped me out. Not Jack Bonnie; he was not my client. I never spoke to him at all, except in open court. Carlo died at fifty-eight, about two months after Billy, of a heart attack in bed. His own bed. Carlo was not my client either, and anyway he never told me anything at all. So I betray no privilege where those gentlemen are concerned.

Teddy is a different matter. I got permission, full waiver. I asked Teddy Franklin if it was all right to tell this story, and Teddy said: "Go right ahead. If somebody asks me, did I get Ryan's case tanked? I'll tell them: 'Of course I did. I have got connections. Now, you want an Eldo GT? Nice cherry Coupe de Ville? And what color would you like? You know lawyers. They tell stories. Ever had a lawyer? They tell stories in the office, tell you stories on the phone, biggest buncha bullshitters God ever put on earth. And alla time the clock is runnin'. Then they bill ya for it.' And then, when what you write comes out, and someone comes after me, I will call you, and pay you, and you will tell them: 'Teddy forgot something. Forgot to tell you that he lies.' And then you will bill me for saying that.

"And nobody will believe you, or me, when we tell them

those things. They will say about me: 'There's Teddy for ya. Never changes. Always fulla shit. Got a great line, that guy has. Talk-talk-talk, talk-talk.' And I, naturally, will say the same thing about you. Just like the man that was the man when Carlo was not the man. Now and then someone, I heard, someone would say to him: 'Hey, huh? What is this with the Carlo shit? We all thought you was the man. Isn't you the man?' And he would say: 'What is this "man?" Of course I am a man. I was a boy, I am a man. "The man?" Just what is "the man?" He's just another man. World is full of men.' And then the real man would buy a paper, have a cup of coffee, maybe, some pastry or a doughnut, and go on about his business.

"It's all business, you know?" Teddy said. "That's all it is, is *business*. You do a thing, you do a thing, you do another thing. You say a guy: 'Hey, I need this,' and he says: 'Hey, okay.' And then he goes and does it. So, you use him once, and he comes through, you call him up again. You say: 'Now I need this other thing.' So he goes: 'When?' You say: 'Tamarra.' He says: 'I can't do it then. Gimme Thursday. I'll be there.' You say: 'Thursday. You got it.' Thursday he is there. And he has got the thing.

"Now that is what I mean," Teddy said. "It's *business*, all right? Everybody's doing business. 'Everybody' includes you. You, and me, and all the guys. Everyone with balls. Including Billy Ryan, who's a dead guy I don't know, but when he was alive, he knew a friend of mine, helped me out a lot of times, or I would've been in jail. So this friend of mine calls up, and he's helping Billy Ryan, and so I figure: 'Okay, lemme see what I can do.' And I do it. That is all. We all help each other out. That's really all I mean."

"I didn't call you that night," I said. "You called me."

"Doesn't matter," Teddy said. "Doesn't matter at all."

It probably doesn't. When the angel comes, and says that it is time, it's time. Which may explain why Billy went off hushed, not crying, to his chosen lullabye.

OUTLAWS

George V. Higgins

In the 70s a dazzlingly successful series of armoured-transport robberies completely stuns Massachusetts law enforcement. There are no links with any of the usual criminal fraternity. No solid clues. Nothing.

Assistant Attorney General Terry Gleason is recruited to take on the case. It is not what he expected. It proves to be a five-year challenge of his professional endurance. The robbers were not as expected either. They are well-born, brilliant, talented, renegade scions of the American establishment – now turned thieves and murderers. In this exceptionally well-created and explosive novel, Higgins shows how the establishment, protecting itself against vicious defectors, takes its revenge.

'A hell of a story from a hell of a storyteller'
Daily Mail

'A picture of traumatised society. Its voices, caught here, have a disturbingly truthful ring'
Guardian

'Higgins' technique of building events only through the conversations of those affected by them makes him a concentrated, difficult read. The rewards are tremendous, however, and it is good to think that with a bit of luck we have another fifteen or so Boston novels to come from him'
Standard

IMPOSTERS
George V. Higgins

Contemporary Boston is a winner's market-place, jostling
with well-dressed, well-fed and mostly well-off imposters
... slick deceivers concealing their corruption so effectively
that they fool themselves as well. Outwardly – and
insistently – respectable, the Imposters suddenly find
themselves on collision courses when what looks like an
open-and-shut homicide case threatens to blow up into a
wholesale scandal exposing events of twenty years ago in
a sleepy seaside town. Who covered what up? For how
much money?

George V. Higgins helps his readers to eavesdrop on the
Imposters as they select their masks and doublecross each
other to surprising ends, in a world where sex is the
ultimate weapon, scruples are a sham, and the only thing
that matters is getting what you want.

'. . . One of the best novelists alive'
Sunday Times

'Higgins writes some of the best dialogue going, with pit-
of-stomach laughs or a cold gasp of dawning implications'
Observer

'That master of dialogue, George V. Higgins, has
produced another compelling novel. Powerful stuff'
Financial Times

PENANCE FOR JERRY KENNEDY

George V. Higgins

Though the taxman is fingering his collar and his everloving wife isn't speaking to him right now, trial lawyer Jerry Kennedy remains a hopelessly nice guy in a business where most of the operators have three rows of teeth. But then his old friend and book-keeper Lou Schwartz is hauled before Judge Maguire on account of having appended his signature to certain questionable tax declarations, and asks Jerry to defend him. The case is hopeless; it is, as Jerry says, a truly shitty way to make a living ...

'He is the le Carré of classy sleaze, and that is classy indeed'
Ed McBain/*New York Times*

'Higgins is almost uniquely blessed with a gift for voices, each of them – judge, car thief, D.A., wayward daughter, devoted but combative wife, drug pusher, wife beater, tricky accountant, I.R.S. investigator, clerk, secretary, flunky – as distinctive as a fingerprint, and the events they relate illuminate only too real a world ... In every respect a fine novel'
New Yorker

'Some of the scenes are the richest, raciest and funniest things Higgins has done ... He is a novelist of extraordinary intelligence and originality'
Julian Symons/*Sunday Times*

KENNEDY FOR THE DEFENSE

George V. Higgins

Jerry Kennedy (no relation) is the richest sleazy criminal lawyer in Boston, even if his wife does say so. Pimps, car thieves, druggies – all look to Kennedy to get them off. Sometimes he even manages it. Sometimes he doesn't. Sometimes there is trouble . . .

'A novelist of extraordinary intelligence and originality'
Sunday Times

'Seamlessly plotted and told almost entirely in dialogue as raw, and fresh, as uncut meat. Funny, too. Brilliantly done'
Matthew Coady/*Guardian*

'Evoked with all Higgins's splendid skill in capturing the actual sound of people talking. It's Runyon-x-Rabelais'
H. R. F. Keating/*The Times*

'George V. Higgins writes very good books. *Kennedy for the Defense* is one of his best . . . He has created a genre of his own, in which the people are so real that it doesn't matter what they're doing or how they go about it; just being in their company is pleasure enough. He is the Le Carré of classy sleaze'
Ed McBain/*New York Times*

☐	Outlaws	George V. Higgins	£4.99
☐	Imposters	George V. Higgins	£4.99
☐	Penance for Jerry Kennedy	George V. Higgins	£4.99
☐	Kennedy for the Defense	George V. Higgins	£4.50
☐	Wonderful Years, Wonderful Years	George V. Higgins	£4.50
☐	Trust	George V. Higgins	£4.50
☐	Victories	George V. Higgins	£4.50
☐	The Mandeville Talent	George V. Higgins	£4.99

Warner Books now offers an exciting range of quality titles by both established and new authors. All of the books in this series are available from:

Little, Brown and Company (UK) Limited,
P.O. Box 11,
Falmouth,
Cornwall TR10 9EN.

Alternatively you may fax your order to the above address. Fax No. 0326 376423.

Payments can be made as follows: cheque, postal order (payable to Little, Brown and Company) or by credit cards, Visa/Access. Do not send cash or currency. UK customers and B.F.P.O. please allow £1.00 for postage and packing for the first book, plus 50p for the second book, plus 30p for each additional book up to a maximum charge of £3.00 (7 books plus).

Overseas customers including Ireland, please allow £2.00 for the first book plus £1.00 for the second book, plus 50p for each additional book.

NAME (Block Letters) ....

....

ADDRESS ....

....

....

☐ I enclose my remittance for _____

☐ I wish to pay by Access/Visa Card

Number ☐☐☐☐☐☐☐☐☐☐☐☐☐☐☐☐

Card Expiry Date ☐☐☐☐